Also by Leland Shanle

Project Seven Alpha: American Airlines in Burma 1942
Vengeance at Midway and Guadalcanal

ENDGAME

IN THE PACIFIC

a novel by

LIEUTENANT COMMANDER LELAND C. SHANLE, JR. USN (RET.)

p7A Aviation
Saint Louis, Missouri

Published in the United States by p7A Aviation.

Cover design by Kristina Blank Makansi, Treehouse Publishing Group LLC
Cover art by Ron Cole, Coles Aircraft, www.colesaircraft.com

Library of Congress Control Number: 2013920655

ISBN: 978-0-9837107-2-1

www.project7alpha.com
www.treehousepublishinggroup.com

To Laura Lynn

ENDGAME

IN THE PACIFIC

CHAPTER 1

1943
19:18 Local, 04FEB (08:18 GMT, 04FEB)
New Georgia Sound, Solomon Island Chain

Plunging into a cloud layer, the flaming FM-1 Wildcat quickly began to disintegrate. Ensign David Brennan struggled to escape as fire started to breach the cockpit. He grasped the canopy handle and jettisoned it, releasing his harness and violently kicking the control stick full forward with his right foot. The negative G it produced ejected him out of the cockpit and into the pure white overcast sky. He narrowly missed the tail as he tumbled past it, and the static line ripped the cover off of his parachute. The slipstream activated it with a spine-numbing jerk.

He got a single swing in the chute before slamming into the hard surface of the New Georgia Sound. The impact knocked him semiconscious, but a moment later, the sting of salt water on his open wound and burns revived him. The parachute collapsed behind him and began to fill with ocean water and sink, dragging him below the surface. He flailed at the harness releases with blistered hands.

Ensign Brennan's lungs burned in warning as he was pulled deeper by the silk anchor. Finally, he clawed himself free and ripped at the darkening water until he burst out of the liquid prison. He kicked furiously to keep his head out of the sea, capturing each uncontrolled exhale in the fill tube of his May West life preserver. Once the vest held enough air to keep him afloat, he assessed his situation between exhausted grunts for air.

It was dire: burnt hands and arms, abdomen wound, and while fighting to get free from the grasping claws of Davy Jones, he had released and lost his raft and survival gear. Worst of all, it was getting dark. He knew he had two chances of survival: slim and none.

No doubt his hands would become useless soon, so he prepared himself as best he could to survive the night. He could not dress his wound, but he hoped that by tugging the white-hot bullet fragment out of his side—burning his hands—he had cauterized it. It was now all he had: hope. As the sun slipped below the horizon, dark grew rapidly.

Brennan's flight lead, Lieutenant Bruce Stutzman, had tried to follow him through the overcast but was jumped by two more Japanese Zeros. By the time he could disengage and penetrate the cloud layer, it was dark underneath.

Brennan could hear the Wildcat and knew it was Stutzman, but he could also hear the low murmur of a patrol craft. He couldn't take a chance—if it was Japanese, he knew what his fate would be. He decided to gamble on making it through the night. Ensign David Brennan, the U.S. Navy's newest ace—having shot down his fifth Japanese aircraft as he went down—steeled himself for the toughest test he would ever face.

Overhead, his fuel exhausted, Stutzman headed for Henderson Airfield on the Island of Guadalcanal. VF-27's Air Group had been forward deployed in support of the Marine's Cactus Air Force, while the carrier task force had withdrawn beyond the range of Imperial Japan's bombers. In the darkness, he searched for and found his new home.

Landing on the rough perforated steel plate runway (PSP) was no easy task in the light of day, let alone the dark of night. Stutzman's wings were immediately folded by mechanics after he bounced to a halt and cleared the makeshift runway. Already crowded before the arrival of CAG 27, it was now as tight as a ship's flight deck. Overworked USMC mechanics would be pushed to the limit with the added aircraft. However, the spare parts transported in the bellies of the dive-bombers were a rare and welcome commodity.

Stutzman shut down his Pratt & Whitney R-1830 and jumped from his Wildcat. A young plane captain was chocking his wheels.

"Lance Corporal," he said to the marine, "where is your HQ?"

"We don't really have one, sir. Closest thing is the operations tent."

After getting quick directions, Lieutenant Stutzman jogged to the tent. He found his commanding officer in a crowd and reported to Lieutenant Commander Steve Jasper.

"Skipper," he said, "Brennan is down."

A few men faced him but the busy atmosphere did not abate for the announcement of yet another casualty.

"Any chute?" asked Jasper.

"No, sir. He went into a layer over the slot. I was engaged two against one and could not get under the clouds to look until it was too dark."

"Any flares?"

"No, sir. But that doesn't necessarily mean—"

"Bruce," interrupted Jasper, "he's gone."

"No, sir. I don't believe that."

The lieutenant commander spoke quietly.

"We lost four aircraft today. I know he was your student and you were close—"

"Skipper, I know he's alive—"

"Bruce, he's gone. We have a strike tomorrow. Get some sleep. That's an order."

Stutz hesitated, prepared to argue more, but the skipper ended the discussion with a hard glare.

"Aye aye, sir."

Across the tent, Colonel Sean "Thumper" McDonald, the Marines Air Group Commander, overheard the conversation. Lieutenant Stutzman turned slowly and left the tent, dejected. The colonel followed.

"Lieutenant," he called after him, "hang on a minute."

Stutzman stood fast at attention as the colonel approached him.

"Relax, Bruce. I'm a reservist pressed into position by circumstance."

"Yes, sir."

"Call me Thumper," said McDonald. "This Brennan kid, he wasn't from Texas was he?"

"Yes, sir."

"David?"

"That's him."

"Damn it. DAMN IT!"

Thumper rubbed his temples with his index fingers as if a migraine had instantly gripped him.

"Obviously, you knew him, Colonel."

Pausing to collect himself, Thumper finally spoke.

"Yeah, I was in China with his father and brother on Project 7 Alpha. They didn't make it back."

Stutzman nodded in silence. Both men stood for a moment, and then Thumper turned slowly back for the tent.

"I've got to go send a message."

Stutzman called after him.

"He was an ace when he went down."

Colonel McDonald didn't turn around. Shoulders slumped, he started a slow walk through emotional quicksand toward the message center. *His mother won't care,* he thought.

"Okay, thanks," he called back. "I'll pass that along."

CHAPTER 2

05:05 Local, 04FEB, (10:05 GMT, 04FEB)
Air Transport Command, Washington, DC

An upright and meticulously manicured orderly silently marched into General C.R. Smith's office. He stood quietly as the general pored through mounds of paper. C.R. had, until recently, been the president of American Airlines. FDR had personally asked him to set up the air transportation branch of the US Army Air Corps.

Unnoticed, the orderly finally spoke. "General, a personal message for you from Guadalcanal."

C.R. looked up, startled. "From the Canal to me—are you sure, Sergeant?"

"Yes, sir. You are addressed in the familiar." C.R. took the message and read it.

UNCLASSIFIED

DTG:4FEB43 1001Z
TO: COMTRANSCOMUSAAC
FROM: COMMARAIRGROUP25
SUBJ: PERSONAL
TEXT: C.R.,
D BRENNAN SHOT DOWN THIS PM OVER THE SLOT. MIA.
WENT DOWN FIGHTING AS AN ACE.
THUMPER SENDS

UNCLASSIFIED

C.R.'s hand went involuntarily to his mouth. His face was drawn in anguish and guilt.

"Oh, no...."

He set the message softly on his desk and began to fidget. A man of action, he needed something to busy himself with immediately. Coming to a quick conclusion, he gave two orders.

"Sergeant, send the following response ASAP."

"Ready to copy, sir."

The orderly held notebook and pencil at the ready.

"Go find him."

"Is that all, sir?" asked the sergeant, flipping his notebook closed without writing.

"No. Please have an aircraft ready to fly to Dallas within the hour."

"I meant the message, sir."

"That is enough for Thumper McDonald."

CHAPTER 3

21:15 Local, 04FEB (01:15 GMT, 04FEB)
New Georgia Sound, Solomon Island Chain

Floating aimlessly in the black abyss, David Brennan started to expel the portions of it he had swallowed as the ocean swelled and heaved. He had been in the water for three hours and began to chill, even though the water was warm. It was still below body temperature, and in his weakened state, it was pulling down his core temperature. He had done all he could to preserve body heat: his canvas flight helmet was on and buckled, the collar was up and the sleeves down on his Navy-issue flight coveralls.

10:22 Local, 04FEB (10:22 GMT, 04FEB)
Kate's Manor, Bowdown House, Greenham Common, England

Colonel J.T. Dobbs, Commander, 10th Transportation Wing USAAC, wept as he handed the message from C.R. to his wife, Kate. Her eyebrows rose in shock: *Oh my God, poor Laura, not again,* she thought. Kate choked down her fear, deciding to be positive for her husband's sake.

"It says MIA," she said. "That's missing in action, not dead—right?"

Unable to speak, J.T. nodded and walked out to the garden. He was racked with a gnawing guilt. He had watched David's father and brother die under his command. To make it worse, Charles Henry Brennan had been his best friend. J.T. had been there the night David was born.

22:00 Local, 04FEB (11:00 GMT, 04FEB)
New Georgia Sound, Solomon Island Chain

David Brennan tried to pull his knees up into the fetal position to conserve body heat, but the pain from the bullet hole in his side wouldn't let him. He was spent from blowing air into his May West to maintain buoyancy and from being pounded by the swells. A second bout with nausea dehydrated him. By midnight he had a fever, but was shivering from the tepid water. David began to lose lucidity. Above him the overcast had dissipated, revealing a sky laced with stars. He gazed up at them and prayed he would make it through the night.

11:03 Local, 04FEB (11:03 GMT, 04FEB)
Kate's Manor, Bowdown House, Greenham Common, England

A soft knock at his door woke Lieutenant Colonel James 'Irish' Meyers. He and J.T. had been up all night, planning for the invasion of Europe.

"Enter!" he bellowed.

Kate walked into the lavish bedchamber toward the large, canopy bed. Irish unconsciously pulled up the heavy bedding, covering his bare chest. Kate found his discomfort amusing.

"My dreams are answered, dear lady," said Irish. "However, I happen to know your husband has a nasty temper and a loaded pistol."

"Take it easy, Romeo. I'm here on official business. I'm afraid it is not good news." She handed Irish the message.

"Shit," he swore, reading. "Where is he?"

"The garden."

"Get out of here so I can get dressed."

"My, aren't we shy! Put him to work, Irish—and no whiskey," Kate added, pulling the door closed as she left the room.

04:08 Local, 05FEB (17:08 GMT, 04FEB)
Henderson Field, Guadalcanal

Thumper shook awake his plane captain, who was sound asleep on the wing of a Wildcat.

"Hey, Corporal," he whispered. "Wake up. I need your help for a few minutes."

Billy stifled a yawn.

"Sure, Colonel. What's up?"

"I'm going to borrow the Navy's Duck."

"Okay sir—where are you going?"

"To get a friend, Billy. To get a friend."

Stealthily, the two marines made their way to the Navy's flight line. They found the Duck sitting at the end of a row of Navy birds. "Duck" was the common name for the Grumman J2F-5, derived because, like the waterfowl, the J2F-5 could land on a runway, water, or a ship. And the small bi-plane looked amazingly like a duck. Its fuselage float extended out and below the propeller, turning up at the end like a duck's bill. While a fine utilitarian aircraft, the Duck was a slow, fat, lumbering target. It had a pilot seat and observer seat in tandem, and the large float could also hold passengers or cargo.

Thumper slid quietly into the cockpit and flipped on the battery switch. A low hum, produced by instruments and gyros spinning up, seemed like a piercing alarm in the pre-dawn silence. He turned on a map light and quickly checked the plot on his chart where David had gone down.

Billy stood on the wing, looking at the map.

"You are going to need someone to pull him in the float," he said. "After spending the night out there, he's liable to be a mess."

"Thanks, Billy," said Thumper, "but this is going to be a risky mission."

The young plane captain looked at his wing commander with a look that could best be described as sarcasm.

"Sir, with all due respect, I live on the Canal."

Thumper couldn't argue with that.

"You have a point, Corporal. Okay, open the aft canopy and get it ready. Man the fire bottle. Once I fire up this ugly duckling, jump your ass in. The Navy may take exception to us borrowing their aircraft."

Sparking to life at 04:18, the nine cylinders of the Wright R-1820 Cyclone gave a thunderous wake-up call to the entire base. Thumper didn't wait to see if anyone answered it. He immediately gassed the Duck out of its parking spot as Billy clambered into the rear observer's cockpit.

04:18 Local, 05FEB (17:18 GMT, 04FEB)
New Georgia Sound, Solomon Island Chain

David was delirious, no longer able to control his thoughts, which raced incoherently. He was losing his battle, surrendering to the pain and fever.

David, David—wake up.

He opened his eyes, which centered on a bright star rising in the east.

Your time is not now.
"Dad?" he asked the night.
You have to hang on, son.
"I can't."
You have to.
"Okay."
Good boy.
"I miss you...."

David's voice trailed off to a whisper. He stared intently at the star and focused his entire being on it, drawing strength and warmth from its brilliance.

04:21 Local, 5FEB (17:21 GMT, 4FEB)
Henderson Field, Guadalcanal

Illuminating the PSP runway with the Duck's takeoff lights, Thumper jammed on full power as the aircraft rumbled off the steel-matt runway. Its wings lifted it into the air quickly, and Thumper snapped off the lights before Japanese gunners could draw a bead on the lumbering plane.

"Cool," came over the intercom system (ICS).

"What's that, Billy?"

"I said it's pretty cool," shouted the corporal. "I've never flown before."

Thumper laughed to himself as he trimmed up the aircraft and turned it toward The Slot, thinking, *I sure hope it's not your last flight, young man.*

05:43 Local, 06FEB (18:43 GMT, 04FEB)
New Georgia Sound, Solomon Island Chain

Thumper navigated to the coordinates that Stutzman had given him and began an expanding box search pattern. It wasn't yet dawn, but the crimson horizon told him it would be soon. He was hoping to see a flare, land on the open ocean, snatch the lad up, and be gone before the first Japanese combat air patrol (CAP) was on station. Not likely. Plan B was to expand the search box, then collapse it at daylight.

Daylight came before a flare. He began to shrink the search box. He also started to scan the horizon, especially behind him, for Zeros.

"Billy," he called through the intercom, "there's some binoculars in the map case back there."

"Already got them, Colonel."

"Excellent. Look for a yellow May West. I suspect he did not make it into his raft, otherwise we'd have gotten a flare."

Hours passed. Thumper knew he was really hanging it out now. Each passing minute invited the presence of a Japanese Zero. And his fuel was reaching a level that would force his return.

Billy's excited voice was regenerated in Thumper's earphones.

"I've got him!"

"Where?"

"Port side—one thousand yards!"

The Duck was already at low level and slow. Thumper chopped the throttle and began a landing approach. Gaining a visual on the floating fighter pilot, he violently crossed-controlled the ponderous aircraft by deflecting full rudder and opposite aileron. The crossed controls caused the Duck to plummet toward the ocean. At the last second, he neutralized the flight controls, held a stabilized attitude, and mushed onto the surface.

Fifteen thousand feet overhead, Lieutenant Yoshi Yamaguchi saw a splash below his flight. Signaling his wingman to follow, he dove his Zero for the ocean below.

Thumper taxied the Duck right up to the unconscious pilot, bouncing him off of the float while Billy dropped through the trap door into the float. He popped open the external door just in time to grab the downed aviator by the collar of his May West. With all his might, the little New Yorker pulled Ensign David Brennan into the float. As David's boots disappeared into the cabin, Thumper cobbed the power.

Billy sprawled onto the deck of the float from the sudden acceleration and fought to untangle himself from David. Plumes of water surged into the belly through the open hatch. Finally slamming it closed, he hung onto the bulkhead as the Duck began to bounce up to speed.

Thumper struggled to get the bi-plane onto the front half of the float on the open ocean. The front half was raised, allowing the aft half of the float to rise out of the water and break the suction. He had to get it on step or the Duck would never get to flying speed.

Yamaguchi dove through eight thousand feet, spotting the fat target as it bounded into the air. Flipping on his gun sight, he armed and charged his two 20-millimeter cannons and two 7.7mm machine guns. At a range of four thousand feet, he centered the piper of his gun sight on the Duck as it desperately accelerated in ground effect until a safe climb speed could be reached.

Thumper held the nose of the aircraft down to maximize the rate of acceleration. Suddenly, the ocean erupted in furious waterspouts as the Zero's bullets splashed all around the Duck. Thumper instinctively snapped on a max performance break turn, nearly dragging a wingtip in the wave tops.

Yamaguchi did not expect an effective evasive maneuver out of the seaplane—most of his rounds missed.

Pulling the bi-plane into heavy buffet, Thumper continued to extract all the lift he could out of the two fat wings. He converted that lift into turn rate, almost getting a head-on pass. With nearly four hundred knots of closure, the Zero blew past without another shot fired. Thumper reversed his turn, pulling back into Yamaguchi as he blew past.

He couldn't run away and didn't have guns to fight. All he could do was maneuver, forcing the Zeros to miss, hoping they would run out of ammo. Unlikely, he knew, but an aviator always had to have hope. He leveled his wings and nearly bent the throttle, pushing it forward to extract all 1,050 horsepower from the R-1820-54 engine. He waited for the next attack.

Thumper didn't have to wait long. *Here they come!*

Rolling in from an abeam position, the Zeros attacked with discipline—slower this time, in sequence. Patiently, Thumper waited. When the fighter lead reached the edge of the guns' effective envelope, Thumper wrapped the Duck up into a steep turn and pulled into the lead as hard as he could. Again, the closure and angle did not allow an effective burst from the Zero's guns.

Yamaguchi's wingman now took his run. Thumper was out of airspeed and ideas. It would be a head-on pass but he was now so slow from bleeding airspeed while maneuvering that he was, indeed, a sitting Duck. Again, he waited.

Inexplicably, the wingman's Zero suddenly exploded before loosing a single round. A dark blue streak flashed over Thumper's canopy. Twisting around so he could see what it was, he recognized it as an FM-1 Wildcat. It attacked and downed the Zero lead before he knew of its presence. As the sky rained fire and Zero parts, Thumper turned toward the Canal.

In the float, Billy was finally able to get off the deck. Not sure of what had happened, he assumed it wasn't good but was relieved they had also survived it. Quickly, he pumped overboard the salt water that had flooded through the open hatch on takeoff. He next turned his attention to their new passenger.

Stripping off David's soaked May West and coveralls, Billy was startled when he saw the wound. He yanked a first aid kit off the bulkhead and dressed it as best he could, wrapping the injured ace in blankets, and got on the ICS.

"Colonel," he called, "this guy's alive but not by much. He's lost a lot of blood, has some burns, and most definitely is in shock."

"Get him to talk, Billy," came the reply. "You've got to get him to talk."

Thumper flipped on the heater and began to pump warm air into the cabin while climbing to altitude. He glanced to his right and saw the Wildcat join on his wing. Lieutenant Stutzman pushed his goggles up onto his canvas helmet and signaled 2-5-5-4 with his fingers. Thumper dialed up frequency 255.4 on the UHF radio.

"Is he alive?" asked Stutzman.

"Barely," was the curt response.

Billy's voice came over the intercom again.

"Sir, I'm no doctor, but I think this ensign needs to get to a ship's medical, not the Canal's."

"Roger that." Thumper passed the word to Stutz, who nodded agreement and began a climb to increase the range of his radio.

"Red Crown, Red Crown—Raven 101."

"Go ahead, Raven.'" Stutzman was surprised to get a response so quickly. The Enterprise had come north to launch supplies to Guadalcanal.

"Red Crown, Raven 101 is a flight of two—one Wildcat and one Duck with a rescued aviator that needs immediate medical. Request pigeons to mother."

"Stand by, Raven."

Stutzman had asked for the bearing and distance to the ship. He knew the ship would be in no hurry to share that information and give away their position.

"Raven, Red Crown—say your posit."

"In The Slot. Bangor to Jacksonville."

He had told them that they were over the Saint Georges Sound, flying south. He hoped his makeshift code would be accepted.

"Continue," was the one-word reply.

Stutzman rejoined with the Duck and they continued down The Slot for thirty-eight more minutes, when suddenly four Wildcats blew past them, two on each side. After buzzing the Duck flight, the Wildcats reversed and rendezvoused on them. One section broke off and began a Thach tactical weave overhead the flight. The lead section joined on Thumper's left wing.

The lead asked for a fuel check from Thumper with a hand signal. He had just calculated his remaining fuel and returned a signal in minutes, tapping his watch so there was no confusion. Having leaned the engine's mixture as much as he dared, he hoped that he had enough to reach the ship. Thumper turned to Stutz and kissed him off so he could return to Henderson Field. Stutz saluted and then rolled off of Thumper's wing, turning northwest to the Canal and thinking, *If I hurry, I can make the strike and maybe the skipper won't court martial me.*

Closing in tight, the Wildcat Lead hand signaled 1-5-5 with a point of his finger and then 7-5. Thumper turned to a course of 155 degrees and did the calculus for seventy-five miles. It would be tight but they would make it. He passed a thumbs-up to the lead, who nodded acknowledgment and then moved out to a tactical position.

Billy popped up through the trapdoor to get a breath of cool air.

"Hey, where did they come from?" he asked over the ICS.

"Friends escorting us to the ship's medical, as ordered, Dr. Corporal."

"Hey, I'm no doctor."

"How's your patient?"

"Still out of it, sir. I did get him to drink some water. He also opened his eyes a couple times. Looks like he had a rough night."

Billy dropped back down into the cabin through the trap door. He checked on David and then went through the first aid kit to see if there was anything else he could use. In it, he found a bottle labeled "medicinal alcohol." He got back on the ICS.

"Hey, Colonel, what's medicinal alcohol for?"

"Drinking. It's brandy."

"Really?!"

"I'll trust your discretion with that information back on the Canal. See if you can get the ensign to drink some."

Billy twisted off the top and took a swig. Moving next to David, he yelled over the noise of the R-1820: "Hey, Ensign, join me for a cocktail?"

12:38 Local, 04FEB (18:38 GMT, 04FEB)
Fort Worth, Texas

Laura Brennan was in her kitchen brewing coffee when she heard a knock at the door. She glanced at the clock on the wall and went into the living room. Peering through a curtain, she saw a strange car at the curb and a man in uniform on her doorstep. Laura swallowed hard and opened the door.

"Hello, C.R., what brings you to Texas?" she asked bravely.

"Laura, I'll get right to it."

C.R. Smith was choking back emotion and not doing a very good job of it.

"Your boy was shot down. He's listed missing in action."

Laura led him into the kitchen and slowly poured two cups of coffee. Handing one to C.R., she added, "Don't worry, he'll be all right."

"Geez, Laura, I'm supposed to be comforting you."

Both of them laughed uneasily.

CHAPTER 4

08:35 Local, 05FEB, (21:35 GMT, 04FEB)
Henderson Field, Guadalcanal

Lieutenant Stutzman bounced to a halt on Henderson's PSP runway. Turning into the fuel pits, he hot-refueled with the engine running, taxied his Wildcat onto the VF-27 line and shut down. His skipper and Thumper's operations officer were waiting.

"Where's the Duck?" asked the skipper.

"On the way to Enterprise."

"And Brennan?"

"In its belly," Stutz replied.

"Alive?"

"Yes, sir."

Lieutenant Commander Jasper rubbed his chin in thought. He turned and began to walk away.

"Okay, Bruce," he called over his shoulder, "we're even. Launch is in twenty minutes. Get briefed."

Standing fast, the operations officer asked, "Is Colonel McDonald in the Duck?"

Stutz nodded and the marine started to walk off, then stopped and turned.

"He didn't happen to have a plane captain with him, did he?"

Stutz smiled.

"He had someone with him," he answered.

08:52 Local, 05FEB (21:52 GMT, 04FEB)
USS Enterprise, Admiral Halsey's Flagship, Solomon Sea

It wasn't until he rolled out on final approach that Thumper realized he had not landed on an aircraft carrier since his two passengers were in diapers. Gear and hook down, he was committed. *I hope I don't screw this up.* He fought off the urge to watch the pitching deck and concentrated on the paddles held by the LSO. The landing signal officer drew a line across his throat. Thumper answered the signal by cutting the throttle to idle.

Settling onto a wire, he felt the welcome tug and looked up to see a flurry of activity. A yellow-shirted crewman was jumping up and down, trying to get his attention. After receiving the international signal to "pull your head out," Thumper remembered, *Oh yeah, he is a handler.*

He followed the Yellow Shirt's directions and taxied over the dropped barricade. It snapped back into place immediately after he crossed it, as a Wildcat rolled onto final approach.

Pulling forward until given a stop signal, Thumper shut down the engine and unstrapped himself. Corpsmen had already gotten David Brennan on a stretcher and an IV in his arm. With two carrying the stretcher and one holding the IV bottle high, they disappeared into the tower. A sailor was waiting for him when he climbed down off the Duck.

"Sir," said the sailor, "Admiral Halsey would like to see you on the flag bridge."

"You'll have to lead me," Thumper shouted over the din. "I'm a jarhead, not a squid."

"Follow me, sir."

As they climbed the ladders to the flag bridge, they came across a message center.

"Stand by there a second, shipmate," Thumper said. He entered and quickly scrawled a message to C.R., handing it to a Navy chief.

"Sir, you don't have release authority—" the chief protested.

"C'mon, Chief, it's to tell his momma."

"Colonel, they will have my ass."

"She has already lost a husband and son in this war," Thumper said. "She has suffered enough, don't you think?"

The chief signalman hesitated and then took the message.

"I'll mix it in with the hourly traffic," he said. "It goes out in five."

"Thanks, Chief!"

"Sure thing, Colonel. Will you be a witness at my captain's mast?"

"Done, shipmate. But I doubt you'll want my endorsement."

16:15 Local, 04FEB (22:15 GMT, 04FEB)
Fort Worth, Texas

Laura and Jon, one of the 7Alpha guys, were putting another leaf in the dining room table to accommodate the growing number of friends who had just "happened by." Not surprisingly, a stifling tension hung in the air. They all jumped in unison when the telephone rang. Laura almost laughed at the reaction of the grown men, but couldn't. She looked at Jon and registered alarm in his eyes.

"Jon," she said quietly, "get that for me, would you, please?"

Kaitlyn and William, her youngest two, poked their heads into the room as Jon reached for the phone. He nodded once, not speaking to the caller, and cleared his throat.

"It is for General Smith," he said.

The room fell silent as C.R. crossed it to take the phone. He glanced to Laura, clearing his throat and put the receiver to his ear. His expression changed to shock and he let out a Texas-sized yell.

"Hot damn, Thumper found him!"

The crowd erupted in cheers.

"Stand by, stand by!" C.R. shouted them down, trying to listen. "'Fished him out of The Slot this AM. Currently on USS Boat. He's banged up but OK. Thumper sends.'"

Laura looked down. She had pulled the tablecloth into a knot. She snapped it out over the table before anyone noticed.

"See, I told you, C.R.," she said, calm. "Nothing to worry about."

Captain Tim "Roper" Smith, another member of the 7Alpha crew, fell forward in a chair he had been leaning against the wall.

"Well, I'm going to get some Budweiser," he said. "This wake just turned into a party."

C.R. thrust a handful of bills in Roper's hand and slapped him on the back.

"By the way, everyone, David's an ace now. Like father, like son."

Looking at each other, Kaitlyn and William mouthed WOW to each other. They would have serious bragging rights in school now. Laura pretended not to hear, knowing the dreams that would come with that status. Kaitlyn turned to her brother.

"Flying is hard enough, Willy," she boasted, "but to be an ace…"

Roper widened his eyes in fear and gave Kaitlyn a subtle shake of the head. He had secretly been teaching her to fly.

10:38 Local, 05FEB (22:38 GMT, 04FEB)
Flag Bridge, USS Enterprise, Solomon Sea

Admiral Bull Halsey stood on the wing of his bridge watching the last of the Wildcats recover. He had let Thumper stand for the better part of a half hour. Finally the sailor escort couldn't take it anymore and spoke.

"Admiral, Colonel McDonald is on deck, as requested."

Halsey turned and looked curiously at Thumper.

"Full colonel, a wing commander at that, rescuing an ensign," he said. "Kind of unusual."

"I've known him since he was born, sir," Thumper replied.

Halsey nodded and then looked down onto the flight deck at the Duck. Painted clearly on its fuselage was USS Enterprise in block letters.

"That Duck looks familiar."

"I didn't think you'd mind if I borrowed it, Admiral."

"Really… looks like it has some holes in it."

"It will be fine, sir," Thumper assured him. "Nothing a bit of ordnance tape can't fix."

Halsey snorted and then turned to face Thumper. He stared at him for a five count, and then spoke slowly.

"Okay, Colonel. We were up here to launch another Duck with some spare parts in the cargo bay. We will just put them in with you… if that's not too much of an inconvenience?"

"Not at all, sir. I'd be happy to."

"Wish you could stay for lunch," said the admiral, "but subs are in the area. We are running south. We won't be able to turn into the wind. We will catapult you off the hangar deck. Dismissed."

"Thank you, sir. Have a good morning."

Thumper fled the flag bridge without waiting for a reply. He flew down the ladder to the hangar bay, where he found the Duck coming down a ship's flight deck elevator. On the elevator with the Duck was Billy, smiling big and eating a sandwich out of a box lunch.

"Look, Colonel," he said, "real food!"

"Looks great, Marine. Let's get the hell out of here before I end up in the brig."

"Weren't too thrilled with ya borrowing the Duck and gettin' it shot up, huh, sir?" Billy added through a mouthful of sandwich.

"Not really," replied Thumper. "You got another one of those?"

Billy held out the box and watched the Navy boys pick up the Duck with a crane and put it on a catapult. Strapping it into place, the launch officer waved Thumper and Billy over.

"Where we going?" he asked.

"For a nice little ride, Marine. You'll love it."

23:07 Local, 04FEB (23:07 GMT, 04FEB)
Kate's Manor, Bowdown House, Greenham Common, England

Kate walked unnoticed into the cavernous dining room. Long ago, it had been converted into a planning room. Irish and J.T. had papers and charts spread all over the expansive table. They had been hard at work planning the air invasion of Europe, but even more so at forgetting the day's events.

She held a magnum of champagne in one hand and three long-stem champagne glasses in the other. Still unnoticed, Kate clinked the glasses by subtly shaking her hand. Both men looked up.

"C.R. just called," she said, smiling. "Our wayward naval aviator was plucked from the Pacific by none other than Thumper McDonald."

J.T. flopped into one of the oversized dining room chairs. Irish threw a handful of paper into the air and yelled, "Pop that damn cork!"

11:28 Local, 05FEB (00:28 GMT, 05FEB)
Hangar Deck, USS Enterprise

Thumper sat on the steel lattice of the catapult and cranked up the R-1820 Cyclone engine. Idling steadily, he gave a thumbs-up to the catapult officer. The Cat O signaled his crew and the entire apparatus rotated under hydraulic power until it was pointed out of the hangar bay door. Thumper sat calmly, looking at the engine's instruments. Behind him sat a very nervous corporal.

"Colonel, are you sure this will work?"

"Oh, it will work, all right. Make sure your goggles are down."

"Why? Do you think we are gonna hit the water?"

"No," Thumper replied, "but when this baby fires, we will go from zero to seventy knots in twenty-five feet. This aircraft is going to move but anything not bolted down is not. And that includes all that Guadalcanal dirt and sand!"

Ready for launch, the Cat O signaled Thumper to run up the power. Thumper pushed the throttle through the gate and set full emergency power. The Cat O signaled his crew to put the Duck in tension. Vibrating and shaking as if it were coming apart, the Duck fought to get free. When put in tension, the aircraft squatted. Billy mistook the bump for launch and keyed the ICS as Thumper saluted and the Cat O signaled launch. The catapult fired just as Billy tried to speak. The acceleration was so violent it knocked the air out of Billy's lungs, so all that came through the ICS was a pitiful groan. Thumper tried to laugh when he heard it but couldn't.

Thumper let the heavily loaded Duck settle off of the Cat as it tried to figure out if it was flying. Its wings and propeller finally caught up to the launch as it actually decelerated before digging in.

Staying low, Thumper turned toward the Canal. After catching his breath, Billy spoke from the rear observer's cockpit.

"Man, I can't wait to write the folks about this!"

CHAPTER 5

08:52 Local, 6FEB (18:52 GMT, 6FEB)
Ford Island Family Housing, Pearl Harbor

The sun rose over the Pacific as it had almost every day of her life, beautiful and big—announcing the potential of a new day. But this day would be like no other. Its bright potential would crash on the rocks like the Pacific surf. Theresa Jameson, daughter of Captain Paul Jameson, commander of "The Cactus Striking Force," would never be the same.

Her father had put to sea leading a destroyer squadron, created by Admiral Bull Halsey, in support of Guadalcanal operations. As a senior officer, he rated a much larger base house, but after his wife died it was just the two of them. He thought the smaller house would be easier for his daughter to maintain. She had insisted on taking over household duties after her mother's funeral. Besides, Theresa loved the ocean view, especially from the rose garden.

Her morning chores done, Theresa sat in her garden trimming stems. She intently studied the roses: each blossom intrigued her, with its complexity of structure as well as diversity of color and form. A familiar voice broke her concentration.

"Theresa, dear."

She looked up to see her father's best friend, Commodore Mitchell Pierce. With him was his aide, a navy lieutenant and the command chaplain, a full commander. All three were in service dress white uniforms.

Theresa dropped her clippers, her eyes wide with fear, filled with tears. The men needed not speak. Their very presence screamed over the pounding surf that she was now alone in the world.

Theresa wept among her roses. She didn't hear how her father's Task Force 67.5 had been instrumental in finally pushing the Japanese off Guadalcanal. She didn't hear that his flagship DeHaven DDG-469 had been lost with 167 hands on board. She didn't even hear how her father was hailed as a hero—he had always been a hero to her. All that mattered to Theresa was that he was gone.

06:52 Local, 07FEB (17:52 GMT, 07 FEB)
Sick Bay, USS Enterprise

David opened his eyes. Standing over him was a large blond-haired, blue-eyed man. *Shit!* he thought, *I'm a POW and this German is going to interrogate me.*

"Hey, shipmate," the man said, "how're we doing today?"

David looked around the white room, confused. Then he raised his bandaged arms and stared at them.

"You should have kept those sleeves down."

"It was hot," he rasped. "Where am I?"

"Sick bay, USS Enterprise. I'm Doc Schneider—Jim."

"How long?"

"You've been in and out for a couple of days."

"How—?"

"You were rescued by Duck."

David squinted, lost in thought for a moment.

"I had a weird dream," he said. "An old friend—"

"That was no dream," said the doc. "A marine colonel borrowed a Navy Duck, went out, found your butt and brought it here."

"Where is he?"

"He beat it back to the Canal two days ago."

"I need to get back, too," David said, trying to sit up. "I need to get back to my squadron."

Doc Schneider put a hand on his shoulder and gently pushed him back.

"Not any time soon," he said. "You have a rather large hole in you and some nasty burns."

"Look, Doc, I need to get back to my squadron."

"The battle is over. The Japs pulled out. We are all headed back to Pearl to lick our wounds."

"That bad?"

"Pretty rough, Ensign. We lost a lot of ships and thousands of sailors. They renamed Savo Sound, 'Iron Bottom Sound' because of all the ships on its bed."

"Thousands?"

"Fifteen hundred in a single night: two admirals, and the scuttlebutt is five brothers died too."

"What about the Canal?"

"The Navy shut down the Tokyo Express. We held the line. And the Marines pushed the Japs off the island."

Two beefy medical corpsmen joined them. Each un-bandaged an arm and then held it firmly. David looked around wondering what was going on, and then he saw the scrub brush in the doc's hand.

"Is this going to hurt some?"

"No, this is going to hurt like hell."

CHAPTER 6

18:58 Local, 28FEB (18:58 GMT, 28FEB)
Kate's Manor, Bowdown House, Greenham Common, England

A blustery winter storm whipped the Berkshire countryside. Dark and gloomy as the weather was, it could not dampen J.T.'s mood. Kate smiled from across the library. She was pleased to see him closer to his old self. He was reading an old book and whistling a happy tune when there was a heavy knock on the door. He went straight for the door, not waiting for the staff. Kate watched him walk. His slight limp, she knew, would never go away.

Standing in the pouring rain, his hat and trench coat drenched, was Captain Mark Hass, US Army Air Corps—and like J.T., an American Airlines pilot on military leave. Also like him, Hass had lost his best friend during Project 7 Alpha.

"Hass-man," J.T. said, surprised, "get out of the rain. What brings you here?"

"You owe me a beer."

J.T. laughed and pulled the diminutive Hass-man into the entrance hall. Taking his hat and coat he turned to Kate.

"Look what the wind blew in."

The three talked for an hour of old times and new. None of them touched on 7 Alpha; all were too deeply scarred.

Hass-man was assigned to a P-47 Thunderbolt outfit a half-hour away. He would soon be escorting B-17s on daylight missions.

"So how do you like fighters?" asked J.T.

Hass let out a low whistle.

"I'll tell you what, the performance of the 47 is incredible! Those eighteen cylinders pumping out 2,100 horsepower—"

"If you boys are going to talk airplanes," Kate interrupted, "I'm going to rustle up some dinner. Mark, I'll have a room made up for you."

"I don't want to impose, Kate."

"Irish lives here too," she said, smiling. "You can't get more imposed upon than that. He is currently attempting to deflower the local village damsels."

"Well, in that case, I have a forty-eight-hour pass."

"Good, I'll have a room made."

"Hass-man, tell me more about the Thunderbolt," asked J.T. eagerly.

"You boys and your toys." Kate shook her head and left the study

10:28 Local, 28FEB (20:28 GMT, 28FEB)
Ford Island, Naval Air Station Pearl Harbor

"For gallantry above and beyond in aerial combat, even after being grievously wounded, Ensign David Brennan is hereby awarded the Navy Cross. This is the nation's second-highest honor."

Admiral Bull Halsey pinned the medal on David's dress "choker" tunic, next to an air medal and Purple Heart, as well as two campaign medals.

"Not bad, kid. Keep up the good work. But if you get your butt shot down again, tell your friends to steal someone else's airplane."

David grinned sheepishly. When Skipper Jasper heard the admiral call David "kid," he smiled almost imperceptibly—a call sign was born.

"Yes, sir," replied David. "I'll try to remember that."

By 11:00 the men of VF-27 were well on their way to inebriation inside the Ford Island Officers' Club. Jasper added to the bedlam by ringing a ship's bell that was bolted to the bar, the penalty for which was buying the bar a round. All hands cheered "Jazz" as they rushed the bar for free booze. He jumped on the bar and raised his hand for silence.

"Gentlemen, gentlemen," he announced, "Admiral Halsey was not able to join us but asked that I buy you all a round for him."

The men cheered again.

"We also have something else supplied us by the Bull," said the skipper. "Brennan! Front and center."

Squadron mates, careful of his arms, pushed David forward.

"Gentlemen, we have what I believe to be a flag officer decree. I give you

Kid Brennan."

The crowd went wild. Kid Brennan looked a little sick. He had been trying to look older than he was since joining the Navy. This would not help. Bruce Stutzman laughed and pushed him up to the bar where he ordered two McLaren scotches and two glasses of water. After carefully pouring the water in equal amounts into each glass of scotch, he handed one to the newly nicknamed Kid.

"Scotch is a concentrate," Kid, Stutz said solemnly. "You have to properly release its flavor with an equal amount of water."

"I was hoping for something a little better—"

"There is no better scotch!"

"I mean the call sign."

Stutz clinked his glass and took a long sip, savoring the flavor. He then turned to Kid Brennan and smiled. He let out a satisfied "Ahh," and smacked his lips slightly.

"It could be a lot worse, Kid."

David thought about that. His father's friend, Two Dogs, came to mind. "Two Dogs" was short for "Two Dogs Fornicating"—as in, he was as ugly as....

Indeed it could be worse.

Ensign David "Kid" Brennan USNR snuck out of the O'Club and began to wander around the base. His head was swimming—laced with beer and fine scotch. Snippets of terrifying moments from his brief combat career started to flash through his mind. He decided to walk them off.

David came across a small park full of children from the Navy chapel nursery school. Mesmerized by their joy and innocence, he sat on a bench and watched. He smiled at their ability to ignore the horrific events that raged around them. He thought of the tragic impact the war had already had on his family. His father and brother were gone, his mother and the little ones were alone. He began to weep, as much for the loss of his own innocence as for the loss of his family.

Across the park, Theresa watched him as she shooed children back onto the playground. She recognized the naval aviator wings and medals hanging from his tunic, and knew he had already seen intense combat. *He's no older than I am,* she thought.

Her fellow nursery school teacher walked up next to her.

"Uh-oh, he looks drunk," she said, eying David. "We'd better call shore patrol."

"No, Betty," said Theresa. "He will get written up. I'll drive him to the BOQ."

Betty looked at her much younger friend and then at David.

"He is kind of cute, but I'd suggest the hospital. Look at his side."

A small spot of red was beginning to grow on his white tunic.

"I better get him out of here," Theresa said, concerned. "Can you get the kids back to the chapel?"

"Sure, honey. But listen, that's no hurt puppy over there—more like a wounded snake."

"Betty, don't be silly. He is a boy."

"Sweetie, he didn't get that Navy Cross acting like a boy."

"I'll be fine. I know how to handle officers."

"You be careful, and I want a call in fifteen minutes at the chapel, or I will call the shore patrol."

Theresa relented.

"Okay, okay. I'll call or be back by then."

They lined up the kids, who still had not noticed Ensign David "Kid" Brennan. With all her ducklings in a row, Betty led them toward the chapel, a short block away. She turned back to Theresa, put her hands on either side of her chin and made fangs by extending her index fingers, and nodded to David, who was now sound asleep, still sitting upright on the bench. Theresa laughed and waved her away.

She studied him closely as he slept. A boy in a man's uniform, she thought. A lock of hair had fallen on his forehead, accentuating his youth. She knew he would be a handsome man, but his baby face only allowed for cute now. Yet there was something about him; she felt a tingling across her body as she stood so close. Inexplicably, she got the notion that this boy would be her man. She couldn't shake it. It made no sense. She had never even seen him before. The stirring inside of her rose and would not be shouted down by reason. Gently, she touched his face with the back of her hand.

"Ensign, wake up."

"Let me sleep, Mom. I'll do the chores later...."

Theresa began to giggle. She calmly composed herself and then used a sharper tone.

"Ensign, on your feet!"

He jerked awake, looking around confused.

"Where am I?"

"Fantasy Island." Theresa smiled.

"What?"

"We are in a park on Ford Island. Come on, we have to get you to your BOQ."

"I don't have a room; I'm on the Suwannee."

"Well, you can't go up the gangway like this."

She knew it was a lie. More drunk sailors had gone up that gangway in the last few days than you could count. Theresa didn't know why she said it, but she felt no remorse. As she pulled him to his feet, he winced. The red spot was growing. She tried to take his arm, but he jerked away in obvious pain. He tried to steady himself by holding onto the park bench. When Kid reached out and his sleeve hiked up, she saw the bandages on his arm. Not knowing where to grab him, Theresa caught his high choker collar.

Once she had him underway, she marched him toward her car. Holding him up by the collar, she opened the passenger door and pushed him in. Immediately, David passed out again. Theresa positioned him on the high-backed Chevy seat and then fumbled through the glove box until she found a pair of her father's sunglasses. Carefully, she put them on his face to cover his closed eyes and then shut the door. Next, she expertly closed the convertible top, hooked it in place, and jumped in the driver seat. *Now what?* she thought.

Nervously—excitedly—she drove through the family housing area. Glancing down at the blood spot on his tunic, Theresa decided to end her adventure at the hospital.

CHAPTER 7

Irish found J.T. at the dining room table studying their plan. Looking up from the charts, he smiled at Irish and winked.

"Home so soon, Romeo?"

"Damn Brits, they close their pubs so early it's hard for a man to—"

J.T. held up his hand, laughing. He sat down, poured two glasses of scotch, and slid one across the massive table. Irish caught the glass before it fell off the other side.

"It doesn't work, you know."

"What?" Irish demanded incredulously.

"The plan. It doesn't add up."

"Yes, I know," he responded, clearing his throat. Irish took a long pull of his scotch, swirled it around, and then took another. Letting out a loud sigh, he leaned over the plans, shaking his head, and asked, "Now what?"

Both men sensed a presence and looked up to see a nondescript man: average height, average brown hair, and grey eyes. He stood at the head of the table with rain dripping off of his coat, plinking on the floor to announce him. J.T. subconsciously began to cover the classified documents strewn across the table. Irish moved slowly toward a .45 caliber pistol lying on the corner of the table.

"It's okay, gentlemen. Agent Shanower, OSS." He held out a wallet with a badge and new type of picture ID.

Irish was quite obviously unimpressed.

"So what can we do for the Office of Secret Spies?" he sniffed.

"It's Office of Special Services, actually." Then, realizing Irish was yanking his chain, Shanower got to the point: "I need transportation."

"Where to?" snapped Irish.

"Europe, parachute drop, undetected. Obviously low level, and at night."

"Well, la-di-da," Irish quipped.

"General Smith thought you could help me," Shanower continued. "Apparently, he was wrong."

"C.R. sent you to us?" J.T. asked.

"That is correct, Colonel Dobbs. He also mentioned you might be able to accommodate me discreetly. I have a letter."

He handed a sealed letter to J.T., who opened it. He had no doubt the spy had already read it. After he finished, J.T. handed it to Irish. The OSS officer smiled as Irish had to hold the letter at arm's length under a candelabrum.

Dear J.T. –

Sorry to drop this on you unannounced, but obviously, it is a security requirement. This is strictly on a need-to-know level. All I can tell you is that this young man is headed for a world of hurt. The President asks that you do us a favor and take care of him. I don't think he is long for this world!

C.R.

PS: Great about the Brennan kid—he will have a story to tell.

Kate entered the room, pushing a cart of coffee and sandwiches. She was startled at the presence of the stranger.

"Kate, this is Mr. Shanower, he is with—"

"Navy Supply Corps, Ma'am."

She nodded, uneasy, as he smiled at her.

"He will be with us a few weeks," said J.T., "at C.R.'s personal request."

"Welcome, Mr. Shanower. I'll have a second guest room prepared."

"Dan. Please call me Dan."

Kate nodded while she maneuvered the wheeled cart to the far end of the table. As she poured two cups, she whispered to J.T. and Irish. "Supply Corps, my ass."

"Why, Mrs. Dobbs—such language," Irish tsk-tsked.

"Shut up, Irish," she whispered back.

"Mr. Shanower—ah, Dan," she said, turning to him, "please join us for a snack."

"Wait a minute," said Irish. "You said a second guest room."

"Boy, nothing gets by your Gaelic intellect," she replied. "Mark Hass is upstairs drying off."

"What is this, a barracks?" he demanded.

11:28 Local, 28FEB (21:28 GMT, 28FEB)
Ford Island, Naval Air Station Pearl Harbor

Theresa sped down the street to the base medical facility. Turning into the parking lot, she came bumper to bumper with a shore patrol jeep. They were wrestling a drunken sailor out of the back. He had been in a fight and not done well. She backed up quickly before they noticed her. Remembering what Betty told her, she glanced at her watch. *Oh, no. Seven minutes!*

Theresa gunned the engine and drove away, headed for a pay phone—any pay phone. She searched her purse but couldn't find a nickel.

"Ensign, do you have a nickel?" she asked her passenger. There was no response.

Glancing at her watch again, she noted that five minutes were left. Out of time and ideas, Theresa drove to her house. Luckily the garage door was open. She bounced up her drive and screeched to a stop, banging Kid off the dash just before hitting the back wall. Jumping out of the car, she quickly yanked down the garage door.

She left David in the car and scurried around her little house, snapping closed the drapes. Then she sprinted for the phone on the kitchen wall, dialing as she looked at her watch. Thirty seconds to spare. Betty picked up after a single ring.

"You like to cut it close, girlie. I was calling shore patrol!"

"I told you I would be fine." Theresa tried very hard to control her breathing. "This entire event has kind of gotten to me. If you don't mind, I'm going to call it a day."

"What are you up to, Theresa?"

"What? Don't be silly. The last time I saw that boy, he was passed out."

Satisfied, Betty hung up. Theresa went back out to the garage. David had not moved except to slump onto her side of the seat after her rough landing. He was sleeping peacefully. She had planned to leave him there, but saw now that the wound was really bleeding. *Oh, no. I must have done that!*

Struggling to get him out of the car, she finally realized if she pulled him under the arms, he wouldn't yelp. Once inside, she got him into her father's study where she put him on a leather couch. A picture of her father, in the same choker white uniform, was on an end table. Theresa placed it face down.

A thought entered her mind and she acted on it immediately. Running back to the phone, she pulled the white pages from a shelf and frantically paged through them. She stopped on Honolulu General Hospital and called the Emergency Room, asking to speak to the head nurse.

"How may I help you?" came a warm voice through the line.

"Hi… ah… my name is Mrs. Smith. My husband just returned from the Pacific. He has a wound in his side and some burns. He has started to bleed, a bit, but won't go to the hospital. I just want to make sure."

"Okay, sweetie—I mean Mrs. Smith—you need to take a look at it."

"Take a look?"

"Sure," said the head nurse casually. "Just pull off the dressing and see what type wound it is. If it is a bullet wound, it will be stuffed with gauze. A shrapnel wound will be stitched. Both will give off a bit of discharge with, ah…activity. Check it. As long as it is not bleeding profusely or the stitches ripped, you will be fine. Keep the burns clean and covered."

Thanking her, Theresa hung up and got her father's first aid kit out of the trunk of the car. She entered the room and kneeled next to the couch. With trembling hands, she released the large brass buttons of the young ensign's uniform, revealing his thin, muscled body. Because of the tropical heat, David had not worn a T-shirt under his tunic.

A feeling of erotic wickedness swept over her as she un-hooked the three clasps on his collar. She touched his chest. It felt cool as her blood coursed hot.

CHAPTER 8

19:48 Local, 01MAR (05:48 GMT, 01MAR)
Ford Island Family Housing, Pearl Harbor

As a gentle sun set over the ocean, Theresa waited for a green flash that never seemed to come. Watching it slip below the horizon, her thoughts turned to her young ensign. He slept quietly, but her tormented mind raced out of control.

She decided to distract herself with activity and went inside to make a nice dinner. She pulled two Kansas City strip steaks—her father's favorite—out of the small freezer and unwrapped them. She ran cold water over the raw meat, reviving her senses.

Theresa got busy setting the table, not even conscious she had put out the fine china. After placing two big potatoes in the oven, she sprinkled the steaks with garlic salt and ground pepper. She put them on a heavy pewter tray and set it on top of the oven to finish thawing.

Moving with an awkward urgency, she prepared fresh asparagus and a simple salad of greens and tomatoes. Theresa turned to go outside and start a fire. David stood in front of her, stripped to the waist.

"Uh, hi," he said, looking around, trying to hide his confusion.

"Hi." Her voice quivered slightly.

"Where am I ... how did I get here?" he asked, and whispered under his breath, "This is getting to be a habit."

"I found you in the park. I didn't want you to get in trouble."

She opened the cabinet and took out a glass, filled it with water from a pitcher in the refrigerator, and handed it to him. He eagerly accepted it.

"Thanks," said David. "Where's here?"

"You are in Captain Jameson's quarters. I'm his daughter, Theresa."

Ensign David "Kid" Brennan USNR, recipient of the Navy Cross, involuntarily spewed cool water across the kitchen. Theresa giggled.

"It's okay," she said. "He's ... he's not here."

"At sea?"

"He was."

"Your mom?"

"She died a few years ago." Her voice trailed to a whisper. "We are alone."

Theresa knew she should have felt vulnerable. She didn't.

"I'm sorry about your mom." He was quiet for a moment. "What do you mean, 'he was at sea'?"

"He was killed in a naval battle near Guadalcanal."

David looked up suddenly.

"What ship?"

"The DeHaven."

He looked back down slowly, nodding his head knowingly.

"Were you there?" she asked in a voice so hushed, he could hear the clock tick.

Without looking up, in a voice nearly as quiet as hers, he merely replied, "Yes."

After a moment he continued, "I lost my father and brother in China last year."

They stood silently staring at each other, not with awkwardness but with shared experience—shared pain—neither knowing what to say to the other but somehow drawing comfort from it.

"Do you know what happened to my uniform?"

"I'm sorry. I was washing the blood out."

Somehow she found it very funny and laughed. David joined in.

"I'll get it," she said.

When she returned with his uniform, David gingerly pulled it on over the bandages on his arms. He checked the fresh dressing on his wound before he buttoned it, feeling the warmth from the cleansed area that had been ironed dry.

"Did you do this, too?" he asked.

"Yes."

"Thanks, it's a good job."

"Are you hungry … what is your name?"

"David, and yes, ma'am, I'm hungry. I don't think I've eaten today."

16:08 Local, 01MAR (08:08 GMT, 01MAR)
Mindoro Island, The Philippines

Butler leaned back, basking in the soft rays of the sun, absorbing their serenity. He thought of his home in Arkansas for the first time in weeks. He longed for it, knowing it would be as foreign when he returned, as this land had once seemed to him. What he really longed for was no responsibility, no life or death in his hands. No more blood on them. He longed to just be.

"Captain."

He did not respond, too far away in his own thoughts to hear."

"Captain Butler."

With his mind so far away it did not recognize a surname let alone rank.

"Dave!"

His mind did recognize his first name. He looked up to see Sergeant Paul Donnelly, Regular Army, from south Boston.

"Sorry, Paul," Butler said, coming back to the present. "What's up?"

"We just got an action order from the Supreme Commander, South West Pacific Area."

"MacArthur himself? What for? Why us?"

"Shit, sir, I don't know. Some radio station needs to be blown up. I guess we are the only suckers that answered the call."

22:41 Local, 01MAR (08:41 GMT, 01MAR)
Ford Island Family Housing, Pearl Harbor

Candlelight flickered in Theresa's eyes. David was drawn to the reflected light and what was behind its distraction. Neither spoke much during dinner. They explored each other's eyes and facial features in the soft light instead. They were comfortable in each other's presence. In fact, they reveled in the pure joy of being with another person and the excitement and anticipation of sexuality.

Forced to grow up in their teens and accept the tragedy of adulthood, they hungered for the joys. They craved companionship, each sharing a lonely past. There was no need to speak. They would move toward an uncertain future together—at least for a night.

Later, David stood alone in the study, looking at the rising moon through the wall of open casement windows. A breeze of perfect temperature caressed his body. He heard a single clink of glass on glass behind him and turned. His eyes fell upon Theresa, her perfect body covered only by moonlight.

"Champagne?" she asked.

22:48 Local, 02MAR (14:48 GMT, 02MAR)
Mindoro Island, Philippines

Captain Dave Butler, US Army, watched the moonlight glisten off the Sibuyan Sea from his mountain perch. The shimmering body of water outlined the individual islands of the Philippine chain. It was hard to imagine violence in the presence of such tranquility. He was trying to comprehend the entire world at war: the unspeakable cruelty that throbbed across the globe, that he had both seen and done. Sitting on this peaceful spot, it seemed impossible, all of it.

Butler and Donnelly squatted over the communal rice bowl, eating with their hands. One other American, three Filipinos, and four aboriginal Negrito tribesmen joined them. Through mouthfuls of rice and fish, they discussed their mission.

"At least it's close, Captain."

"Yeah, I guess that's the good news, Kowalski."

"How important could it be, Sibuyan Island? It's in the middle of nowhere," Sergeant Donnelly said, shaking his head.

"Maybe that's exactly why," Butler replied.

All those who could speak English turned toward him.

"Look," he said, "it is in the middle of all the islands. If you wanted to reach the most troops, you'd put it in the middle."

He pointed to a map hanging on the wall.

CHAPTER 9

06:45 Local, 04MAR (06:45 GMT, 04MAR)
Over the English Channel

B-17 Flying Fortresses stretched out for as far as the eye could see. Hundreds of them, in battle formation, flew toward the enemy. A thousand fingers waited to release a million rounds of .50 caliber in their defense.

Around-the-clock bombing had seemed like a good idea on paper. However, it meant someone had to do it in daylight. The Americans had drawn the short straw. Hass-man found himself in the middle of the gargantuan formation, leading a division—chosen by rank, not experience, because no one had much time in the Thunderbolt and none in combat.

Blue, crystal-clear sky wrapped the earth, its only impurity the long, man-made clouds streaming from a thousand engines. Contrails, created by cold, moist air hitting hot engines, pointed an accusing finger at each aircraft in the formation. Hass-man knew it wouldn't be long before a German reception would show up.

Crossing over France, he waited nervously for the black dots that would grow into Me-109s and Fokker 190s. Nothing was on the horizon. Then without warning, forty Me-109s slashed through the formation from the rear quarter, their guns and cannons blazing. So quick was the attack, no one saw it coming. Giving chase, the Thunderbolts dove after the Germans. Hass-man's heavy P-47 accelerated so suddenly at emergency power that he almost overshot the trailing Me-109.

Not knowing what else to do, he pulled the trigger, igniting his eight M2 Browning .50 caliber machine guns. His target flamed dramatically as he flew past the debris. Hass-man found himself in the middle of a large German formation. They were as surprised as he was at his predicament. Forty against four was not good odds, especially with the combat experience on the side of the forty.

A swirling dogfight raged over the peaceful French countryside. Joined by the rest of the squadron, Hass's division fought like tigers. But the Germans were good, too good. First one, then a second of his wingmen spiraled to the earth in flames. Above them, a second wave of German fighters attacked the bombers unmolested. Falling B-17s began to fill the airspace between the bomber formation and the farm fields below. Parachutes blossomed as the Flying Fortresses spilled their warriors across the sky. Not all would escape: some spun while others exploded in mid-flight, taking their crews with them. The slaughter was staggering.

Confusion reigned. Hass-man, in a fight for his own life, continued to bend his Thunderbolt to its structural limits. There were so many aircraft in the morning sky that a midair collision was the biggest danger. He would turn hard, dodge another Thunderbolt, shoot at a 109, and then turn hard again as tracers streaked over his canopy. Aircraft were everywhere, all of them trying to kill or evade.

Then, just as suddenly as they had appeared, the 109s vanished. Fuel expended, the surviving Thunderbolts turned for home. Navigation wouldn't be necessary; a trail of carnage marked the way. Black plumes rose from the earth, marking where the airborne violence had smashed the peace of the countryside.

With the safety of Dover's white cliffs in sight, Hass-man looked around, counting his squadron. Many were gone. *What a disaster,* he thought, and then he remembered the unescorted bombers still over France. He wouldn't be surprised if none of them made it back.

17:38 Local, 05MAR (17:38 GMT, 05MAR)
Kate's Manor, Bowdown House, Greenham Common, England

A storm had swept through the English countryside with such fury that the electricity was still out. J.T. and Irish, surrounded by heavy silver candelabras, worked on in spite of the outage. A large fire crackled in the oversized stone fireplace. J.T.'s concentration was broken by a rhythmic drip on the floor. He looked up to see Captain Shanower, OSS, soaked head-to-

toe. His wool suit clung to him, accentuating his slender build. J.T. couldn't help but laugh.

"I thought all you spies wore trench coats."

"They give us away."

"For God's sake," Irish bellowed, "look at the waif! With that fedora, the skinny bastard looks like a railroad spike."

Shanower shook the rain off of his hat, looking at the laughing pair in annoyance.

"Ha ha, very funny. Any chance we can go tonight?"

"In this shit?" snapped Irish.

"Yes, it would help my... situation."

J.T. gripped Irish's wrist, cutting off the conversation.

"Okay, Spike," he said, bestowing on the secret agent his brand new nickname. "We can drop you in tonight. Care to tell us where?"

Spike spread a map of France on the table and pointed to a remote field deep inside German lines. J.T. and Irish looked at each other with raised brows.

"Son," Irish asked finally, "do you expect to live through the night?"

08:45 Local, 05MAR (18:45 GMT, 05MAR)
The Island of Oahu, Hawaii

They were inseparable. They had roamed the island of Oahu, its mountains, beaches, and waterfalls, making each place their own. Enthralled with the mere presence of each other, titillated by touch, they had lived and loved more in the last five days then most would in a lifetime.

"David, would you get that?" Theresa called from the kitchen.

David stood, dumbstruck, trying to register why a commodore, an admiral's aide and his own commanding officer were standing on the doorstep. Before he could come to any conclusion, the commodore punched him in the nose.

Theresa had peeked out of the kitchen just in time to see the impact. She ran to his rescue.

"Stop it!" she shrieked.

"Stay out of this, Theresa," warned the grizzled senior officer. "This scallywag has taken liberties, and he shall pay for his transgressions."

He stalked forward for further action.

"We are *married!*" she shouted.

Theresa held up her hand, displaying a simple gold band, and then reached down to hold up David's. He lay stunned on the floor, bleeding from his left nostril.

Commodore Pierce stopped.

"Oh!" he said. "My apologies—I mean congratulations. When did this happen?"

"Yesterday, Commodore, at the base chapel."

"Well, the goddamned chaplain could have told me!"

"Sir, your language," whispered the aide.

"Oh, yes. Excuse me, Theresa," said the commodore, collecting himself. "Lieutenant Commander Jasper, schedule a proper reception, tonight 18:00."

"Yes, sir," replied Jasper. "Done deal."

"Excellent. Let's leave the newlyweds alone until then, shall we?"

"Yes, sir," both officers replied in unison.

As the commodore and his aide made their way to the staff car, Skipper Jasper helped Theresa get David off the floor.

"Thank God you did the right thing, Kid," he said. "He was going to hang you from the highest yardarm in Pearl! Eighteen hundred, mister, full dress whites. Do NOT be late."

Still stunned David gave a weak reply. "Aye aye, sir."

01:18 Local, 06MAR (01:18 GMT, 06MAR)
The English Channel

Bathed in red cockpit lights and buffeted by hostile air currents, J.T. struggled to keep the wingtips of the C-47 out of the frothing surf.

"Geez, Spike, could you have picked a worse night?"

"Radar can't see us through all this bad weather." Shanower motioned toward the windscreen with his chin. "Cliff ahead."

With his attention redirected forward, J.T. heaved back on the yoke, barely clearing a coastal village and the cliffs of the Brittany coast. Headed south, they buzzed the German position in Brittany. Then they turned hard to the east, coming to a course of 120 degrees, knowing that their position and relative course would be reported as over Brittany, headed south.

ENDGAME

16:45 Local, 05MAR (02:45 GMT, 06MAR)
Ford Island Officers Club, Naval Base Pearl Habor

In four short hours, the main dining room of the Ford Island Officers Club had been transformed into a formal reception hall. White wedding bells hung from each of the chandeliers. Magnolia centerpieces were on each of the white linen-covered tables. A hastily baked, four-tier wedding cake was on its own small table, centered perfectly in the room. An unsheathed sword lay on the table, waiting to cut the cake.

Commodore Pierce's wife had been close friends with Theresa's mother; she had sprung into action after being informed of the situation by her husband. A mother of four boys, she also knew this would be her only opportunity to plan a wedding correctly. She and the commodore had also eloped; this opportunity would not be squandered.

The commodore's aide had also executed an immediate action plan. He called all the commands in port, requesting the presence of their officers and wives—a not-so-subtle demand. Wives scurried all over the Pearl Harbor complex, searching for dresses, shoes, and wedding gifts. Husbands hurried home to ready dress white uniforms.

03:48 Local, 06MAR (03:48 GMT, 06MAR)
In the Air Over France

Updating his navigation plot, just north of Orleans, J.T. turned eighteen degrees farther south, hoping to further complicate any attempted tracking of their route. He plotted a course that would take them between Lyon to the south and Dijon to the north, and sweetened up the course for a small farmer's field outside Saint-Amour, France. It was not lost on the aviators that they would be twenty-five miles from the Swiss border. Less than an hour later, they approached the drop zone.

"You better stand in the door, Spike. We are five minutes out. Good luck!"

"Roger that, J.T. Save me a bottle of McLaren."

Spike disappeared into the dark cabin of the C-47.

J.T. focused outside the cockpit, looking for a directional light—a bright light in a tube. The tube allowed the French resistance to point the light at them, and no one on the ground would be able to see it.

"Two minutes," Irish called out and then flipped on the yellow pre-jump light in the cabin next to the door.

"How high are we?" asked J.T.

"Three-to-four-hundred feet above the ground... there!" Irish pointed to a pinprick of bright light as J.T. climbed a couple hundred more feet. Irish flipped on the green light.

Spike plunged into the night and the unknown. A180-mile-per-hour wind hit him in the face as it swept him past the tail. A static line attached to the back of his T-10 parachute fed out, popping free of rubber-band holders. Too low for an emergency backup chute, Spike's only thought was, *I hope this works.* Snapping to the end of its travel, the static line snatched off the parachute's cover, deploying with a tremendous jolt. All ear-shattering noise from wind and aircraft abruptly stopped and the canopy blossomed with a loud pop.

Hanging in the silent air, Spike listened to the drone of the C-47 trail away. *Well, I'm committed now.*

18:00 Local, 05MAR (04:00 GMT, 06MAR)
Ford Island Officers Club, Naval Base Pearl Habor

Mrs. Pierce had demanded that LCDR Jasper arrange for an arch of swords, and upon arrival in the commodore's staff car precisely five hours and fifteen minutes later, the couple stepped under the arch. Eight of David's squadron mates, four on each side of the sidewalk, stood at attention, holding swords overhead at arm's length. The tips touched, forming an arch of steel.

Theresa wore a white gown borrowed from a newly-arrived wife of the same size. The two young newlyweds walked tentatively through the arch, embarrassed at the sudden attention. On the steps, Mrs. Pierce had arranged the crowd perfectly. They were clapping as the final two swords slowly lowered, blocking the path for the couple.

Lieutenant Stutzman, the next man back on Theresa's side, swung his sword, swatting her on the bottom with the broadside.

"Welcome to the Navy!"

Polite applause turned to cheers.

04:00 Local, 06MAR (04:00 GMT, 06MAR)
In the Air Over France

Spike released the bag of gear strapped to his harness. It fell ten feet until a lanyard yanked it to a halt and held it in place below him. The heavy bag helped stabilize the parachute as he continued to descend. As he dropped below the tree line, darkness rose up from below. Spike knew the ground was close. He got in the proper PLF (parachute, landing, fall) position: feet and knees together and slightly bent, elbows in, fists in front of his face. He heard the gear's impact, *ten feet!*

On impact, Spike swiveled his hips and twisted his upper torso in the same direction. He made contact with his calves, thighs, and the muscles of his back. Rolling immediately to his feet, in one motion he grabbed the parachute, deflated it, and froze, listening. No sound. Quickly he unsnapped his harness, dropping it silently to the ground and pulled a Walther PPK out of his shoulder harness.

A challenge came out of the darkness, "Viva?"

"Lafayette," was Spike's whispered response.

French resistance members swarmed around him, grabbing the equipment and gathering up his parachute rig. They moved quickly to the edge of the field where they threw the parachute in a pre-dug hole and buried it. Spike noticed it was big enough for a man. They would be putting his body in the hole now, had he given an incorrect code word. At first light, the field would be plowed by a trusted French farmer.

Without a word spoken, the group disappeared into the night.

CHAPTER 10

The jungle welcomed him back. Like a lover once spurned, it was changed. Antagonistic, not indifferent, it seemed intent on claiming him this time—for all eternity. Captain Butler felt intimidated; he too had changed. He glanced back at the Bonka boat as it quietly slipped away from the shore. Tentatively, he led his men into the dark foliage. He peered at the radio station through binoculars that magnified the moonlight as well as the objects in them. He shook his head and handed them to Sergeant Donnelly. "Ever see anything like that?"

"Not in my life," replied Donnelly. "I suspect that is why they want it blown up."

Corporal Kowalski had crawled up on his belly next to them. He glanced over the ridgeline without the aid of binoculars. "Radar," he whispered confidently.

"Excuse me?" Butler asked.

"Yes, sir. I saw it in *Popular Science*. Right before it all hit the fan. This radar can see aircraft and ships hundreds of miles away. By using Doppler Shift as a measurement, it basically pulses an RF signal out, bounces it off the target, and then times the return, for distance."

Both Butler and Donnelly looked at each other dumbfounded and then turned back to Kowalski.

Donnelley spoke softly. "Any idea how to blow it up?"

"Sure, Sarge," Kowalski replied. "The antennae are the key, and that small control room. Take those out and it's useless. All the other buildings are to house generators, transmitters. Run-of-the-mill stuff, easily replaced."

"There are a lot of antennae over there," Butler replied, looking through the binoculars. "I don't know if we have enough TNT."

"Oh yes, sir," said the corporal. "More than enough. All we really have to do is bend them up; it will mess with the frequency attenuation. They will be just as useless as if we had blown them to smithereens."

Kowalski slithered away to count the sticks of dynamite, leaving both of his superiors to stare at each other in disbelief.

10:27 Local, 06MAR (10:27 GMT, 06MAR)
Kate's Manor, Bowdown House, Greenham Common, England

Irish and J.T. sat at the kitchen table, still in flight jackets and rumpled uniforms. They were eating bacon and fresh eggs, sipping cool milk. Kate walked in and greeted them casually.

"Hello boys, how was your night with the supply corps?"

Their bloodshot eyes did not see the humor, causing Kate to laugh.

"You two knuckleheads are way too old for this. Here—" she handed them a sealed envelope. "Your favorite supply officer left this for you."

"What is it?" J.T. grumbled.

"I suspect an invitation to another nocturnal adventure."

J.T. slowly took the held-out letter and opened it. Slipping on his "cheaters," he read it twice. With a grimace, he slipped it across the table to Irish, who read it quickly and then consulted his chart.

"Holy sh—"

"Language!" warned Kate.

"Yes, dear," Irish sighed. "So sorry, dear."

Irish slid the chart across the table so J.T. could see the point he had his finger on. It rested at the foot of the Alps, near the Swiss border.

"Long way, my Irish friend."

"Yes, and getting just a smidge off course would not be good. Spike is really beginning to get on my nerves!"

00:30 Local, 06MAR (10:30 GMT, 06MAR)
Ford Island Officers Club, Naval Base Pearl Harbor

David and Theresa had sat all evening at the head table. They were at the place of honor, in the middle. Commodore Pierce and his wife were on Theresa's right. To the left of David sat Lieutenant Commander Jasper and Lieutenant Stutzman. They were truly an odd couple: Jazz, small with a red mustache and crown of hair, and Stutz, tall with a full, unruly head of brown hair. Every time Theresa looked over at them, she giggled.

Formal and proper, more due to the presence of the commodore's wife than himself, the party ended at half-past midnight. The newlyweds were escorted to the waiting staff car that now trailed strings of cans. As Theresa got in, Betty caught her eye. She was making the same fangs as before, in the park. It seemed a lifetime ago. Theresa laughed out loud and fell into David's lap in the backseat. She leaned out the window and kissed Mrs. Pierce, thanking her, as the car began to move. "Your mother would have been so proud," the older woman gushed, eyes welling.

"Let the kids go," Commodore Pierce snapped, pulling his wife away from the car.

Finally alone except for the driver, Theresa spoke to David for what seemed like the first time that night. "Now, where do we go, David?"

"I don't know—"

"Sir, if I may interrupt?" said their chauffeur.

"Please do, Petty Officer."

"Your commanding officer directed me to take you to the Royal Hawaiian Hotel, compliments of the Fighting Twenty-Seventh," he said, handing an envelope back to Theresa. "Ma'am, this is from the commodore and his wife."

She opened it and began to cry.

"What's wrong, Theresa?" David asked, alarmed.

"It is from Housing. They've assigned my dad's house to us."

"Well, that is good news, not bad. Why are you crying?"

"I'm just so happy!"

David traded a quick glance in the rearview mirror with the petty officer, who returned an almost imperceptible shrug.

"Last week," Theresa went on, partly to herself, "I had nothing and no one. Now I have everything."

19:33 Local, 06MAR (11:33 GMT, 06MAR)
Sibuyan Island, The Philippines

Butler made his way through the tropical forest, more a part of it than an intruder. Even though his presence had an underlying feel of hostility, he seemed to float silently like the Negrito tribesmen alongside him. Butler moved effortlessly toward the target, deeper into the jungle's heart again.

A platoon of Japanese marines guarded the complex. Their tactical deployment verified that they, too, did not understand radar: the antennas were left unguarded; the marines' perimeter encircled the buildings.

Butler's men moved around the Japanese defenses and toward the ignored antennas. Once in position, they waited for the total darkness that the setting of the moon would bring.

01:33 Local, 06MAR (19:33 GMT, 06MAR)
Royal Hawaiian Hotel

When David and Theresa arrived in the bridal suite, they found it full of flowers, chocolates, and champagne. They walked out onto the balcony, hand in hand, and watched the moon set. Both realized they would never be alone again. Neither feared the future, even the war. They would face it together.

Late that night they slipped down to the beach, wearing only the robes they had found in the room. After walking to a secluded spot, they went for a skinny dip—not returning until just before dawn.

03:33 Local, 07MAR (1:33 GMT, 06MAR)
Sibuyan Island, The Philippines

Like a prehistoric skeleton of a long fallen beast, the antennas jutted out of the tropical underbrush. Kowalski weaved among its bones, placing charges. They had decided—actually, Kowalski had decided—that blowing up the control room was too risky of an approach. He reasoned that without the antennas, it would be useless. After rigging the explosives, he made his way back to cover.

At 03:48, they moved out of hiding again. The few Japanese troops that were awake focused on the tree line of their free fire zone around the buildings. Overlooking the sea, the antennas were well away from the rest of the facility. It would allow for an easy escape. Donnelly decided to rig an insurance policy with the TNT intended for the control room; he set a booby trap on their intended escape route.

Precisely at 04:00, Kowalski pushed the plunger. Six explosions violated the pre-dawn silence. The men moved quickly down the trail, away from the Japanese position, stopping only to set the tripwire on a grenade taped to the excess TNT. Eight minutes later, an explosion rattled the jungle, causing her creatures to howl in approval. As human screams mixed in, the warriors melted back into the dark forest.

11:30 Local, 06MAR (21:30 GMT, 06MAR)
Royal Hawaiian Hotel

David answered a soft knock at the door. A bellman handed him a large manila envelope and vanished before he could find a tip. He checked the contents as Theresa walked up and hugged him.

"What is it?" she asked.

"Pictures and a note," he replied, showing them to her.

The note said,

Kid,
You better send these home or your butt will be in a sling.
- Stutz
P.S. Shore leave expires at 22:00 tomorrow, enjoy.

"I know we are young," Theresa said, "but I don't think it is right they keep calling you a kid. After all, you are an officer and a naval aviator."

He looked a little sheepish as he turned to her.

"Well, actually it is my radio call sign—a nickname, kind of."

"My dad told me you airdales had funny names." Theresa giggled and then suddenly looked very serious. "Your mother is going to hate me."

"Nah, she'll love you. Me, I'm not so sure!"

CHAPTER 11

Captain Mark Hass sat inside a hastily constructed Quonset hut, the operations building for the 56th Fighter Group. On the stage was the wing commander of the 56th, a very young colonel whose senior rank contrasted with his youthful appearance. It was something that Col. Mark Berry, as well as the rest of the Army Air Corps, had gotten used to.

"Gentlemen," he began, "today we will put up a maximum effort fighter sweep for a classified raid. The sky is forecast to be crystal clear. We can expect a similar response from the Luftwaffe."

He let it sink in for a moment, taking note of those who smiled in anticipation. They would be his tigers and flight leads in the future.

"Secure all doors and windows," he said.

All around the room, men rose and closed all the windows and pulled heavy, dark curtains across them. Behind Berry, a strange-looking picture flashed onto the screen. Antennae jutted out from a large lattice steel frame, mounted to a pivoting base.

"This brief is top secret," he continued, "and this is how they keep getting in our knickers."

He went on to explain the basics of radar and ground-controlled intercept—how the Freya radar could see them, even in clouds, and then radio the German fighters onto their six. After the briefing, the crews hurried out of the room so they could brief their flights and ready their aircraft. Hass waited for the room to clear and moved to the stage.

"Sir," he said, "a moment."

Colonel Berry turned to face the captain, older than himself.

"A very quick moment, Captain," he replied.

"Yes, sir," said Hass. "Do we have the control frequencies?"

"Why?"

"I speak German."

The younger officer looked sharply at Hass-man. "How well?"

"Fluently. English is my second language."

Berry turned to his intel officer.

"Get the frequencies and give them to Captain—"

"Hass, sir."

"Captain Hass, pull your division out of the gaggle and form on my left wing. If you get actionable intel, take the lead. No radio transmissions. Maybe we can surprise them for a change."

22:36 Local, 06MAR (04:36 GMT, 07MAR)
Aviation Officer Candidate School, Naval Air Station Pensacola

Sergeant Major M.L. Paillou, United States Marine Corps, sat at his desk, tapping a pencil mindlessly. Inactivity was the ultimate enemy of a true warrior. He worked out twice a day and was back in peak physical shape, wounds fully healed. However, Paillou felt his combat skills fading; he needed to get back in the fight. His wish was answered with a knock on his doorjamb.

"Paillou, you old devil dog, what in the hell are you doing slacking off with a bunch of squid airdale wannabes?"

He looked up to see his old commanding officer from the China Burma campaign, Jim Russell. Glancing at his uniform, Paillou noticed the rank of Lieutenant Colonel; when he last saw Russell, he was two ranks junior.

"Were you a major all of a week, Lieutenant Colonel?" asked Paillou.

Russell closed the door behind him.

"About the same amount of time you were a first sergeant," he replied.

Paillou smiled his wicked smile. "Touché, Colonel."

"It's still Jim with a closed door, Mike. We've been through too much together."

Paillou smiled and nodded. He got up, shook Russell's hand, and gave him a bear hug. He went back to his desk and pulled out two glasses and a bottle of scotch. Reaching behind his desk for a water pitcher, he filled each glass a quarter full and then added an equal amount of scotch.

"What's up, Jim?"

"I need someone I can trust."

"Do tell?"

"I've been given a battalion, Second of the Twenty Ninth, Sixth Marine Division."

"Operation Iceberg?" asked Paillou.

"How the hell do you know about that?"

Paillou shrugged and flashed his most devious smile.

Russell shook his head in disbelief. He couldn't believe the sergeant major was even aware of the code name of the Okinawa invasion plan. He also knew instantly that he had made the right choice.

Paillou downed his scotch, poured another and asked, "And—?"

"I need a battalion sergeant major," said Russell, "one I can trust to tell me when I'm wrong."

"I'm in."

Russell held up his hand. He swirled the glass of brown liquid as he contemplated his next words. Deciding on the truth, he downed the scotch and came to the point.

"Have you noticed the female marines?" he asked.

"The BAMs? Who could miss them?"

"Do you know why there are so many?"

Paillou shrugged, pouring both men another scotch and water.

"They look good."

"That they do," said Russell. "Plan is for eighteen thousand of them."

That number got Paillou's attention; the glass froze inches from his lips.

"Not the damn paper pushers!"

It was Russell's turn to shrug. However, his smile was more sickly than devious. The women were indeed replacements for the corps admin troops, so the men could go to war. There was a long pause before he spoke.

"They are emptying offices around the US. We will get thousands of them."

"You have got to be shitting me, Jim." Paillou put down his drink. "Against hardened Japanese troops? Fighting on their home turf for the first time?"

"I won't hold you to it...."

Paillou rebuffed the thought with a wave.

"No. What we need is a plan to sneak in as many war dogs as we can."

"Outstanding," replied Russell. "I thought you'd get on board so I took the liberty of cutting you some orders. We leave for Pendleton in five days. Is that enough time?"

"We will be drinking beer for three of those days." Paillou raised his glass to his lips.

"Excellent." Russell stood up. "Can I bunk with you? I hate the BOQ here—full of drunken aviators raising hell all night."

"Absolutely. I have a hut on the beach—within walking distance of a nice little watering hole called the FloraBama."

06:17 Local, 07MAR (06:17 GMT, 07MAR)
Over the English Channel

An American air armada stretched for miles behind him; Hass-man looked over his shoulder, marveling at the sight. Looking forward, he could not recall ever seeing a clearer day—a good day for the hunters. He looked around again. With the armada and channel behind him and the French coast stretching in front of him, the vista was spectacular. Bits of color jumped out at him from the aircraft and the ground. It was as if he could see forever.

He knew he would never see anything like it again in his life. Mankind was capable of incredible achievements—unfortunately, many of them were made during war. He began to concentrate on the sky ahead, knowing he was not the only pilot to enjoy the visibility.

Hass-man glanced at his briefing card and dialed in a Luftwaffe intercept frequency. He clicked from one to another until he heard directions. The German controller was using simple slang and a crude code that a classically trained linguist would not pick up. Hass-man smiled as he instantly deciphered, "Caesar crosses the Rhine." No doubt it meant the armada was "feet dry" over France.

Their code utilized small German towns referenced to Berlin as the center of the grid. Obviously, Berlin was the armada, the small towns the Luftwaffe. By calling out the small town, it gave the relative location of the bombers. Hass-man quickly reversed the process and drew a rough plot of the Germans' location.

Pushing the throttle up on his Pratt & Whitney R-2800 Dual Wasp engine, Captain Hass fed all eighteen cylinders, that in turn pumped out

ENDGAME

2,100 horsepower. Transformed by the four-bladed Curtis constant-speed propeller into thrust, the twelve-foot disc pushed Hass-man's P-47 past the wing commander.

Colonel Berry relinquished the fighter lead with a silent hand signal. Hass-man accepted the position with a returned signal. Turning the fighters to the northeast, he first accelerated, passing over the top of the bomber formation. So expansive was the B-17 armada, it was like flying low over a landscape of green fields instead of molted green vessels of war.

With their superchargers in high gear, the Thunderbolt fighters quickly climbed above the heavy bombers. Those crews watched jealously, condemned to holding position while their little friends maneuvered to survive and to fight.

Hass-man deciphered and interpolated the course corrections from the German ground-controlled interception (GCI). He knew they were close, and he signaled the rest of the air wing by jettisoning his auxiliary fuel tanks. Drop tanks extended the fighter's range and were shed when they engaged the enemy to increase maneuverability. Glancing in his rearview mirror, he saw the indescribable sight of hundreds of shiny aluminum tanks tumbling to the French countryside, flickering in the morning sun as they fell.

A group of dots appeared, ten o'clock and low, moving away from the fighters toward the B-17s. Without hesitation he snapped his P-47 inverted and pulled hard toward the dots. He centered the nose on the attacking wing of the Luftwaffe fighters. He reached down to his armament panel, toggled the master arm on, and then charged all eight Browning .50 caliber guns with a thump.

Rolling his wings level, Hass centered the piper of his gun sight on the middle of the pack. His intent and duty was to break up the attack. The best way to do that was to fly into the middle of the hornets' nest. Dots grew again into ME-109s as he closed the distance. Angles and lead pursuit allowed him to overtake the Germans. Sweetening up his aim point, he placed the piper on the lead of a four-aircraft division. With the subtle hand movements of a surgeon, he steadied the piper on the wing root as distance closed to two thousand feet.

Careful not to disturb the control stick, he gently pressed the trigger, releasing pandemonium onto the morning. A high-octane-fueled explosion announced the arrival of the 56th Fighter Group. At least ten more 109s flamed as the entire group opened fire.

Completely caught by surprise, the Germans initially made no counter moves as the 56th slashed through their formation, guns blazing. Hass-man blew through, pulling off high and setting up for another attack. Outmaneuvered, the Luftwaffe attempted to dive away in a split-S.

Hass-man rolled, inverted, and gave chase. The heavy Thunderbolts ran down the ME-109s, using gravity and horsepower. The closure rate on the second attack was much more controlled. Hass-man held his fire until fifteen hundred feet before flaming another German. Turning hard left, he engaged the German air wing's leader, who broke left in a maximum G turn. Giving chase, Hass-man matched his eight G pull. By the time they completed one circle, the entire sky was filled with a swirling dogfight. For some reason, his mind noted that the 109 had a yellow tail.

Over one hundred twisting aircraft seemed to fill every square foot of morning air. Grunting hard and contracting stomach and leg muscles, Hass forced blood back into his brain. Even so, his vision began to tunnel as centrifugal force pulled his blood toward his feet.

He got a quick burst at his foe but missed aft. Leveling his wings, the German pulled up. Hass-man matched his move, but before he could get into a firing solution, the German reversed and then rolled inverted. He gave chase as the German flew into the middle of the fur ball of fighters.

Suddenly a P-47 flashed in front of him, flying into its wingtip vortices and causing Hass-man's Thunderbolt to buffet on the edge of control. The wily German escaped. Regaining control of his aircraft, his brain abruptly lost focus as his senses were bombarded by the noise and the tremor of impact. Totally disoriented, he was inside a trashcan being beaten by thugs with baseball bats. Heavy, 20 millimeter cannon fire pummeled him for a fraction of a second more before, out of instinct, he just pulled.

Not knowing exactly where his enemy was, Hass just kept pulling until the noise stopped. Jamming on full emergency power, he desperately looked for his hunter. Leaning all the way back, as far as physically possible, his head was past the headrest—between it and the canopy. He was literally looking behind the aircraft. Finally, he got a tally.

He could see that the 109's nose was not in a position to shoot. However, its position was very offensive. With no other option, Hass-man entered a defensive death spiral, a constant maximum G descending turn; the 109 followed. By descending in the turn, each aircraft could maintain its best turning speed. If either slowed from the best speed, their turn rate would decrease. If they got too fast, the size of the circle they made through the sky would increase. Either case would allow their foe to turn tighter and to get behind them. That would result in a kill.

Round and round they went, circle after circle, each unable to get an advantage. The constant eight Gs pulled the mask off of Hass-man's face—it came to rest under his chin. It didn't matter. With each turn, they lost altitude; soon he wouldn't need the oxygen. He felt the ground getting closer. Taking a quick scan of his altimeter, he saw it pass five thousand feet.

The physical strain was like being in an endless wrestling match. The ground approached. French fields began to reveal trees and houses. They rose slowly from the surface, growing in warning: *Low*, he thought, grunting hard, *I can't hold it much longer!*

Locked in a game of chicken, both knew whoever stopped descending would also slow their turning—and ultimately die. Hass-man gingerly manipulated the controls. Even at high G, especially at high G, the smoothest pilot would win. Unless, of course, he was the first to run out of altitude and thus energy. Big trees came into his peripheral view. Hass-man looked down on the 109—he was winning!

Easing his turn, the German dodged a tree. Hass-man pounced. With engine howling, he buried the stick in his lap—literally pulling for his life. Seeing his move, the 109 pilot made a last-ditch effort to escape by leveling his wings and running. Hass-man opened fire. They were so close to the ground that he could see the rounds hitting the dirt around the fleeing Messerschmitt. *Something is wrong*, he thought, *all my guns aren't firing!*

Time expanded as the guns seemed to spit in slow motion. He had wondered how the yellow-tailed 109 got on his six so quickly. The answer was in front of him. This 109 did not have a yellow tail.

Even with only two guns firing, he began to score hits. It didn't hurt that the German caught a wing on a stone wall, cartwheeling into a freshly plowed field and spewing liquid fire and parts. Hass-man had to pull up to avoid the wreckage.

Absolutely exhausted, he eased the power back to military power and cracked the cowls to cool the red-hot engine. He scanned the sky above and realized he was totally alone. He felt as if he were the last man alive on the planet. Deciding against a climb, he accelerated and hedge-hopped his way, at redline speed, all the way to the English Channel.

21:59 Local, 06MAR (07:59, GMT, 07MAR)
USS Suwannee, Naval Air Station Pearl Harbor

Ensign David "Kid" Brennan ran up the gangway as the boatswain's mates began to retract it. On the quarterdeck, he saluted the flag and requested permission to come aboard. Before even receiving it, he bolted for the handrail and searched the crowd for his bride.

Theresa was easy to find. She stood leaning against her red Chevy under the soft lights of the dock. She wore the white shorts and red halter he had bought for her the day before. He waved until she saw him. Her hair drifted in the soft breeze as she smiled and waved. For the rest of his life, this would be how he remembered his wife.

08:05 Local, 07MAR (08:05 GMT, 07MAR)
Royal Air Force Station Kings Cliffe

Hass-man slumped forward against his straps, unable to get out of the cockpit. A crew chief unstrapped him, pulled him out and helped him off the wing, sitting him next to a main mount on the soft grass. As Hass-man leaned against the tire, the crew chief handed him a thermos full of Irish coffee. He attempted to unscrew the top, but his hands shook. Taking it from him gently, without a word, the crew chief poured him a cup. Hass-man nodded and the sergeant returned to his duties, shaking his head at the condition of the P-47.

A few minutes later, after inspecting the aircraft, the crew chief let the wing access panel for the guns drop.

"Jesus, Captain, not only do you have about a hundred holes, you broke six of the guns!"

Hass did not respond, taking another sip of the spiked coffee instead.

"Busy day, Captain?"

Hass looked up to see Colonel Berry standing over him with his head leaning on the wing. "How did we do, boss?" Hass-man asked.

"One hell of a lot better than last time!"

05:15 Local, 07MAR (11:15 GMT, 07MAR)
Fort Worth, Texas

Kaitlyn Elizabeth Brennan slipped quietly out the kitchen door, clutching her purse to her chest. Her brown eyes darted left and right looking for danger—the danger of being caught by her mother. In her purse was a high school diploma certifying an early graduation, birth certificate, and a brand new commercial pilot's license. Tightly gripped in her hand was a piece of paper with the address of the Women's Auxiliary Ferry Squadron recruiter. Laura watched from the living room window as her daughter got into the cab.

By noon, it was done. Major Nancy Love, commander of the Women's Auxiliary Ferrying Squadron (WAFS), had accepted her personally and then sent her to be processed by the Air Corps across the hall. Kaitlyn stood in front of a young bomber pilot seated at a desk. He appeared much older than he actually was. His left sleeve's cuff was pinned near the shoulder; he didn't need it. His arm had been severed by flak over Polesti.

Looking up at the striking brunette, he felt uncomfortable; his deformity seemed to amplify in her presence.

"Women flying airplanes," he lashed out, defiant. "I don't think it will work."

Kaitlyn glared back at him.

"I already do fly, Lieutenant," she replied evenly, "and I'm unconcerned with what you think."

Rebuffed, the man awkwardly shuffled a few papers and then stamped them harshly before handing Kaitlyn back the entire stack.

"Oh boy, your instructors are going to have a riot with you," he said.

She snatched the papers out of his hand, turned up her nose, and marched out of the office. He couldn't help himself and smiled.

CHAPTER 12

08:10 Local, 07MAR (18:10 GMT, 07MAR)
USS Suwannee, Pacific Ocean

Kid Brennan tried to slip unnoticed into Ready Room Six, but Skipper Jasper wasn't having it.

"Well, well, well, the prodigal ensign returns! Front and center, Brennan."

David had no choice or escape route, especially after his shipmates started pushing him forward, laughing and cheering.

"My, my. What an import we had, Mister Brennan?"

"Yes, sir. A bit busy."

"Oh, son," said the skipper, "do not underestimate it! I think it might be a top ten—maybe even a top three of all time."

Kid looked sheepish, even a bit sick to his stomach, as Jazz went on with glee.

"Let's review. You received, in the following order: a Navy Cross, a call sign from an admiral, a punch in the nose from a commodore…." He put his finger to his chin in mock contemplation. "There was something else… what was it? Oh yes, a wife."

Ready Six erupted in cheers again.

"Like I said," continued Jazz over the din, "biblical."

One member of the squadron was not impressed or cheering. The new executive officer looked annoyed, in fact.

"Okay, Kid," said Jazz. "Sit. We also have a new squadron member. XO, introduce yourself."

ENDGAME

Kid didn't hear a word the new XO said. Instead, he turned to Stutz with questioning eyes. Stutz subtly shook away the answer, but there was no denying the professional slight: he had been demoted from acting XO. By Jazz's lackluster introduction, it was also equally obvious he was not pleased with the presence of the new officer.

"Okay, gents," Jazz continued after the XO finished, "we are headed back to the action. For those of you who were not paying attention the last few days, which I believe is just about all of you, we have new aircraft—FM-2 Wildcats. Make no mistake: this is a different machine. Much improved, even over the FM-1," he concluded and called up Stutzman to explain.

Stutz came forward and began to hand out new manuals. He avoided Kid's eyes when he handed him his.

"Boys," he said, "there are a lot of changes. All good. It truly is a better breed of cat. More power, more rudder, and best of all, less weight. The skipper and I flew them while you knuckleheads were getting drunk."

General Motors indeed had improved on their first attempt at redesign of Grumman's F-4F, the FM-1. They improved performance by raising horsepower and reducing weight. By increasing the rudder size, they also improved the stability of the aircraft. Grumman had stopped manufacturing the Wildcat in 1943 to concentrate on the new F-6F Hellcat.

After a few more highlights, Stutz dismissed the squadron for self-study. Kid started for the door, bone tired. He just wanted to get some sleep. The new XO intercepted him.

"Kind of irresponsible, don't you think, Ensign?"

"How's that, sir?"

"Getting married so quickly. Seems awfully drastic just to get laid, and now charging off to war? You could leave her a widow."

A hydraulic pump bolted to the wall had cycled off, allowing Jazz and Stutz to hear the conversation. Stutz started for the XO, but Jazz stopped him.

"Get Kid out of here," he said and turned toward the new executive officer.

"XO Burns, a word," the skipper bellowed, stopping the exchange.

Stutzman grabbed Kid by the elbow and escorted him forcefully toward the door. Kid was seething. He turned as Stutz pulled him out the door backward.

"I don't intend to get shot down, XO," he said. "Do you?"

Burns' face flushed at the insolent comment. Stutz pushed Kid out the door and slammed it behind him, leaving Jazz and the new XO behind. Jazz remained silent as the rest of the squadron scrambled out.

"Do not ever do that to one of my pilots again." Skipper Jasper strained to control his voice but his red complexion gave away his anger.

Burns was shocked that Jazz had taken the ensign's side.

"Do what?" he stammered.

"Belittle one of my fighter pilots," said Jazz. "I want these boys to feel like tigers when we throw them up against a more experienced foe in a superior aircraft. The last damn thing I need is my second-in-command kicking the confidence out of my warriors."

His XO stared back in disbelief.

"Do you read me?" Jazz asked a second time with menace in his voice. "Do you read me, Lieutenant Commander Burns?"

Burns swallowed hard and then responded.

"Yes … yes, sir."

Kid Brennan didn't know it yet, but he now had a mortal enemy. The XO would do everything and anything to destroy him. He didn't have the guts to go up against Stutzman even though he outranked him. He certainly would never fight an even battle; Jasper was out of the question. No, he would crush Brennan, and then the rest of the junior officers would get in line.

Bruce Stutzman knew it already. He knew because he was familiar with the XO's backstabbing reputation. It preceded him. He had risen through the ranks on the stacked bodies of fellow officers. All had back wounds.

Kid was still steaming when he keyed the door to the bunkroom. Stutz pulled it back closed, keeping them in the privacy of the secluded passageway. He pinned Kid against the bulkhead by the shoulder.

"The XO is a class-A jerk," he warned, "but he is still second-in-command."

"This is bullshit," said Kid. "You are the XO."

"Not any more. He will be gunning for you. Do not give him any ammunition."

"Why?"

"He's jealous … and a petty man."

"Jealous of what?"

Stutz tapped the ribbons on Kid's chest. "To start with, those. You have more fruit salad on your chest, in less than a year, than he has after ten. And you're an ace."

Kid just stared at him and then shook off his hold.

"Listen to me, Brennan," Stutz continued. "On his best day he is an average pilot and a below-average leader. He gets ahead by destroying the competition—"

"I'm not competition—"

"In the air, you damn sure are! You just got designated section leader of my division and promoted to Lieutenant Junior Grade. We have two nuggets to nursemaid. Act surprised when Jazz gives you the letter."

Kid thought a minute. He calmed down and spoke softly.

"I am surprised—I'm just a nugget myself."

"Not anymore. You are an experienced aviator and an ace. That is why you are a threat to that piece of shit."

Kid met Stutzman's eyes. He'd never heard him cuss before.

"Don't get paranoid on me, Kid. Just stay away from him. Got it?"

"Aye aye, sir."

CHAPTER 13

20:38 Local, 21MAR (20:38 GMT, 21MAR)
Royal Air Force Station Greenham Common

A lone C-47 Skytrain sat on the end of a dark runway; both Pratt & Whitney R-1830-90C Twin Wasp engines were turning. All checks and the run-up were complete. J.T. and Irish watched the clock slowly click off seconds. Irish looked over at J.T. The instrument panel's night lights cast an eerie red pall over his face.

"You know," said Irish, "Kate is right. We are too old for this crap."

J.T. smiled mischievously in the crimson illumination.

"I'll get you a rocking chair when we get back."

A green Aldis lamp flicked on in the tower. J.T. answered the light signal by pushing the throttles to takeoff power. Irish punched the clock, starting elapsed time. Loaded down with extra fuel, the C-47 was slow to accelerate. J.T. eased the control yoke forward, lifting the tail as the momentum increased. At eighty knots, he began to coax the heavy Skytrain off the runway.

"Too late now, Grandpa," he said. "Raise the gear."

08:38 Local, 22MAR (21:38 GMT, 21MAR)
USS Suwannee, Pacific Ocean

Stutz stood at the front of Ready Room Six. Nervous chatter was building to a crescendo when he barked out an order.

"Attention to brief!"

All hands stopped talking and turned to face forward. Stutz looked back at the group calmly. He noted the torqued jaws of the nuggets and began to speak.

"Our target today is the Truk Atoll. The Fighting 27th has been given the dream job of a pure fighter sweep."

Excited chatter broke out at the announcement; they would be free to attack the enemy. No bombers or strikers to escort, just fighters against fighters—what they had all trained and dreamed of.

"We will attack in a classic pincer," Stutz continued. "The skipper will lead two divisions of four fighters each from a southern vector while the XO comes in from the north. We will push the Zeros into the middle and then rip into them from both sides."

He let the big picture settle in.

"XO's two divisions will come in at 130 knots, simulating SBD dive bombers. When the Zeros go for him, he will accelerate and engage as Jazz's divisions show up on their six o'clock."

After breaking up into individual flight briefs, the crews covered frequencies, tactics, and rescue procedures if anyone was shot down. Kid avoided saying anything, letting Stutz correct the XO's numerous inaccuracies.

After the brief, the flight crew got into their gear and waited for the call from AIROPs (Air Operations). Kid was playing a game of acey-deucey with Thor in the back of the ready room when both of the nuggets from his flight approached.

"Kid, can we talk to you?"

Thor did not waste the opportunity to bug out unscathed rather than take the impending pummeling on the board.

"Sure," said Kid, "have a seat."

"Well, you've been out there and—"

Kid laughed, knowing exactly what their concerns were.

"I got you," he replied. "Four rules, guys—that's it. First: keep your lead in sight. Second: once engaged, never stop pulling, never give up. Third: the Zero has no armor or self-sealing tanks, to improve performance. Good for shooting, but do not try to climb with them. Last: if you get a hotshot on your tail, get in the Thach Weave. Let one of us shoot him off your six. You cannot outmaneuver him."

"PILOTS, MAN YOUR AIRCRAFT," boomed over the 5MC speaker in Ready Six.

All sixteen naval aviators scrambled to the flight deck. Each sprinted to his own Wildcat. As pilots jumped into the cockpits, plane captains (PCs) held straps clear and then, once they were in position, helped strap the pilots in. After sliding off the wing, each PC manned a fire extinguisher for engine start.

Fifteen R-1830s popped to life, and then picked up RPM before stabilizing at a steady roar. One did not; it backfired through the carburetor, blowing off the stack to the air filter. Raw aviation fuel ignited in the carburetor. A PC quickly doused the flame with his extinguisher. Regardless, Stutz's Wildcat was done for the day.

Having already been warmed up by mechanics, Jazz was able to launch immediately. His wingmen jammed their throttles forward, following him off the bow, Kid was heads down, finishing his checks when Stutz tapped him on the shoulder and shouted over the Twin Wasp engine.

"You got the division lead. Jazz put me with the XO for a reason. Don't let him kill you."

Kid nodded with dread as Stutz hopped off the wing.

With the last of the XO's division rolling, Kid taxied into a launch position and ran up the power. As soon as the previous Wildcat cleared the bow the flight deck officer launched Kid, who released the brakes and went to full power. With the canopy open, the howl of the Pratt & Whitney was deafening. A steady deck allowed him to get the Wildcat airborne before the edge of the bow.

Jazz had his flight rendezvous and was circling overhead at two thousand feet. The XO was heading overhead to one thousand, his flight still not together. Kid had his heavy section (three fighters) formulated and was chasing down the XO. Once all fifteen Wildcats were overhead, Jazz pushed toward the target.

Inexplicably, the XO did not push. Instead, he continued to orbit. Kid flew up next to him and waggled his wings to get his attention. When the XO looked over, Kid pointed overhead to where Jazz was no longer, then toward the target. Angrily, the XO waved him away, ignoring him.

After another complete circle, he finally pushed for the target—late. A pincer attack depended on timing to ensure its success: they simply had to show up at the same time. Kid kept waiting for the XO to pick up his speed to compensate for the late push; he never did.

Finally approaching the target, Kid nervously scanned the sky. He knew the Zeros would fly away from Jazz's group and toward their slower flight, assuming they were the bombers. Jazz's flight would not be in a position to support them, and they were already down one Wildcat and their best pilot.

Thirty miles north of Truk, he saw black dots high and maneuvering behind them. Again, he flew up next to the XO, signaling many bogeys up and behind, and again he was waved away. LTJG David "Kid" Brennan had witnessed a midair while in training. He'd seen it develop but since he was only a student, he had not interceded. Two men died. He vowed then to never again sit quietly while circumstances got out of control.

Kid jammed on combat power. His new Twin Wasp with water injection answered immediately. *Screw this idiot.* He flew in front of the XO, climbed, and then turned to meet the enemy. XO didn't even notice.

Kid's mouth dried as he counted sixteen Zeros diving on his flight of three. On the good side, he was pleasantly surprised at the increased climb rate from his FM-2 Wildcat. His flight was climbing at 180 knots; the Zeros were diving at 250, for a combined closure rate of 430 knots.

Charging his guns first, he next transmitted, more for Jazz than the XO: "Kid, flight engaged 30 North of Truk. Three versus 16. Kid, flight arm 'em up!"

At two thousand feet of separation, he centered his piper and opened fire. He watched the wings of the Zero sparkle as he answered with the same. Closing at an incredible rate, each twisted, trying to score hits. Exploding just prior to the merge, A6M2 Zero parts littered the air. Kid pushed to dodge the biggest chunks.

His flight was nose high, the Japanese nose low and accelerating. Thus, he had the turning advantage of speed and gravity. Snap rolling inverted, he yanked on maximum G. Reversing course dramatically, he was now behind the Zeros. But they were over 100 knots faster and unconcerned, for now, with Kid.

Eight of them separated and attacked the XO's flight. He was still cruising along, fat, dumb and happy. Slashing through the Wildcat flight, the Zeros scored two kills in a single pass. They split into two divisions; one went left, the other right. Kid, now up to speed, pounced on the division that faded right.

Cutting across the circle, he met them ninety degrees off and let loose with a max deflection burst aimed at the lead Zero. This time, both of his wingmen opened up; neither had fired on the first pass but Kid's aggressiveness was contagious. They now fought like tigers. Three Zeros fell to the ocean in flames. The fourth dove away.

Kid knew that even a max G turn couldn't hack the angles, so he let him go, reversing course to rescue what was left of the XO's division. They were totally defensive in a Thach Weave; Zeros were engaging them, two at a time.

Jazz had cranked his flight to the northeast and accelerated past redline speed, desperately trying to get into the fight. He finally got tally just as Kid's flight attacked a flight of six Zeros. Flying just over the top of the XO's weaving flight, Jazz shot one of the pursuing Zeros in the face. Then, he looked up and saw a Jap division re-enter the fight from the east, jumping Kid. Jazz attacked the attackers.

A massive swirling dogfight ensued—twenty aircraft in a giant circle, one right after the other, each trying to shoot an aircraft in front of him, while defending against any behind. In fighter pilot lingo, it was a daisy chain.

Jazz's flight scored two kills before the Zeros climbed away. Unable to match their climb and with his plan in a shambles, Jazz called for a bug-out north, before the Japanese could turn the tables on them. After reforming, and out of the Truk area, he turned the flight for the Suwannee.

23:43 Local, 21MAR (23:43 GMT, 21MAR)
In the Air Over France

Streaking across the French countryside at four hundred feet in their C-47, J.T. and Irish glanced nervously as far aft as they could see from the side windscreen. A full moon hung over enemy occupied territory. They would have never planned a mission deep into country on a night like this. Unfortunately, they didn't have a choice.

Spike had pre-set the extraction, and he had been behind enemy lines for sixteen days. No doubt, he needed to come out. They continued to thunder toward the French Alps. Navigation was easy with the countryside illuminated. Intermediate checkpoints of bridges and rivers stood out, but nothing like the snow-covered Alps that loomed in the distance. Filling the windscreen, the mountains seemed perilously close as they continued to motor straight at them.

"How's the timeline?" J.T. asked with an edge to his voice.

"Fine, just fine, press!" Irish snapped.

Five minutes later, with the peaks now out of view, they were so close, J.T. asked again.

"Time hack?"

"Two minutes. I'm not asleep, you know."

Each second morphed into a minute as J.T. flew closer to the jagged jaws of the mountains. They were so close now that the ridges and ravines were well defined.

"Mark on top. Turn right, one eight zero!"

J.T. rolled the lumbering C-47 into a thirty-degree angle of bank turn. With the Alps so close to the left wing, he subconsciously tightened the turn, rolling past thirty degrees. Irish instantly corrected him.

"Thirty degrees angle of bank," he demanded.

Skimming along the edge of the mountains, the roar of the R-1820s echoed off their face, denying any gunner a directional cue. They knew that this low in this terrain, no radar could track them, and no fighter would come down to play.

"Hold your course!"

"We are damn close over here, Irish."

"Yea, no kidding. That's how it's planned," he snapped.

J.T.'s stomach was tight, and his sweat glands active when Irish called out one minute and then yelled, "Decelerate!"

Simultaneously, J.T. pulled the throttles to idle, pushed the prop levers to max pitch, and eased back on the yoke, climbing to eight hundred feet above the ground. Irish threw down the gear handle at max extension speed and then feed in flaps as the aircraft slowed dramatically. Both men actively searched the ground for a signal.

Pointing to a sloped farmer's field, J.T. yelled over the engines, "That's got to be it."

Irish was nodding agreement when a series of quick flashes emanated from the center of the field.

"What did it say?"

"S-P-I-K-E," laughed Irish.

"Hang on, Grandpa, here we go!"

Diving toward the field, J.T. watched as smudge pots lit sequentially, marking a rough, dark, runway. Slamming the throttles to idle, J.T. reefed on the yoke, landing with authority and braking hard.

Irish unstrapped and headed for the cabin door as they bounced down the field. If a Luftwaffe fighter was stalking them from a safe altitude, now was when he would strike. Spike was at the door as it swung open—he helped a pretty blonde into the cabin.

"Well, hello, my dear," said Irish. "To what do I owe the pleasure?"

She pushed her way past him.

"Irish, how about some help!" came a voice from behind her.

He turned to see Spike wrestling with a bound and gagged man in his pajamas. Irish grabbed the man by his silk lapels and pulled him into the aircraft as Spike piled in behind him, slamming the door.

"GO!" Spike yelled loud enough for J.T. to hear in the cockpit.

Locking the right brake, J.T. jammed power on the left engine; the aircraft pivoted in place. As it swung one hundred eighty degrees, he released the brakes and brought up the other throttle. Matching them, J.T. smashed both full forward to emergency power. In an instant, the tail was light and he coaxed it into the air. They bounced so violently as the C-47 raced across the field, he couldn't read the instruments. Extinguishing smudge pots marked their progression. Unable to read his airspeed indicator and as the trees at the far end grew too large to ignore, J.T. pulled the aircraft off of the pasture.

Climbing steeply, he cleared the tree line, punched his clock, reset his nose attitude before he stalled the aircraft, and reached over, pulling up the gear handle. Leveling quickly at four hundred feet above ground level, J.T. eased back the throttles, setting a cruise power of 24 inches of manifold pressure and 2,200 RPM on the props.

Exasperated, he looked back into the cabin for Irish as he cycled closed the cowl flaps. What he saw made him laugh out loud. In the dim red cabin light stood Irish, foot up on a seat next to the young woman, leaning close, chatting away.

15:22 Local, 22MAR (04:22 GMT, 22MAR)
USS Suwannee, Pacific Ocean

Sitting alone in the Dirty Shirt Wardroom, XO Burns was enjoying a slider, oblivious to the day's events. He had retreated to the wardroom after his only surviving wingman, a rather tightly wrapped Italian boy from New York City, had to be restrained during debrief. Hammer made very clear his desire to choke the XO to death with his bare hands.

CAG (Commander, Air Group) entered the wardroom, looked sideways at the XO and then sat at another table. Nonplused by the obvious rebuke, Burns collected his plate and a beloved stack of paperwork and moved to

CAG's table. CAG looked up with a forced smile, in an attempt to hide the dread he felt when he saw who was joining him.

"Kind of rough out there today, eh, XO?"

"Yes sir, it sure was. It didn't have to be—"

"What do you mean by that?"

CAG bristled at the XO's feigned restraint, well aware of his reputation. He knew the weasel couldn't wait to knife a squadron mate.

"Well, CAG, I don't like to talk out of school—"

"But you will anyway, right?"

Shrugging off the slight, Burns continued.

"Not without heavy heart."

"No doubt." He could no longer suppress his disgust with this slimy officer. He pushed back from the table and crossed his arms across his chest.

"Well, sir," said the XO, "if LTJG Brennan had stuck to the plan, we would have more Wildcats on the flight deck. He's a real loose cannon."

With his appetite soured, CAG excused himself from the table with a grunt and set a direct course for Ready Room Six. When he banged through the hatch (door), the squadron duty officer called out, "Attention on deck."

Everyone in the space snapped to.

CAG was a warrior who led from the front. He led the second wave himself and had heard the bedlam on the radio. More importantly, he sensed all was not right in Ready Six. Jazz met him at the hatch.

CAG got right to the point. "We got a loose cannon?"

"No, sir, an idiot."

"Well, he's just a nugget. Let's sit him down—"

"Nugget? Who are we talking about, CAG?"

"Kid Brennan, the XO told me."

"Told you what, exactly?" Jazz's voice betrayed his outrage, surprising CAG. Quickly escorting the air wing commander into a small office at the back of Ready Six for privacy, he turned beet red as CAG detailed his conversation with the XO. Jazz then forced himself to calmly explain what really happened.

"I never did like that guy," said CAG. "Your squadron, your call, Skipper."

"Relieve him for cause."

CAG shook it off.

"Technically we can't. He is not in command. I got it." Then, he snapped his fingers and smiled in triumph.

"Ship's admin officer has some tropical funk. We will offer up your XO to replace him."

"Perfect," replied Jazz. "Paperwork is the only thing he is good at."

CHAPTER 14

With the sun's rising, Dover's white cliffs turned orange, visible from miles away. Regardless of color, they were a welcome sight to a weary combat crew. It was a beacon of safety; if you made them, you were home. Spike came forward after knocking out his prisoner with another shot of sodium pentothal.

"Thanks for being on time, lads," he said. "C.R. was right, you boys definitely have your shit wired."

"This is our second war, young man. So who is our guest?" asked Irish.

"I guess you've earned the right to know," replied Spike. "Besides, the Nazis will assume we have him. He's a nuclear scientist, head of the Germans' program."

Both men turned to face Spike with raised brows. He shrugged and continued.

"We got HUMINT. He was going to visit a heavy water facility in the French Alps. They always stay at the same hotel in Morteau. We inserted Agent Smith," he said, gesturing to the woman, "through Switzerland last month. He likes the ladies; too bad for him. The rest, you know."

"What is a nuclear scientist?"

"You don't want to know, Irish."

* * * *

High above the solitary C-47 Dakota, a maximum effort bombing raid was headed in the opposite direction. Eighth Air Forces mission 46: seventy-nine Boeing B-17 Flying Fortresses and twenty-six Consolidated B-24 Liberators, escorted by the 56th Fighter Group, were headed for the submarine pens in Wilhelmshaven, Germany.

Colonel Mark Berry was leading the 56th, positioned above and behind the bomber formation. Periodically, he glanced over at Hass-man, hoping to get a signal from him that he was taking the lead. Each time, Captain Hass shook him off; there was no chatter on any frequency.

Their navigation plot had them pointed directly at Bremen; it was a feint. When they got overhead Oldenburg, Germany, the strike would turn north for Wilhelmshaven and drop on its sub pens.

Hass-man frantically flipped through the frequencies—nothing. Hair was standing up on the back of his neck; he felt them. Where is the flak? *There should be flak!*

Straining eyes looked in every direction for bogeys. At the end of the line, Hass-man watched as the formation turned for the target. He looked ahead, at first thinking it was flak that he saw. Suddenly, he realized the occasional clicks he heard on frequency #2 was code, not static.

"Multiple bogeys twelve o'clock!" he screamed into his mic.

No wingmen heard him. He was on a Luftwaffe frequency. It was too late anyway. The ME-109 and FW-190s turned into the formation's exposed flank as the strikers began their target run. The only warning he could get off was by jettisoning his drop tanks and accelerating ahead of the fighters.

The morning sky filled with shiny, aluminum tanks that glinted in the sun as they tumbled silently to the ground. Howling Wasps pulled Thunderbolts to the enemy, but they arrived too late. One hundred Luftwaffe fighters slammed into the Americans, guns and cannon blazing. A B-17 fell immediately to the onslaught, followed by two B-24s, one taking its crew with it as it exploded in a fireball. Others began to fall out of formation.

The 56th was caught flatfooted and at their maximum range; the Luftwaffe had timed their attack perfectly. Each Thunderbolt pilot had one eye on the horde of German fighters and the other on the fuel gauge. Twisting violently in his seat, Hass-man got sight of a section of 109s about to take a shot. Turning his division hard into the fight as they opened fire, Hass-man's section lead peeled off high to avoid the rounds. Neither German followed him; both stuck to Hass and his wingman.

Nose low at emergency power, Hass-man knew a death spiral was not an option for his wingman, so he leveled the wings and looped. Leaning his head as far aft as he could while he pulled over the top, he watched helplessly as his number two was shot off his wing. He also caught sight of the yellow tail of the 109 chasing him.

Burying the stick into his lap going down the back side of the loop, he went right back into another. Hass-man had read the detailed intel reports on the 109; he knew the wings had leading edge slats. At slow speeds they would deploy automatically, like a flap, to help the fighter turn. They would also increase the drag—he hoped dramatically.

Reaching the top of the second loop, Hass-man snap-rolled upright, and pulled the dual-gripped stick into his lap. The Thunderbolt's nose hung high in the morning air as he jerked the throttle to idle. His trap set, he waited, knowing the 109 could not match his move.

Yellow Tail didn't fall for the bait; his young wingman did. Easing off to the right, Hass watched as the German wingman stalled, trying to pull for the shot. Now out of control, the 109 rolled off to the left as he fell. Hass-man pounced. Jamming full power on the R-2800 engine, he used the torque generated by the massive engine and prop to roll his P-47 behind the 109. A two-second burst at zero range sawed off the German's tail. Easing the power to stop the rolling moment, Hass-man passed between the severed tail and the rest of the 109.

Shit! It's not yellow!

Desperate, he tried to wrestle the bucking Thunderbolt back to the right, knowing what was coming. He didn't have to wait long; streams of 20-millimeter and 30-caliber tracer rounds squirted over his canopy. Simultaneously, Hass-man stomped the right rudder, pulled the throttle to idle, and pushed the stick full forward, drastically slowing the P-47. Passing a mere ten feet below the yellow-tailed Messerschmitt, he exercised his last option: he ran. By pushing, he unloaded the wing to zero G; this eliminated all induced drag on the airframe. Gravity pulled the big nose of the P-47 to mother earth as Hass-man gingerly fed the horses of his Wasp engine.

Pointed straight down at full emergency power, the Thunderbolt screamed through its maximum speed. Exceeding redline by 100 knots, the P-47 began to buffet wildly. Captain Mark Hass was now in a flight regime that would not be understood for many years: sonic flow. Portions of his aircraft were actually supersonic. The shaking he was experiencing was Mach buffet, caused by this phenomenon.

He didn't need to understand what was happening to know instinctively that if he didn't slow down, the aircraft would disintegrate. Surprisingly, the controls were not heavy; in fact they were so light it was as if they were disconnected. Shock waves had attached to the wings and tail, effectively blanking the control surfaces. Not knowing what else to do, Hass-man pulled the throttle to idle, turning the big, thirteen-foot prop into a large speed brake.

Plummeting into the thick air helped, and the big fighter began to slow as the altimeter unwound so furiously he couldn't read it. Gently, he tried some back stick pressure, in an attempt to raise the nose. He felt the elevator nibble at the edge of the airflow. Hass-man was rapidly running out of altitude for a pull out; it was now or never. Feeling the controls returning to normal as the dense air decelerated the P-47, Hass-man fed in as much back stick as he dared; the G-meter began to register a pull. Even with the meter at four Gs, he was plunging toward the forest below. It became very obvious, very quickly, that four Gs, and then six Gs, would not suffice. At eight Gs, he felt the nose rising, and he held it.

16:13 Local, 22MAR (08:13 GMT, 22MAR)
Mindoro Island, The Philippines

Slipping off the Island of Luzon, once again Butler and his men had escaped the clutches of the jungle. A moonless night provided the cover they needed to deny the primordial forest their blood. After a restless attempt at sleep, Butler gave up and climbed his mountain. He was waiting for the sun to set over the majestic Pacific when Donnelly found him.

"We just got an atta boy from HQ in Australia. They say to lay low for a while."

"Roger that, Paul," he replied. "I could lay low right here forever."

"Nothing could make it better?" his sergeant asked, mischief in his voice.

Butler looked sideways at his friend, noticing the canvas bag that was dripping water. He heard giggling and looked past Donnelley at the two bar girls coming up the trail.

"Well, I didn't say it couldn't get better."

Donnelley smiled as he pulled a San Miguel beer out and set the bag down with a clink. He popped the top with a church key and handed it to Butler.

"Where in the world did you find ice, Paul?"

"Never underestimate a good sergeant, Captain," he said with a wink.

07:43 Local, 22MAR (07:43 GMT, 22MAR)
Wilhelmshaven, Germany

Hass-man began to grey out as the G-force pulled the blood from his brain. Slowly, his vision went away until he was blind from the pull, yet his hearing was strangely unaffected. He could not relax the pull. Grunting and flexing his abdominal muscles, he tried to push the blood uphill into his brain. He lost consciousness just as the aircraft cleared the trees in a slight climb. Jerking back to awareness, panicky, he scanned his six for Yellow Tail. The sky was empty. Alone again in enemy territory, Hass-man yanked on four Gs, turning for England just as the engine seized. So violent was its failure, the centrifugal force generated by the propeller twisted the fuselage at the nose when the seizing engine stopped its rotation.

Instinctively he read his instruments; they verified what the large, still prop had already proved. His engine was dead; there would not be a restart. Looking overhead, he saw a long trail of what was no doubt his oil splashed across the morning. Yellow Tail must have thought the trail and the fact he was pointed straight down meant he was done for. Indeed he was. His twisted Thunderbolt was now falling out of the German sky. With no time for self-pity, Hass-man popped up as far as he could before gravity took his remaining speed. He saw a small meadow and established his best glide speed and pointed at it.

Cutting through the tops of sixty-foot pines, he made the edge of the field. At twenty feet, he pulled the stick for all he had, to break the rate of descent. The doomed Thunderbolt crunched into the soggy meadow on its belly. The prop dug deeply into the ground, helping to bring the heavy fighter to an abrupt stop.

Disoriented, he was jolted back to his senses when an ME-109 flashed over his cockpit. Yellow Tail pulled its nose up steeply and executed a perfect victory roll. With his Thunderbolt still on battery power, Hass-man heard distinctively, in German:

"Welcome back to the fatherland."

His blood ran cold and then hot. *Those bastards were hunting me; I've got to get out of here!*

Jumping out of the cockpit, he reached back and pulled the parachute and survival gear out of his seat. He snatched a signal flare out of the kit and tossed it under the raised right wing into an accumulating pool of AVGAS. Sprinting away as it ignited, Hass-man glanced back at his trusty steed engulfed in flames and disappeared into the darkness of the forest.

CHAPTER 15

08:03 Local, 22MAR (08:03 GMT, 22MAR)
Deep in the Forest, South of Wilhelmshaven, Germany

Captain Mark Hass pushed deeper into the forest, seeking its cover and refuge. He resisted the almost uncontrollable urge to head for the coast. He knew they would expect that. Instead, he pressed further into Germany. Although still a bit rattled by the realization that he'd been individually targeted, Hass-man shifted seamlessly into survival mode.

In spite of his strong intent of never getting shot down, he had paid attention to the briefs. He had to go to ground; most evaders were caught in the first few hours after being shot down, wandering around aimlessly.

Shot down, he thought. *Irish is never going to let me hear the end of this.*

Making his way deeper into the forest, he came across a stream and followed it toward the coast, stopping after three hundred yards. Digging through his survival gear, he pulled out a pencil flare and pried it open with his knife. Pouring the contents on a flat rock, he carefully ground the magnesium and gunpowder together. After doing the same with two more, he sprinkled it all on his trail. He jumped across the creek onto a rocky area and reversed course until he found a small, dry tributary, following it further into the forest.

A BMW motorcycle with a sidecar led a small convoy to the crash site of Hass-man's Thunderbolt. At the end of the line was a Luftwaffe staff car. Riding shotgun in the motorcycle side car, two large bloodhounds sniffed at the cool air.

A very large sergeant, sitting upright in the saddle of the motorcycle, raised a clenched fist. The convoy slowed to a halt. Dismounting with surprising ease, the big man stood erect. He was dressed more as a hunter than soldier; in fact, he was a tracker. He wore tall hunting boots and a heavy wool jacket; the only clothing that identified him as a sergeant was his garrison cap.

He slung a bolt-action rifle over his shoulder and began to bark orders.

"Halt! None of you idiots move—you'll ruin my scent."

He whistled twice, and his dogs leapt from the sidecar. Giving three more sharp whistles, he swept his arm to the burnt-out hulk of Hass's Thunderbolt.

The dogs shot toward the P-47, baying as they ran. They circled it numerous times and finally sat. Their inaction caught the tracker's attention as a Luftwaffe major strolled up next to him. Ignoring the officer, he walked briskly to the wreckage. After inspecting the cockpit, he turned to the major.

"This is a clever one, Herr Major."

"How is that, Sergeant?"

"Look, he has taken everything his body came in sweaty contact with: parachute, seat cushion, and charts. Then he burnt his scent out of the metal cockpit," murmured the tracker with admiration. "Wait here, I must find his footprints."

Finding Hass-man's size six boot prints in the soft earth, he whistled for his dogs. They ran up and down the impressions, finally getting the scent. With one whistle, he launched them on Hass-man's trail.

"He's a little one, this wily fox," he said. Turning to face the major, he noted the aviator's own short stature. "No offense, Major."

"None taken, Sergeant. A man such as this has had to rely on brains not brawn. No offense."

"None taken, Herr Major. Shall we search the cockpit?"

"No, he's left nothing of use to us. It is him that I want. Get on with it."

"Jawöhl, Herr Major."

Waving a meaty arm in gesture, the tracker barked orders to the troops, who immediately started after the hounds.

Picking up speed, the hounds got further in front of the pursuing troops. The tracker could hear them baying and prodded his patrol forward in a vain attempt to keep up. At the stream, he stopped with a look of concern.

"What is it, Sergeant?" asked the major.

"He is not the type to run for the obvious. Something is wrong!"

Whistling two short shrill blasts, he attempted to recall his hounds. Too late. In the distance, he heard barking and crying.

"Damn it!" the tracker cursed as he ran toward the ruckus. He found his dogs sneezing and whimpering, pawing at their noses. The tracker knelt and scooped up some dirt. He recoiled after a sniff of the sulfur, magnesium and potassium nitrate from a ground up flare.

"What is it, Sergeant?"

"I told you he is a clever one."

Looking around the area in a single scan, the tracker stood up letting the dirt slip through his fingers. "He's gone."

"Gone, Tracker?"

"Gone!"

"I thought you could track anyone?" demanded the Major.

"So did I. Look, he ruined my dogs for days, maybe weeks. Then our little Fox crossed here—where it is rocky. No prints, no scent; he will be careful not to leave tracks now. He is gone Major. He will go to ground now. We are wasting our time here, we must set a containment perimeter."

Scanning the woods, the Major added to no one in particular, "Even a fox gets hungry, he can't stay in there forever."

It was cooling rapidly with the setting sun. Hass-man knew he had to find shelter and cover. The dense woods would make it difficult for the German searchers, but not impossible. He also knew they would not give up easily.

Coming across a fallen, hollow tree, he peered inside, looking for inhabitants. Clicking on his flashlight, he saw no sign of any animals. Quickly, he gathered up a few fallen branches, lined his new home with his parachute and then slithered into the tree trunk. He pulled the parachute over himself like a sleeping bag and then covered the entrance with the branches. A searching soldier would have to look inside to find him. Not likely during the day, let alone in the darkness.

Fitting his flashlight with a red lens, he took inventory of his survival gear. It was not impressive: two cans of water, two candy bars, a knife, compass, and a small first aid kit. In this cold, I won't last three days, he thought. Then what? Hunkered down with nothing else to do, he forced himself to sleep.

10:43 Local, 22MAR (10:43 GMT, 22MAR)
Kate's Manor, Bowdown House, Greenham Common, England

Spike Shanower appeared at the head of the table and stood silently. J.T. and Irish were intently studying plans for the invasion of Europe. Finally,

Irish looked up with a start at the unannounced presence.

"Jesus, Spike! Would you stop doing that?"

Shanower smiled big; giving Irish a dose of his own medicine was one of his few pleasures in this war.

"What are you smiling at?" Irish gruffed. "Hass-man is down. We aren't in the mood.

"Yes, I know. He was specifically targeted."

J.T.'s interest was now piqued. He looked up from his invasion plans.

"Explain that."

"Well, Colonel Dobbs," replied Spike, "apparently, the Luftwaffe took exception to him listening in on their GCI frequencies. Spies! They are everywhere. That is how I know they don't have him," he added with a wink.

"What do you mean by that, Captain?" demanded J.T.

"All I can tell you is that they are beating the bushes for him."

"Unfortunately, it won't take long," said Irish.

"I've seen his profile," Spike said. "I wouldn't underestimate him."

"He's down behind enemy lines, Junior."

"Actually, Irish, not only is he behind enemy lines, he is down in Germany."

Irish shook his head.

"Well that's it. We will see him after the war is over."

"Want to bet?"

Now irritated, Irish snapped.

"Yes, young captain, I do. One beer—place of my choice."

CHAPTER 16

17:52 Local, 23MAR (08:52 GMT, 23MAR)
Above the Caroline Islands

Circling on his assigned BARCAP (Barrier Combat Air Patrol) for hours with nothing except the monotony of blue sky and water, Kid Brennan was righteously bored. Once down to his pre-briefed joker fuel, he turned his flight of four toward the Suwannee and home.

In the distance he could see a squall line forming. Checking his MOBOARD for the ship's predicted position, he decided that it was more likely to be hiding under the small front. Light rain began to stream up his center windscreen. Glancing side to side, he could clearly see his wingman. Droplets zipping by, even at 250 knots, didn't affect visibility. Rain only restricted vision at the point of impact, where drops would splat. On a Wildcat, that was the flat center windscreen.

His mind wandered from the rain to a rainbow he noticed out of a side windscreen panel. Its colors brightened as he descended through the gentle clouds. Not well defined, the front was not the normal collection of angry thunderheads knotted with turbulence. Able to float among the wispy clouds, Kid weaved his division of dark blue Wildcats around the biggest of them.

He looked over at the rainbow. It had formed a perfect circle, a gate to the Suwannee, a transition point. They penetrated the rainbow. On the other side, Kid's eye detected movement. To a warrior, movement was danger—to a hunter, opportunity.

Eight Japanese "Kate" bombers were stalking the Suwannee. Kid flipped on his electric gun sight, toggled his master armament switch on, and electrically charged his four .50 caliber Browning machine guns. He hand-signaled "eight bandits" to his wingmen and pushed them out into attack formation. Then, he coldly calculated the angle of intercept that would bring death quickest.

Smashing the mixture to full rich and the prop lever to full pitch, Kid slowly eased in full throttle to keep his flight together. With their R-1830s howling at full power, he dove the division below the bombers and then pulled up into the Kate bombers' exposed bellies, guns blazing.

Kid put the piper of his sight on the trailing flight, then sweetened it up by placing it on the wing root of the Japanese lead. He knew they still refused to arm their aircraft or install self-sealing tanks. Squeezing the trigger, he released a mix of HE, high explosive, and incendiary rounds. Tearing open the fuel tanks, the HE would then explode, igniting the fuel with the help of the glowing incendiary rounds. The result was almost boring in its predictability. The sparkling impact of HE mixed with the red tracers collapsed the wing in a flare of flame. Kid didn't even wait to watch the certain death.

Tail guns came alive as they pitched toward the lead division. Instinctive-ly, the four remaining bombers broke left, the strong side. Because military aircraft were flown with the right hand, it was natural—and again, predict-able. Kid anticipated and pounced. His Wildcats clawed at the Kates and then finally sank their fangs, insuring that they joined their squadron mates in the grey water. Just-promoted Lieutenant Junior Grade Kid Brennan calm-ly turned his flight back on course and unarmed his guns. Behind them, the rainbow dissipated to nothingness.

Kid found the Suwannee where he expected it, hiding among the rain showers. They circled overhead in finger four formation until the boat turned into the wind. With a ready deck below, Kid let the nose of his FM-2 Wildcat gently fall toward the water. Now behind the ship, he pulled smoothly in a forty-five-degree angle of bank turn to match its course. Flying up the Suwannee's wake, Kid held up his fist, giving Dash Two the signal to cross under lead and to fill in the gap left for him between Kid and Three. Once in echelon, the three wingmen nestled up close.

Kid flew the tight formation up the starboard side, in close, at pattern altitude. As the bow flashed below him, he kissed off the formation and broke away in a hard, four-G pull. His wingmen continued on ship's course. Reaching the abeam position opposite the ship's course, he cranked down the gear and lowered the flaps. Glancing over his left shoulder, as he sustained his turn, he watched as his wingmen continued to break off, one at a time, for proper separation.

Continuing his level turn to final, Kid completed a circle and was now flying up the wake at fifty feet. He rolled out on centerline and was precisely where he was expected to be. Looking left, he clearly saw the LSO with arms stretched straight out—no correction would be necessary. Approaching the ramp of the Suwannee, the LSO slashed a paddle across his throat; Kid obediently pulled his throttle to idle and held his attitude.

Crunching onto the flight deck, his Wildcat's hook snared the second wire. On board, the cross-deck pennant played out, while below deck the long cable wound through two blocks that were being pulled together. The action pushed hydraulic fluid through a nozzle, increasing friction, which abruptly jerked the aircraft to a stop. Recoiling slightly at the end of the trap onboard, the hook released the wire, allowing Kid to raise it upon the arresting gear officer's signal. Quickly, he unlocked his wings and goosed his engine to taxi forward as the cable barricade, which kept aircraft that missed the wires from piling into parked ones, dropped. His squadron maintainers held his unlocked wings, letting the aircraft's forward movement fold them. After snapping each wing into place on the fuselage, the men scurried across the barricade before it rose.

Kid followed the yellow-shirted handler's directions, turned hard right toward the tower, and then shut down his engine. More men ran to his aircraft, grabbing it wherever they could as the handler gave the signal to push it back. Parked with his tail over the water, Kid's aircraft was chocked and chained to the deck. He now had the best seat in the house to watch flight operations.

On his left, he watched as the last of the CAP replacing him launched. He turned right and watched his Dash Three roll in the groove, as Two taxied clear of the barricade. Watching it snap back up into position, Kid then glanced at the activity amidship. It was alive with colored jerseys darting in, under, and around aircraft. Purple shirts pulled fuel lines. Red shirts, seeing the powder burns on his wings, began to pop the panels on his guns. Blue shirts finished chaining him down, as his brown-shirted plane captain jumped up on his wing with a stencil and paint. Kid held up two fingers. His PC smiled big and began to paint two more Japanese flags under the Wildcat's canopy rail. Bragging rights would be the plane captain's tonight—his pilot was top ace of the air wing.

Kid admired the masterpiece of timing and operation; he couldn't help but smile at its precision. Suddenly, all hands stopped moving and looked aft. Kid turned to the right and saw the LSO leaning way over, signaling a turn back to centerline. Looking up, he saw his last wingman overshoot the wake, already in a steep turn, struggling to line up on the aircraft carrier. His nose was cocked up, way too high. He was dangerously close to a stall. Having seen enough, the LSO waved off his approach.

Ensign Jordan did not see the LSO waving his paddles wildly over his head until the last second. When he finally saw the frantic go-around signal, he over-corrected by jamming the throttle to emergency power and pulling up on the stick sharply. With his wing already dangerously close to stall, the abrupt input tore the smooth air from the Wildcat's wing. With the laminar flow gone, the lift from the wing and airflow over the flight controls dissolved.

Torque took over, generated by the 1,350 horsepower of the R-1820-56 Cyclone engine and Curtis propeller. It slowly rotated the Wildcat left, around its own prop, rolling the aircraft onto its back.

Kid looked up and into Jordan's wide eyes as he passed a mere twenty feet over his own Wildcat. Completely out of control, with landing gear pointed awkwardly to the heavens, the doomed fighter plunged into the ocean, off the port side.

Kid's plane captain ducked, out of reflex, when the dying Wildcat screeched overhead.

"Geez Louise," he yelled. "Lieutenant, what happened?"

Kid was looking past him; the burbling spot of impact was sliding aft off the port beam and out of view. Davey Jones' locker would surrender not so much as a chart. Jordan, his Wildcat, and everything he was or ever would be, were gone.

"AIRCRAFT IN THE WATER, AIRCRAFT IN THE WATER!" boomed over 5MC loudspeakers.

In the Suwannee's wake, the plane guard Destroyer rushed to the spot and deployed a rescue boat. It motored in futile circles, waiting for an aviator who would not appear. On deck, all hands were already returning to their flight deck duties. Kid finished gathering his gear and stood up, stepping onto the wing.

"Sorry, Lieutenant—" his plane captain was fighting back tears.

Kid was without words. He patted his PC on the shoulder, turned, and slid off the wing. Dodging aircraft and propellers, he slipped below deck and out of danger.

Lieutenant Junior Grade David "Kid" Brennan sat slumped in his Ready Room chair, contemplating the day. Lieutenant Bruce Stutzman, the new XO of the Fighting 27th, entered Ready Six and stood behind his chair.

"You okay, Kid?"

"I saw his eyes, XO. He looked right into mine. He was terrified."

"He was dying, and he knew it," Stutz replied softly.

Behind them, the Ready Room door swung open and two LSOs entered.

"Sorry about Jordan, XO," said one of them.

"Nothing you could do, boys—a naval aviator still has to fly his aircraft."

"Roger that, sir," the LSO replied. "Kid—nice pass, a little short in the groove, a grade of OK."

Using the excuse that they had to debrief other pilots, the two men scurried out the door.

"Two kills and an OK approach," said Stutz. "Not a bad mission, Kid. Let's go get some chow."

05:05 Local, 24MAR (05:05 GMT, 24MAR)
Deep in the Forest, South of Wilhelmshaven, Germany

For two days, Hass-man didn't move. His water and both candy bars were gone. Lying in his rotting sanctuary, hunger and thirst began to grip him. He was slipping in and out of consciousness—his thoughts mingling with dreams.

He dreamed of a circling Spitfire, the distinctive howl of its Merlin engine haunting him. Jerking awake, he could see light at the end of his lair. Then he noticed the low hum of the Merlin was still there. *What is going on?*

Moving to the end of the tree trunk, Hass-man slowly pushed aside the cover and poked his head out into the brisk morning. The Merlin's rumble grew louder; it was not coming from the air. It is echoing through the trees.

He scanned the forest for any movement or sound. Satisfied there was no threat, he shimmied out. He was so stiff he could hardly stand at first. He shook it off and made his way toward the sound. *I can't be delirious yet.*

As he closed on the sound, it stopped. He continued in the direction it had originated. Peering from the edge of a clearing, he discovered the source. An ME-109 sat alone, tucked in the trees. It wasn't a Merlin V-12 he had heard but a Daimler-Benz DB 605, also a V-12. A mechanic finished up his daily inspection and then walked down a narrow taxiway to another stashed Messerschmitt. *I'll be damned—they are unguarded!*

Easing back under cover, Hass-man considered his options. He thought about waiting and checking things out thoroughly, to assess the situation, but in the end, he sprinted for the 109. Reaching the aircraft, he squatted, forcing himself to listen. When the mechanic started another ME-109, Hass-man pulled the chocks and jumped into the cockpit. *Now is my chance. He won't hear me and neither will anyone else.*

Hass-man stared at the foreign language on the controls, unable to comprehend it until he cursed to himself in German. He flipped on the battery switch and the gauges jumped to life. He mashed the starter button, intently watching the propeller pass through the 12 o'clock position. Time stretched with each passing blade. After the third blade, he pumped the electric primer button and moved the mixture knob to full rich. Coughing to life, the Daimler-Benz then tried to die; Hass-man wouldn't let it. He cajoled it to life with subtle throttle movements.

The engine roared into the morning air. He steadied it at 1,500 RPM so it could not stall, ran the electric prop pitch to full, released the brakes, and goosed the throttle to get it out of the revetment. Looking left and right for armed guards, he almost ran off the taxiway. Adrenalin was spiking, blood coursed through his veins and pounded at his temples—he could hear it over the roar of the DB-605.

Fast-taxiing past a very surprised mechanic, Hass-man took a hard right on a perpendicular taxiway. The close-coupled and narrow gear wobbled, the tail yawed, and then the 109 ground-looped, swapping ends.

15:05 Local, 24 MAR (05:05 GMT, 24MAR)
USS Suwannee, Caroline Islands

Pitching bow to stern, the flight deck rose, then fell, forty feet in the rough seas. Suwannee was a converted oiler with an added ship-handling quality: a Dutch roll. Its stern moved in a figure-eight motion during high seas.

Kid sat waiting his turn to launch in XO Stutzman's division as number Three. He couldn't believe they were even going to try. Jazz rolled the first division right on time, propelling into the air as the bow pitched up. In sequence the other three Wildcats in his flight launched with the bow at or above the horizon. So far so good.

Stutz rolled. Halfway down the deck, the Suwannee's roll kicked in and the flat-bottomed ship slipped off a wave top, slamming into a trough. Stutz's Wildcat reached the end of the flight deck as a giant wave crashed over it. Incredibly, the Wildcat emerged out of the froth, clawing to get airborne. Rough Ryder started his roll next. Kid pulled his canopy closed.

Looking to his left, he saw the launch officer winding up his flag in a tight circle. Kid saluted. The LSO dropped to his knee and pointed the flag to the bow. Brakes released, with the bow down in a trough, the Wildcat accelerated dramatically toward the ocean. Kid resisted yanking the stick into his lap; he waited, praying the deck would rise. It rose high into the late afternoon sky as he cleared its edge.

Rendezvoused overhead, Kid could see that Stutz was drenched. Against his better judgment, he couldn't suppress a smile when Stutz looked over at him. He got a non-standard hand signal in return.

They pushed on their mission: war at sea. A scout plane had discovered a lone Japanese destroyer, two-hundred-sixty-miles north. No doubt it was a picket ship for a larger force; the task force commander didn't want it snooping around. To fly to it, sink it, and then be back before sunset meant only the speedier FM-2s could be used. Each was armed with a single, five-hundred-pound armor-piercing bomb.

05:06 Local, 24MAR (05:06 GMT, 24MAR)
Deep in the Forest, South of Wilhelmshaven, Germany

Slightly disoriented, and now facing the opposite direction, Hass-man quickly checked the wing tips to see if he had damaged the aircraft. Panic was beginning to creep into his subconscious. Looking forward, he decided he had enough taxiway and would not find the runway in the maze of trees. Without another thought, he jammed the throttle forward, careful to keep the tail behind the nose.

Feeling the tail get light, he raised it with slight forward stick pressure. The little fighter accelerated impressively. He moved the throttle past the gate to emergency power; the DB-605 wailed in protest. He was running out of taxiway. Fumbling around, he finally found the flap handle, moved it a single notch, and then snatched the ME-109 off of the runway, standing it on its tail. Clearing the pine trees, he forced the nose back down and prayed it would not stall. He milked the stick to keep the fighter airborne and cajoled it into steady state flight.

Raising the gear and flaps as the 109 accelerated, Hass-man noticed fighters hidden in the trees—a yellow tailed fighter among them. He knew he should run, but he just couldn't. With a maniacal grin on his face, he armed up the 109's 20-millimeter cannon. Pitching back in a wing-over maneuver, he put the piper of the gun sight on the yellow tail and squeezed the trigger. As an orange and black plume grew behind him, he turned toward England and the Channel, laughing like a madman.

16:46 Local, 24MAR (06:46 GMT, 24MAR)
Above the Caroline Islands

It was right at the predicted position of movement. All eight Wildcats rolled in on the Japanese destroyer in a tight sequence. Its crew did not initially see the attack. Jazz's five-hundred-pounder dropped true, hitting amidship. Stutz also got a hit-alpha (fatal hit). The rest of the young aviators dropped close as the ship maneuvered in its death throes. The strike quickly formed a racetrack pattern and strafed the ship with .50 cal until it slipped below the surface.

Again, the Zeros had not challenged them while they hammered away at the Imperial Japanese Navy destroyer. Kid Brennan already had the reputation of being the best triple-A suppressor in the air wing. He would press the target until he could see Japanese gunners, his own guns blazing. XO Stutzman had already pulled him aside, counseling him on low pullouts. Kid didn't care; he just wanted to kill the Japanese. On this mission, he had concentrated on the ship's bridge.

Three hours later, VF 27 was marshaled above the Suwannee, waiting for the ship to turn into the wind. On schedule, she heeled to port and then steadied on course, pointed into the prevailing winds. Even from his altitude, Kid could see the deck moving as the sun began to set. Signal Charlie was run up the yardarm. Stutz saw the recover signal and let the nose of his Wildcat fall through the horizon without touching the power. His wingmen fell with him as he turned in tight to expedite the recovery as much as possible. They were racing the sun.

Stutz kept it so tight he never rolled wings level over the ship. He merely kissed off the flight, steepened his turn, and pulled for the abeam. His flight continued in sequence, peeling off in order. Approaching the abeam, with 180 degrees of turn to go, Kid glanced at the ship to check his position. He watched in disbelief as the screws (propellers) came out of the water. Concentrating on the pattern, he began his turn to final approach. He rolled into the groove directly behind the ship and chased the Suwannee up her own wake.

He could clearly see the controlling LSO being held up by two kneeling assistants. In his periphery, the ship pitched wildly—from plan form to the back end or ramp, back to plan form. Kid forced himself to ignore the ship and to trust Paddles (LSO).

A cut signal slashed across Paddle's throat and Kid immediately pulled the throttle to idle. Fighting an almost overwhelming urge of self-preservation as he flew toward the ramp and sure death—he held his attitude constant. The ship began to fall away as he approached the in-close position. At the ramp, it continued down and his Wildcat chased it. The ship stopped momentarily before pitching back up, allowing the Wildcat to snare a wire and bang onto the deck as it began to rise again.

Below deck, the arresting gear engine jerked the cross deck pendant as it began to re-wind for the next trap on board of an aircraft. The action let the Wildcat spit the wire, allowing Kid to immediately retract the hook on command as the barricade dropped. He did not need to add power as the ship pitched bow down—gravity again did all the work.

Behind him, his wingman approached but he couldn't surrender fully to the LSO. Paddles emphatically gave him a cut. He delayed just long enough to float over the wires. The LSO waved his paddles frantically trying to get him to go around as the deck continued to fall away. Finally taking his own wave-off, Ensign Robert Wilson clipped two parked aircraft tails that took out his prop. Clearing the deck but unable to climb, he ditched off the port side. Kid watched helplessly as his wingman hysterically fought with his harness straps while the Wildcat sunk.

An hour later, Kid sat in the dirty shirt wardroom pushing pork adobo around his plate with a fork. Stutz sat down next to him.

"You are not going to stop pressing the target are you, Kid?"

He didn't respond; instead, he changed the subject.

"We kill more pilots at the ship than in combat. How long can we maintain this attrition rate?"

"You are a naval aviator, Brennan. You knew the score. You can turn in those wings any time."

Kid shrugged, and neither man spoke for a long pause. Finally, the XO spoke in a softer voice.

"Bobby had a wife, name is Janet." Stutz dropped a stateroom key onto the table in front of Kid. "Go through his stuff. Anything with another female name on the return address, pitch."

Picking the key up and turning it over slowly in his hand, Kid mumbled, "What if it's a married sister or cousin?"

"Not worth the risk. Janet will have enough to deal with. Sanitize it."

"Aye aye, sir."

He got up to leave. XO Stutzman called after him.

"Kid?"

"Sir?"

"I do not want to go through your stuff. Clear?"

Again there was no response.

"I say again, is that clear, Mister?"

"Loud and clear, sir."

Not wanting to go through a dead squadron mate's personal effects alone, Kid pressed Ensign "Rough" Ryder into service. Bobby was squeaky clean; they taped up his boxes with red ordnance tape and took them to the admin office.

After dumping the boxes on a yeoman's desk, they went into Ready Six and started a game of acey-deucey. Neither spoke as the pieces moved around the board with each roll of the dice.

"Kind of puts it into perspective doesn't it?" asked Rough, more to the game board than to Kid.

"Yeah. Two boxes."

Skipper Jasper entered the space and sensed their melancholy.

"Hey," he said. "They need two planners in CVIC, turn two."

"Aye aye," both men responded.

Jazz walked over to the squadron duty officer's desk and picked up a phone.

"Jimbob, Jazz here. I sent two junior officers your way. Give them something to do. Thanks."

Hanging up the phone, he winked at the SDO and pressed a finger to his lips, signaling silence.

06:56 Local, 24MAR (06:56 GMT, 24MAR)
Above the English Channel

A lone ME-109 streaked across the German coast at redline speed. Its pilot did not need to worry about return fuel. Clearing the coastline, Captain Mark Hass eased back on the throttle slightly, bringing down the cylinder head temperature. He stayed low, welcoming the cover of the haze and clouds. He was now outrunning both the Axis and the Allies.

He got sight of the coastline late—almost too late. Standing the 109 on its tail again, he flashed across the coast before the gun positions could open fire. Quickly rolling inverted, he pulled back down to the countryside to hide. After buzzing Kate's house just for fun, he flew to his base at RAF Kings Cliffe. Flying right up the runway, he pitched to the abeam position, lowered the gear and flaps, and was promptly shot down by his own base.

Bellying in for the second time in days, he sat in disbelief until GIs began trying to forcefully pull him from the cockpit. Try as they might, the straps held firm. Hass-man's expletive-laced demand that they cease caused the GIs to back off in surprise.

"Captain Hass?"

09:42 Local, 24 MAR (09:42 GMT, 24MAR)
Kate's Manor, Bowdown House, Greenham Common, England

This time it was J.T.'s turn. He looked up to see Spike standing next to him.

"Damn it, Spike. Stop doing that."

"Yeah," Irish jumped in, "why don't you do something about the Nazis buzzing around the countryside instead of screwing with us?"

Spike smiled his biggest I gotcha smile.

"That was no German, gentlemen," he said. "I give you the Luftwaffe's newest ME-109 pilot."

Hass-man stepped through the door, a magnum of champagne in each hand.

"Irish," Spike added, smug, "you owe me a beer. Paris, Eiffel Tower."

CHAPTER 17

08:30 Local, 07MAY (08:30 GMT, 07MAY)
Royal Air Force Station Kings Cliffe

Captain Mark Hass sat patiently in the wing commander's outer office. Colonel Berry walked out of his private office and poured himself a cup of coffee. Stirring in some cream, he turned to Hass-man.

"Come on in." Moving to his desk, Berry motioned with a small spoon. "Take a seat. I've got good news ... and bad."

"Great," mumbled Hass-man.

Colonel Berry sat quietly, contemplating his response. He was a career officer by profession but a fighter pilot at heart.

"I don't like it anymore than you will," he began. "Unfortunately, top brass got wind of your 109 ride and were duly impressed. They want you in DC for a personal debrief."

"Colonel," Hass-man protested, "I was debriefed by Captain Shanower. I'm no expert, but I know a spook when I see one—"

"I tried that," interrupted Berry. "They then reminded me of the 'shot down and escaped' policy."

Hass-man bristled at the stupidity.

"That's to protect the French resistance," he said. "I was in Germany!"

"I also pointed that out. Their response was curt and issued as an order."

Captain Hass stood and paced, trying to route an escape. He couldn't grasp at anything but the thinnest straw, nothing that would hold back the powers that be. He sat back down in defeat.

"Any other good news before I go pack?" he asked, glum.

Colonel Berry smiled, leaning back in his wooden chair and crossing his feet on the desk.

"Actually, I never got to the good news," he said. "It seems that while our paper-pushing comrades were scouring your record, they noticed you were an airline pilot."

"So?"

"And thus you have a lot of multiengine time and night instrument—"

"Colonel, I'm a fighter pilot, with kills to prove it!"

"Exactly: icing on the cake," Berry continued. "After they are done parading you around DC, you are headed to Orlando Army Air Field, to stand up a new night-fighter squadron."

"Night fighters?"

Berry nodded, sipping at his hot coffee.

"Obviously, it is multi-engine and big. Rumor is—and it is a top secret rumor, by the way—it has onboard radar."

Hass-man stood again and moved toward the door. After saluting, Berry called after him.

"Mark, it's a small price to pay for your own command. Try smiling a little during the parading of the beef. You don't have to mean it."

Captain Hass let out a laugh as he pulled closed the door.

CHAPTER 18

15:05 Local, 20JUN (05:05 GMT, 20JUN)
USS Suwannee, South Pacific

W eeks had turned to months; the missions became as monotonous as combat can be. It had become apparent that the Suwannee and the rest of the escort carriers were the second string. Fast-attack carriers like the Lexington and Enterprise were ripping around the South Pacific, taking on the Japanese toe-to-toe.

By contrast, the Suwannee and her air group had taken on the duty of escorting the transports and supporting ground forces on various islands of the Solomons. It was not duty fit for a hard-charging fighter pilot. The air war had moved on, and they had not been invited. The tally of Japanese flags on the fuselages of their FM-2 Wildcats had come to an abrupt halt.

Fighting 27th was chomping at the bit; even XO Stutzman was getting pissy. A final insult came when half of their Wildcats flew to the Lexington to reinforce her air group—then the pilots suffered the humiliation of being shuttled back in the belly of Ducks.

They were reaching their collective boiling point. Jazz was trying to keep his indignant warriors in check when a reprieve was passed down from command: a port visit at Pearl Harbor. No one was more ecstatic than Kid Brennan.

17:05 Local, 03JUL (03:05 GMT, 04JUL)
Naval Air Station Ford Island

Even though he had not slept in two nights due to a raging case of channel fever, Kid was wide-eyed and full of energy as he cranked down the landing gear of his Wildcat. Because of the war, their movement was classified. With no ship pulling into Pearl to announce the squadron's arrival, VF 27's presence was anonymous.

LTJG David Brennan stood breathlessly, watching his bride through the window of the back door. Theresa was picking at her dinner, sitting at the small dinette set alone. Kid paused. It suddenly struck him as very sad. Humans were communal, and nothing was more communal than eating a meal. To see his wife sitting alone made him want to cry. It confused him—especially in light of all the deaths he had seen. But none of those tragedies elicited the guilt he felt now. Gently, he tapped on the glass and then opened the door.

"David!" Theresa screamed.

Jumping up from the table and into his arms, nearly knocking him over—she seemed to ask ten questions all at once. He held her tight, unable to answer a single one.

For five days, they spoke to no one but each other. Even the fireworks on the Fourth were not a distraction.

20:38 Local, 04JUL (20:38 GMT, 04JUL)
Royal Air Force Station Greenham Common

Row after row of C-47s were parked on the thick, grass tarmac. The setting sun gave strange coloration to their molten green camouflage paint scheme. The aircraft outnumbered the crews, who were as green as the paint. J.T. and Irish had more flight time than the rest of their crews had, combined. To make things worse, the men had been trained as single-ship pilots with very little formation experience, and almost none in the C-47. As if that wasn't enough, fuel was critical and the bombers had priority. Their allotment had already been cut in half twice.

J.T. sipped at a cup of coffee. The steam roiled off his face, rising from the hot liquid. Irish watched, amused, as a smile formed beneath the vapor.

"Flight hours don't mean squat," J.T. said.

"Really?" asked Irish with a smile.

"Yes, really," said J.T., irritated at Irish's expression. "It is sorties that matter. Drilling along on the autopilot at altitude doesn't give you any more experience than sitting in this chair."

"I'm listening," Irish responded.

"Okay." J.T. leaned forward. "First, have the chief disconnect all the autopilots. Second, no more day flights; we will be going in at night, and in large formations. So third, no single-ship flights, either."

"From now on," he continued, "we will train like we will fight. Last item—fuel all flights for 1.5 hours. No more wasting gas at altitude. Takeoffs, landings, and formation work only. Everything else is a waste of time"

Irish set down his coffee, smiling.

"Roger that, Skipper. I'll get on it."

15:38 Local, 04JUL (20:38 GMT, 04JUL)
Army Air Base Orlando, Florida

Major Mark Hass, Commanding Officer of 348th Night Fighter Squadron, sat in the hot and humid cockpit of an XP-61 while technicians worked on the finicky SCR-720 radar. The initial testing on the Black Widow had thus far been a disaster. Overheating engines and constant radar failures were just two of its problems. Not only was it almost impossible to employ tactically, it was a handful to fly, having already picked up the nickname Widow Maker.

It could be worse, he thought, *I could be in D.C.*

CHAPTER 19

06:05 Local, 07SEP (16:05 GMT, 07SEP)
USS Suwannee, Pearl Harbor

Tugs pushed the USS Suwannee free and it began to ease out the channel of Pearl Harbor. Ford Island was in the background on her right. In the foreground, rising from the shallow water was the superstructure of the USS Arizona. Sparks popped all over her exposed carcass, cascading to the water below, snuffing on impact. Hot torches cut into her like carrion feeding as she decomposed on the water's edge—a ghostly reminder that fortified Navy crews with vengeance as they sortied to the Pacific and the enemy it held.

Kid hardly noticed; he was manning the rails with the rest of Suwannee's crew, glistening in their dress uniforms. They formed an unbroken ring of pure white to pay honor to fallen comrades. Kid Brennan was on the starboard side, facing Ford Island and the Arizona.

His head was motionless, but his fighter pilot eyes darted about scanning the shoreline; finally, they registered movement. Standing near the edge was Theresa in a red dress she had bought the day after they were married. She raised her hand in a small wave of good-bye. Kid broke military bearing and returned it.

13:30 Local, 07SEP (18:30 GMT, 07SEP)
Army Air Base Orlando, Florida

A radar blip appeared on the small pilot repeater that was centered in

Major Hass's instrument panel. He banked hard in its direction and pulled four Gs. It was gone in an instant, just like every other practice intercept before this one. Pulling as hard as he could, Hass-man couldn't bring the guns to bear. The target P-40 sped away unscathed.

Later, during the squadron debrief, Major Hass sat quietly at the front of the ready room as his men went over the multiple runs. He had ironed out the targeting problems of the guns by taking them out of the wing and putting them on centerline. Wing-mounted guns were set so their bullets would come together at fifteen hundred feet. By getting rid of convergence, the effective range of his Black Widows doubled and the targeting was made simpler. But it wouldn't matter if they couldn't get the weapons pointed at the bad-guy aircraft. He stood facing his handpicked crews.

"This is not working, boys," he said. "Any ideas?"

One of his ROs (Radar Operators) spoke softly from the back row.

"It's just a geometry problem."

"Define that," demanded Hass.

"Well sir, it is a problem of geometric angles. We are trying to solve the equation with one step."

"Show me." Hass-man held up a piece of chalk.

Second Lieutenant Jim Stoneman made his way to the chalkboard. He was tall, blond, and blue-eyed, impossibly young-looking with a smattering of freckles across the bridge of his nose. He broke the chalk in half and drew two diagrams simultaneously, his long arms stretched out wide. He now had the attention of the room. When he had finished, a J-hook diagram was on the left and a series of angular lines, forming half an octagon, was on the right.

"The problem is," he said, turning to the men, "we are trying to get it all in one turn. What we need to do is offset laterally and keep our nose on the target through a series of thirty-degree course changes. We must start turning way before the merge—"

An experienced fighter pilot spoke up from the back.

"Hold on there, Stony. That turns us belly up to the enemy."

"It will be night."

Major Hass held his hand up to silence the room. "Continue."

"By making small course changes," said Stoneman, "we keep our speed up. By early turning, we can time our arrival at the bandits' five or seven o' clock position, with the firing solution solved."

Hass-man studied the diagram intently, nodding his head.

"It's like pulling lead in a high-G fight," he said.

"Exactly, just spread out over a series of moves."

"Congratulations, Lieutenant," said Hass-man. "You are now the tactics officer and in my crew."

13:00 Local, 02OCT (21:00 GMT, 02OCT)
Naval Air Station North Island, California

After an uneventful crossing from Hawaii to San Diego, VF-27 spent a few days on liberty and then got mired down in administrative duties. Commander Jasper formed up his grumpy aviators at quarters for the word of the day. And then, much to their horror, he marched them from the Suwannee's pier across the base to North Island's airfield. They protested under their breath the entire way. After calling a halt on the tarmac, Jazz centered on the formation and called out facing maneuvers.

"Squadron ... left face!"

Mutiny was nigh.

"Squadron ... about face!"

They pivoted 180, facing away from Jazz, wondering what they did to deserve the drill sergeant-style abuse.

"Boys," he said, "this is the little surprise I told you about."

Twelve brand new F6F-3 Hellcats glistened in the midday California sun. Their dark blue paint was resplendent and fresh. Still confused, the formation of VF-27 aviators held fast. Jazz spoke again from behind them.

"Knuckleheads, the Hellcats are ours. Go pick one. Fall out."

Letting out a loud hoot of joy, the pilots sprinted to the world's greatest carrier-based fighters. Watching them run in and around the F6Fs, Jazz lit two cigarettes with a Zippo, handed one to Stutz and smiled at the men's enthusiasm. Their warriors looked like children scurrying around the tree on Christmas morning.

"Do you think they will let us keep them, Skipper?" asked Stutz.

Jazz shrugged and took a long drag off of his Camel.

"I hope so, Stutz," he responded, exhaling blue smoke. "I hope so."

Suwannee was one of only a few escort carriers that could handle the bigger F6F-3. The rest of the escort carrier fleet would fly the Wildcat for the duration of the war. Even if they didn't keep the Hellcats, they had them now, and because of that, they were invincible.

For the next ten days, Jazz had his boys in the air three times a day, every day. The complaining stopped. They loved their Hellcats. Compared to the Wildcat, it wasn't a step up—it was two. Powered by a Pratt & Whitney R-2800-10 Double Wasp engine, the Grumman Hellcat had 650 more horsepower than the Wildcat. Two thousand horsepower pushed the Hellcat through the air more efficiently due to improved aerodynamics. Even though the Hellcat was forty-five-hundred pounds heavier than the Wildcat, its slick design and bigger engine gave it twice the published climb rate. In reality, it was three times better.

It handled like a dream even at high speed, and top speed was seventy miles per hour better. Even with all the performance and handling improvements, LTJG David "Kid" Brennan's favorite feature was the landing gear. Instead of manhandling a crank through twenty-six-and-a-half revolutions, he could simply grasp the handle and raise it to the up position—pinky finger out, as if sipping tea. Hydraulic pressure did all the work.

VF-27 was out of the bush leagues now. They felt like frontline, fast-attack carrier pilots. They were sure, as they chatted away in the I-Bar, the Suwannee would now be attached to the main force.

Hidden in the bachelor officers' quarters on NAS North Island, the I-Bar was one of a kind and born out of necessity. Naval Air Station North Island was the first NAS. Naval aviator #1, Spuds Ellyson, had learned to fly on NAS NI. Home of AIRPAC, a three-star admiral billet, it was more formal than most air stations of the time.

Set in a Spanish style, each building had an ornate courtyard, and the entire base was set on the north end of the Silver Strand Beach. Down the Strand sat the stately Hotel Del Coronado.

North Island was host to a large number of senior officers and their wives. Aviator antics, fueled by cheap booze, were not welcome at the officers' club. AIRPAC, not wanting to loose his aviators on Coronado every night, ordered a bar built in the BOQ.

Modeled after an 1800's wooden ship, it had a very low ceiling, large, dark beams, and wooden walls constructed to emulate a ship's planked hull. In the center was a circular bar, and hanging over it was the only sign of the twentieth century: model aircraft hung from fish line, dangling over the patrons' heads.

Tables were tucked into the nooks and crannies created by large timbers holding back an imaginary ocean. Jazz and Stutz sat at a table, sipping ice-cold Budweisers and watching their boys roll dice for a round of drinks.

"We won't be joining the main force, will we?" said Stutz.

Taking a pull of his beer as the leather dice cup slammed on the bar, spilling its contents, Jazz waited for the hoots of joy to die down.

"Nope," he replied. "The Suwannee is too slow. Halsey won't slow down the strike force by adding us."

Rough Ryder slammed down a five-dollar bill, protesting the roll loudly.

"But let's not tell them," he continued.

"Roger that, Skipper."

"Shall we join our Hellcats and show them how to roll?"

18:07 Local, 12OCT (04:07 GMT, 13OCT)
Ford Island Officers Club, Naval Base Pearl Harbor

Theresa sat at a table on the veranda overlooking the Pacific. She nervously sipped a cocktail and repeatedly checked her watch, rhythmically tapping a swizzle stick on a glass ashtray. Finally, Betty arrived and joined her.

"What is so important, Theresa?" she asked. "Is David okay?"

"Sit down, Betty, sit!" replied Theresa. "David is fine—"

"Then what is so—?"

"I'm pregnant."

Betty threw back her head in laughter.

"Shhh!" Theresa begged her.

Patting her on the hand, Betty stifled her laughter. "Honey, that is what married people do."

"What if he doesn't want a baby?"

"Well it's a little late for that, don't you think?"

"I'm serious, Betty."

"Okay, okay. Haven't you two talked about kids?"

"No, not really. We're so young. I guess I just assumed it would happen later."

"Well, sweetie, you guessed wrong. Time to tell Romeo." Betty reached over and took the cocktail out of Theresa's hand.

06:00 Local, 13OCT (14:00 GMT, 13OCT)
Quayside, North Island, California

VF-27's officers stood at ease on the pier while their shiny new Hellcats were loaded onto the Suwannee behind them. XO Stutzman counted heads, and then reported all hands present to Commander Jasper. Jazz quickly dismissed the aviators to allow them to board the carrier.

Kid loitered, waiting for the crowd to get up the gangway. He didn't want to stand in line with heavy bags and a throbbing head. Through his self-inflicted fog, he contemplated how much his life had changed since he last stood on this pier. Not even a year. *Man, I miss Theresa—*

"Well, well, well. Look who finally got a Hellcat," a familiar voice rang out with the clarity of a bell in the fresh morning air.

Kid spun around and there stood his two oldest Navy buddies. The three had ridden the train together to Pensacola. He grabbed both around the neck and hugged them.

"Cue-ball, Andy, what are you guys doing here?"

Cue-Ball Bement puffed his chest, showing off the shiny wings of a naval aviator and nodded to Andy's.

"You are looking," Andy said, "at the U.S. Navy's newest—"

"And finest—" added Cue-ball.

"Yeah, sure, Cue—"

"And finest!"

"Okay," Andy relented, "and finest dauntless dive bomber pilots."

"Excellent," said Cue-ball. "So, David, you had better sweep the skies clean so that we can get to the real work."

"Roger that, Cue," David replied.

04:18 Local, 14OCT (09:18 GMT, 14OCT)
Army Air Field Orlando, Florida

Major Mark "Hass-man" Hass sat by himself at a picnic table contemplating his squadron's progress. As he sliced into a juicy Kansas City strip steak, he thought about Second Lieutenant Stoneman's tactics. They had proved effective, once the pilots trusted them. In fact, Hass-man had ordered his pilots to comply. The intercepts were getting the night fighters into position to fire on their targets.

He further prepared his crews by inverting their body clocks. Fighter Squadron 422 flew by night and slept by day. They didn't even schedule day flights anymore. And Hass-man had a screened-in lean-to built, with a barbecue pit and tubs of beer, for nocturnal steaks and post-flight Happy Hour.

"Atten-hut!"

The order was shouted over the music of Tommy Dorsey's band emanating from a large console radio.

Hass-man turned on his bench to see just who in hell was disturbing his dinner. He was quite surprised to see the two stars of a major general. Major Hass came to attention and saluted, while a perfectly manicured lieutenant colonel spoke.

"Officers and enlisted men eating together, Major?"

Hass-man, with registered irritation on his face, looked on the man's tunic where campaign ribbons should have been.

"This is a squadron bar, Lieutenant Colonel," he replied. "A gun squadron. We fly and fight together, maybe even die together. I think it appropriate we break bread together."

"Thank you, Lieutenant Colonel, that will be all."

The general dismissed him with a wave. He sat down at the table, inviting Hass-man with a hand gesture to join him. Hass-man sat down slowly, wondering what was coming.

"What can I do for you, General?" asked Hass-man.

"Well, Major, I'll be honest with you. I'm getting some heat to get you boys into the fight. How close are you?"

Hass-man thought about the question before answering.

"General, we've ironed out the engine problems with Northrop and Pratt & Whitney. We are getting a seventy percent reliability rate out of the radar. Tactically, we have had a breakthrough, but—"

"I need a date, Major."

Again, Hass-man was introspective, not rushed by rank.

"February," he said at last.

"I need you in place," the general replied.

"Where?"

"England. The 422nd will go against the V-1 flying bombs. You realize the political ramifications if you are late, of course."

"We will be ready."

"I will hold you to that, Major."

Major Hass shrugged as if unconcerned. *What will they do, send me back to American Airlines?*

Major General Hoffman studied this diminutive officer. He was definitely a warrior, unlike that peacock he had sent outside. He had also read Hass's official and unofficial record. It wasn't the first time he had run into one of the 7Alpha guys. They all had the same attitude.

"You got another one of those steaks, Major?" he asked.

"Absolutely, how would you like it, sir?" replied Hass-man.

"Rare."

"Is there any other way?"

"Not in my book, Major. By the way, just in case you are wondering, it won't be the airlines you get shit-canned to. It will be Adak, Alaska, as the BOQ officer."

Hass-man glared back, incensed by the threat.

"Fine with me," he said. "I love to fish and they don't shoot back."

Both men locked eyes, each attempting to evaluate the mettle of the other. Finally, the general smiled in genuine amusement.

"I hear there is a woman behind every tree."

Hass-man laughed out loud. He knew the punch line. There were no trees on the island of Adak.

CHAPTER 20

08:15 Local, 20OCT (18:15 GMT, 20OCT)
USS Suwannee, Pearl Harbor

Theresa anxiously wrung the coral-colored gloves she held tightly. Her thin, feminine hands began to match their hue as she subconsciously squeezed them. She was determined to tell David as soon as she could. She just couldn't keep the secret any longer; it grew faster than the child inside of her. But unlike the baby, it would not wait. She had to let it escape to save her sanity.

Mooring lines were put into place at an excruciatingly slow rate. She rose to her toes, scanning the throng of white-clad sailors as they streamed down the gangway. Rising to her toes to look over them, her heels came out of the patent leather pumps. Panic rose in her throat. *Where is he? Does he already know?*

"Theresa!"

David's voice both startled and revived her. She turned to see three aviators, with David in the middle. Theresa threw her arms around his neck and squeezed, almost knocking him down. Laughing, he lifted her out of her shoes. Cue-ball gave a nod of approval as he looked on.

"I want you to meet a couple of old friends," David told her, "Paul 'Cue-ball' Bement and Andy Levine."

"The boys from the train?" she asked.

"The very same," offered Cue-ball.

"I asked them over for the weekend," said her husband.

"Oh, sure." Theresa forced the edge out of her voice.

"That's okay, ma'am." Andy sensed her trepidation. "We will be fine on the boat."

"No, absolutely not," she said. "I'm not only a Navy wife—I'm a brat. I could feed my dad's entire wardroom at the drop of a hat. Two new friends are easy and welcome."

"Didn't I tell you she's the greatest?" David beamed.

22:48 Local, 20OCT (22:48 GMT, 20OCT)
Royal Air Force Station Greenham Common

Intense training had continued for six months and yet the staff of the 10th Transportation Wing felt like they were trying to hold back the tide. New crews showed up every week, needing the same training as the crews before. And the old crews needed to stay current. Irish cracked the operational whip and the chief kept the planes flying. J.T. was kept busy with the daily hassles of a rapidly expanding command.

On this dark night, the air wing's luck ran out. A brand new crew collided with their lead. Two flaming masses of metal lit up the sky like meteors as they fell to the English farmland. Four pilots, two navigators, two radiomen and two air crewmen were incinerated on the way down.

Irish burst into J.T.'s office.

"Skipper—"

"I heard the sirens," said J.T. "Full crew?"

"Yes, sir. Two."

"Chutes?"

"None."

J.T. sat quietly for a moment. *Ten letters to write, and we haven't even been in combat yet.*

"We're lucky," said Irish. "The damned fighters are dropping like flies—"

J.T. slammed his open hand on the desk.

"No! NO! I do not accept that. We are training. Combat losses are one thing. But I will not accept training losses. Is that clear?"

"Yes, sir," a startled Irish responded. "Very."

"Assemble the entire wing."

"Now, Skipper?"

"Right damn now! Everyone—crews, mechanics, even the admin guys. Get them in formation in the main hangar."

Two hours later, at 01:00, J.T. strode into the hanger and marched between the two halves of his air wing's formation. He ascended the three steps of the dais deliberately and stopped in front of a microphone. Colonel Dane "J.T." Dobbs tapped the microphone once and then spoke a single, measured sentence.

"Do not crash any more of my aircraft."

He then strode out of the hangar the way he had come in.

17:22 Local, 20OCT (03:22 GMT, 21OCT)
Ford Island Navy Housing

Steaks crackled on the grill, their wondrous aroma beckoning the emaciated aviators. Their thin waistlines were more a result of ship food quality, not deprivation. Unable to resist, they began to cut off pieces of the thick sirloins, eating them right off the grill. Theresa watched from the window and called out.

"You three are going to get sick."

Already well on their way to inebriation after three beers on empty stomachs, the three stooges began talking with their hands. It continued through dinner. Theresa's apprehension grew as her interest in the conversation waned. She began to reach her breaking point as the conversation turned dark.

"Hey what happened to Skinny?" asked David.

"Didn't you hear?" Andy said.

"Hear what?"

Cue-ball entered the conversation. "He augured in behind the boat."

"Beats burning to death," David replied.

"Nothing is worse than that," added Andy.

"Surviving a couple days as a crispy critter—that sure would be—"

David didn't finish his sentence; Theresa had had enough. She stood without a word and walked out of the house. Cue-ball watched her closely; when David made eye contact, he jerked his head toward her. Kid got the message and followed her outside. He found her staring at the barbecue pit as the remaining fat burned off of the grill. Sensing his approach, she walked toward the beach. David chased her, finally catching her by the arm.

"Theresa, stop, I can't keep up," he said. "What's wrong?"

"Crispy critters, for one thing! I've seen them, you know. I was here, I held their hands while they died."

"I'm sorry, it was stupid."

"Do you think I don't have nightmares about just that?" She began to weep.

"Theresa, don't cry," he begged. "We are going to be relegated to the backwaters. We'll be safe. Baby, we survived the worst of it. What could be worse than what we have already been through?"

Theresa began to sob heavily.

"You not wanting me anymore ... I'm pregnant."

David said nothing; he scooped her up off the sandy beach and carried her back to their house. She clung to his neck, fearing it would be the last time, not noticing he held her just as tightly. David kicked open the back door and walked into the kitchen, cradling Theresa.

"Cue," he called, "there is a cigar humidor in the study, grab three. Andy, I saw a bottle of champagne in the fridge. Open it and grab four glasses out of the cabinet over the sink."

"What are we celebrating?" Cue-ball shouted from the study.

"Boys, I'm going to be a daddy!" David leaned to Theresa's ear and whispered, "And I couldn't be happier."

23:31 Local, 20OCT (04:31 GMT, 21OCT)
OSS Headquarters, Langley, Virginia

Major Dan "Spike" Shanower sat at his desk, studying debriefs. His German scientist was lying to him, and he knew it. They had drugged their prisoner, slapped him around and kept him in a wet basement for months. Spike was running out of time and patience, mostly time. In a snap decision, he picked up one of four phones on his desk.

"Get me a C-47 and crew, fueled for Alamogordo, now." He picked up a second phone as he set down the first in the cradle. It rang without dialing. "Bring me the Nazi."

Standing defiantly in front of him, in the same silk pajamas he had worn the night he had been snatched, the German elicited a smile from Spike. It was ridiculous, and it was time to break him. Before his prisoner could speak, Spike pistol-whipped him to the floor.

"No more lies," said Spike. "We are going on a little trip."

A red line appeared on the horizon at Langley Air Field as the sun began its daily cycle. It matched the thin line of blood that ran out of the left nostril of the German's nose. Shackled, he was unable to wipe it away, just as he was unable to wipe away this nightmare. Spike dragged him toward the

C-47 cockpit by his soiled, silk collar. Stopping him between the seats, he unshackled the Nazi.

"Put him in the co-pilot seat," he told the pilot.

"Sir, I don't like—"

"I don't give a damn what you do or do not like, Captain—launch."

Sitting quietly as they plunged deeper into America, the German knew there was no resisting. He assumed he would be tortured and then executed at their destination.

Bumping through the afternoon air, the C-47 churned across the United States. The deeper they flew into the country, the more depressed the German grew. Its expanse overwhelmed him. The size of the Mississippi River was astounding. His father had been a river barge captain on the Rhine. He had spent many years on his beloved Rhine; it was a creek by comparison.

He had also done enough navigating to realize just how big the United States was. Shanower had tossed a chart on his lap so he could follow along. Distance and scale was not lost on him; two-and-a-half hours just to cross Texas. He could have flown from Paris to Berlin in less time.

Colonel Gerhardt scanned from horizon to horizon; Alamogordo's desolation matched his mood. Seeing him looking south toward Mexico, Spike interrupted his melancholy.

"Forget it. We won't be staying."

Spike left the shackles off his prisoner. In fact, he seemed to be not paying much attention to him at all when he barked out orders to the crew.

"Captain, be fueled and ready for departure in two hours."

"But Major, we need to rest."

Shanower nodded toward the lieutenant who had slept most of the way.

"Let him fly," he said, "he's rested. We will be back in two hours. The engines will be turning and the galley stocked. That is not a request, are we clear?"

"Yes, sir—very."

09:14 Local, 21OCT (19:14 GMT, 21OCT)
Ford Island Navy Housing

All three aviators awoke to the smell of maple-flavored bacon. It popped cheerfully in its own grease, the sound announcing a new day. Drawn to it like moths to a flame, they rendezvoused in the kitchen.

Theresa had four frying pans going simultaneously over the gas flames. One held the bacon, two held eggs. The larger of those sputtered with grease, the smaller with butter. In the fourth pan was a steak left over from the night before.

"Good morning, boys. Andy, I prepared a steak and eggs cooked in butter for you."

"That's not necessary, Theresa," he replied.

"Yes it is. I went by the Base Exchange, first thing. I got each of you a swimming outfit."

All three looked in unison at the table where she pointed with the spatula. Matching Hawaiian shirts and swim trunks taunted them from the Formica.

"You three are taking me to the beach. Go on, get dressed. Breakfast will be ready soon."

Cue-ball shrugged and grabbed the biggest matching outfit and headed for the bathroom to change. The other two followed obediently.

16:48 Local, 21OCT (22:48 GMT, 21OCT)
Naval Air Station Glenview, Chicago, Illinois

Halfway to Chicago, the German scientist broke, weeping for hours. What had broken him was a not-so-chance meeting in Alamogordo. He had recognized a former German colleague and whispered "traitor" to him in their native tongue. His fellow German's response unnerved him: "As will you be, Hans. Do you think after being showed this place you will ever be allowed to return?"

His tormentor then laughed and walked away, leaving him to deal with his new reality.

Puffy-eyed and shivering in his thin pajamas, the scientist had slipped out of the cockpit and back to the cabin. He stood in front of Major Shanower.

"What is it you want?" he asked.

Spike handed him a suitcase packed for travel. The German pulled out a wool suit and fresh undergarments. While his prisoner dressed, Shanower spread out a chart of Germany on the deck.

"Hans, I need to know where every nuclear facility is."

Colonel Hans Gerhardt stared down at the map and then met Spike's eyes.

"So that you can kill my friends? I have changed my mind. You can have back the suit."

"Colonel Gerhardt," said Shanower, "no doubt you are aware of the atrocities of the SS?"

He did not reply.

"I also suspect you are not a true believer."

"I am a scientist—"

"Then, surely you can deduce that the war is lost?"

"What does it matter now, Major?"

"I'll tell you: accountability."

"I don't understand...."

"Hans," said Spike, "as we speak, a tribunal is in place. It has been given the charter of trying and then executing, of course, Nazis. I offer you immunity, no more."

Hans Gerhardt sat down on the wooden slat bench along the fuselage. The drone from the engines seemed to hypnotize him, to throb through his very soul. He had nothing and yet everything to lose. His family was still in Germany. He remembered Germany between the wars; they would not survive without him.

Spike continued.

"In exchange for a detailed list of facilities, I will further direct the strikes at a time that minimizes casualties."

Hans looked up at Spike. The offer surprised him.

"Here is the best part, Colonel," Shanower went on. "After the hostilities cease, I will get out a team of your choosing."

The German's eyebrows lifted as he jumped at the opportunity.

"Families too!"

"Now wait a minute, Hans..."

"I will put the entire program behind by eighteen months with a single strike," promised Gerhardt.

Shanower looked down at the chart. Eighteen months. It would give the American program time. They could win the war. But families—hell, that would be like herding cats!

"Eighteen months?"

"One strike," responded Hans.

"Okay, Hans, you have a deal."

CHAPTER 21

07:00 Local, 20OCT (17:00 GMT, 20OCT)
USS Suwannee, Pearl Harbor

Again the Suwannee got under way, again the crew rendered honors to the Arizona, and again Theresa waved to David from the pier. What was different now was that a family stood in front of him while a Hellcat crouched behind. Kid felt a strong gravitational pull from both. He waved subtly to her as the big ship eased silently from quayside toward the channel and war.

On 5 November, they dropped anchor at Espiritu Santo to replenish stores and re-fuel. A week later, she sortied to participate in the Gilbert Islands operation. By the 18th, Task Force 52 was in position: seventeen aircraft carriers, twelve battleships, twelve cruisers, sixty-six destroyers, and thirty-six transport ships holding thirty-five thousand marines and soldiers.

20:00 Local, 20NOV (08:00 GMT, 20NOV)
USS Suwannee, Gilbert Islands

VF-27's young tigers sat in excited anticipation during the next night's brief. Commander Jasper stood next to an easel with butcher paper pages clipped to it. All hands present were certain they would be a part of the fighter sweep because of their new F6F-3s. They would take their Hellcats, guns blazing, to the enemy and defeat him.

It was not to be. When Jazz flipped the first page, the diagram clearly showed that they would be in the Southern Force. CV-27 and her air wing was part of Operation Galvanic. They would fly close air support for the

2nd Marine Division while the Northern Force would engage the Zeros over Makin Island. With moans and groans building to a crescendo, Jazz laid down the law.

"Belay that whiney bilge or I will keel haul the lot of you!" His thunderous retort shocked the naval aviators into silence.

"The purpose of a naval vessel," he continued, "is power projection—specifically, power ashore. We are the primary; the Northern Force is support. We may not see any Zeros but we damn sure will fight! And some of you will not make it back to Pearl. So you had better all pull your heads out and prepare for battle."

Commander Jasper turned the brief over to the XO and stalked out of the subdued ready room. An hour later Stutz, knocked at his stateroom door.

"Enter."

Stutz closed the door behind him as Jazz handed his second-in-command a scotch and water. Jazz had a large grin on his face.

"Too much, Bruce?"

"No, Skipper, just right," Stutz replied. "They have their heads back in the game."

VF-27's commanding officer took a sip of his drink, shut his eyes, and leaned his back against the bulkhead, exhaling audibly.

"Well, for the record," he said, "I share their frustration."

"Me too, Skipper, me too."

* * * *

Spikes of radiation began to show in the pre-dawn sky. In the east, the sun began to consume the darkness. Thirty aircraft sat on Suwannee's deck, propellers turning. The entire air wing crouched in the dark as the Suwannee turned into the wind. CAG's SBD Dauntless lumbered down the short deck as she steadied up on course. Right behind him, his wingman rolled, coaxing the heavy dive-bomber into the air. The section leader rolled on time, with his wingman close in succession—but something was wrong.

Number four did not have enough right rudder applied as the engine ran to full power; torque pulled him to the left side of the dark deck. Careening off a gun emplacement as he lunged over the port side of the ship, a wing tank was torn open. It flared slightly at first and then erupted brilliantly into a blinding light, until impact with the black water snuffed it.

Without pause, the launch continued until the entire remaining air wing was airborne. The death flash had been reduced to a glint of memory to be snuffed too, like the actual flames—compartmentalized, to be taken out at a later time, but not now. Now, a strike had to be flown.

Black ocean turned purple, revealing dark islands not yet able to absorb the dawn's light. Artificial light danced across them as sixteen, eight- and five-inch shells flashed on impact. The shell's blue-white illumination was normally obscured by the power of the sun. Tarawa was alive with the fight of dark versus light until the sun pierced the horizon, ending the struggle profoundly.

Lieutenant Junior Grade David "Kid" Brennan was alive with anticipation of the fight. The scene enthralled him: fourteen SBD Dauntless dive-bombers bracketed by sixteen Hellcats, all moving as one entity: a strike. The word alone was aggressive. After checking in on frequency, the radio came alive with directions.

"Strikers orbit twenty south Red Beach 1, angels one five."

First to go in, at 06:10, were the SBDs; they hit pre-planned targets near Red Beach 1. After expending all of their .50 caliber rounds, they RTF'd (returned to fleet) to the Suwannee. Hours passed. The Hellcats had leaned out to minimum burn, but they were quickly approaching joker fuel. When they hit that point, they would have to RTF Suwannee.

Something was definitely wrong. Kid could see that the Higgins boats were coming to a stop on the reef, while the tracked LTVs continued. *The tide isn't high enough!*

Continuing on through the eruptions and geysers of water and shrapnel, the LTV's formation was now completely a mess. Even so, they began to reach the beach. Kid watched as the marines were pinned down at the sea wall in the lagoon. Bodies began to stack up in the shallow water of the lagoon's Red Beach 1.

"This is FAC-Alpha, FAC-Alpha: fire mission one, how copy," crackled over their radios from the forward air controller, who was on the beach.

"Stutz flight is checking in with four Hellcats, one five-hundred-pounder per and fifty; read you loud and clear."

"Roger that, Stutz; I need the five-hundred-pounders on the first line of vegetation, fight center. Target two type 97 tanks, how copy?"

"Copy all; give me a flare and call posit off same. Stutz flight is in hot."

Having moved over Red Beach 1 after the naval bombardment; Stutz merely rolled over on his back and let the heavy Pratt & Whitney R-2800 pull him toward the target. He saw the flare.

"Tally ho mark."

"Target one hundred yards inland from mark."

"Roger; get your heads down."

His wingmen had followed at five-second intervals. Stutz selected bomb on his rotary and toggled the master arm switch. His pickle switch, under his left thumb, was now hot. Placing the piper on a general location, he waited to get closer so he could see the target.

Stutz maintained 250 knots by easing back his throttle; at forty-five degrees nose down, the island was growing rapidly. He waited patiently, cross-checking his altimeter. At eight thousand feet, triple-A began to fly by the windscreen. He held his attitude and dived. At five thousand feet, he saw a muzzle flash and centered on it. At precisely three thousand feet, he jettisoned his bomb. Feeling it release, he snapped on four Gs and began a hard right turn as he pulled out.

"Shack, shack; nice hit."

Rough Ryder had already released, but Kid was still in his dive.

"Call second tank's posit off first," he radioed.

"Fifty yards, five o-clock."

Kid pushed his nose even steeper, placing the piper in the vicinity of the call. Already below his safe release altitude, he pulled the throttle to idle to buy a few seconds. *There!* At the same time, he put the piper on the tank and "pickled" the bomb by pressing the release button. Counting to one, he pulled for his life. Just as the nose came up, he clipped a couple of fronds from a coconut tree. Then, he yanked on a turn to follow Ryder. Dash Four dropped on Kid's smoke and followed him.

"Good hits, Navy. Give me some fifty parallel to the skirmish line."

Stutz didn't answer; he was busy pulling hard to align ninety degrees out from their first run and reset the mils for his gun sight to strafe. He then selected guns on his armament panel, charged his Brownings, and let loose hell from his six M2 Browning .50 caliber guns.

"Let it all go on one run, boys; we are joker."

Stutz's wingmen followed in a ten-degree dive, guns blazing. Strafing was done up close and personal—the pilot could see the troops scatter and fall in front of his guns. It was also very risky to the pilot because it brought him within range of every gun on the ground. Fuel critical, Stutz came off target, turning directly for the Suwannee and climbing to conserve. His three wingmen chased him down and rendezvoused.

They were lucky; the Suwannee was turned into the wind and they recovered immediately. Once on deck, Kid stared into space, trying to get a second wind. He knew it was going to be a long day. A hard thump penetrated his thin canvas helmet; it instantly infuriated him. He jerked around, expecting to see Cue-ball's smirking face, but instead XO Stutzman was standing on his wing with two boxes. He dropped one in Kid's lap and pointed the guilty finger between his eyes.

"Here's breakfast," Stutz said. "One more low pullout and I'll ground you!"

Ending all discussion, he jumped off the wing and stalked back to his own Hellcat, leaving Kid to rub the forming bump on his forehead. Man, he thought, the XO has hard fingers.

14:12 Local, 20NOV (19:12 GMT, 21NOV)
OSS Headquarters, Navy Hill, Washington DC

Deep in the bowels of the OSS headquarters building, Major Spike Shanower sat at his desk consumed in thought. He rhythmically tapped a mechanical pencil against a front tooth. Finally, he set the pencil on the desk, carefully pointing it at the Air Corp officer sitting across from him.

"So what you are telling me, Lieutenant Colonel," he said, "is that you cannot hit the target."

Flushed with anger, the officer visibly strained to control his voice.

"Negative," he replied. "What I'm telling you is it cannot be hit."

"Oh, I think I know a couple of old war dogs that can."

"It cannot be done—impossible."

Spike spoke softly as he retrieved his pencil from the desktop.

"Difficult," he said, "but not impossible. You may go, Lieutenant Colonel."

"A major does not dismiss a lieutenant colonel. I would remind you that I outrank you."

Shanower laughed. "Not here, Lieutenant Colonel. Good-bye."

02:45 Local, 21NOV (14:45 GMT, 20NOV)
USS Suwannee, Gilbert Islands

A string of dim white lights floated in front of him. The ship's movement gave them animation. Kid thought of Theresa and how she would nervously tug at a pearl necklace he had bought her, as if she were a child secretly trying them on, afraid of being caught. He smiled into the darkness. A rapidly waving flashlight wand demanded his attention. It forced all thoughts from his mind except the mission at hand.

Kid Brennan ran the power up on his R-2800, setting takeoff power. The string of lights momentarily brightened as the launch officer touched his coned flashlight to the deck. Kid could easily follow the illuminated trail toward the black abyss. When they disappeared under him, he eased the stick aft and brought his view into the cockpit.

Scanning the artificial horizon, he leveled the wings and held the big nose of the Hellcat ten degrees above the horizon line. He quickly cross-scanned his other instruments as he raised the gear handle. Verifying a steady state climb on the VSI, he saw his airspeed was already at best rate of climb, and eased the nose up two more degrees to hold it.

His altimeter began to wind up as he moved away from the black ocean below. At five hundred feet, he began a turn to the northwest. Rolling out on the exact course of three hundred thirty-five degrees, he used his RMI to hold it. Kid felt confident, comfortable, barely scanning the balance ball to ensure he was trimmed and in balanced flight. Kid Brennan didn't need to—he could feel it.

In just a few hundred hours, LTJG David Brennan had become one with the Hellcat. He fit in the cockpit perfectly. The R-2800, mated to the marvelous aerodynamic qualities of the aircraft, made it the best fighter in theater. Kid knew it. He felt invincible in his Hellcat. He felt as if he could do anything.

In his youth, he had not been an especially good athlete. He loved sports but didn't excel at them; he was happy to be average. In his Hellcat, he was anything but average, even among his fighter pilot peers. His aviator skills were superior; the command had recognized that fact. It is how he found himself airborne, alone at 02:45, heading for a CAP position 150 miles northwest of the Southern Force.

His mission was to find and kill any reconnaissance aircraft. Known as Recce birds, they would radio the fleet's position, and bombers would follow. Kid climbed into the stars. At ten thousand feet, he switched on his oxygen and snapped the mask in place. After seven minutes and forty-eight seconds, he reached twenty thousand feet and fired up the cockpit heater. By thirty thousand feet, the heat it radiated was not adequate and he pulled up the mouton fur collar of his G-1 flight jacket.

Control movements, which could have been measured in centimeters at lower altitude could now be measured in millimeters. To get the maximum performance from his Hellcat's wing, his controls had to be moved at a minimum. Kid checked the super-charger control lever on the throttle quadrant with his left hand, ensuring that it was set for max boost. Sliding his hand aft and outboard, he double-checked that the cowls and oil intercooler were set fully closed, to keep the temperature within the operating limits of his R-2800.

He moved his hand slightly inboard and placed his palm on the horizontal trim wheel. His thumb naturally fell on the vertical wheel of the elevator trim tab, and his forefinger on the electric aileron trim switch. Trim tabs are small control surfaces that move the opposite direction of the main control surface. If a pilot wants to put in a left rudder correction, the tab will move to the right, causing aerodynamic pressure to push the rudder left.

Tabs also hold the control surface in place. It is the equivalent of being able to align the wheels of a car while it moves down the highway. Kid was now flying the Hellcat with just subtle movements of the trim tabs. In fact, the trim wheels had slack in them; he was using the slack to minimize movement by tapping inputs against the resistance. So subtle were his bump corrections that even another pilot wouldn't have felt them.

These minimal movements and perfect aerodynamic balance allowed Kid to climb above the 37,300-foot maximum ceiling of the Hellcat. As he delicately balanced his F6F-3 by touch, he reached up and dimmed the cockpit lights. Turning them to the absolute minimum, the soft red lights barely emitted illumination.

He thought back to that night a year ago when, as a newly winged naval aviator, he tumbled out of control from altitude. Kid nearly ended it all that night. He had learned so much since then and seen even more. Not even twenty-one years old, and yet he had experienced more than billions of humans who came before him.

Darkness granted unfettered access to the heavens. No light from the ground or moon interfered. David Brennan felt a part of the stars. He felt his father and brother as he floated among them. He felt Theresa and the child that grew inside her. This night was his.

"Watch Dog 1, this is Red Crown: your bogey bears, zero-three-zero, for three-five, angles forty, speed two-hundred, heading one-six-zero."

His radio broke the silence and demanded undivided attention. The ship had radioed an unknown aircraft 030 degrees and thirty-five miles from his location. It was at forty thousand feet heading southeast toward the Suwannee with a speed of two hundred knots.

"Red Crown, Watch Dog 1: Declare," Kid demanded to know its status; friend or foe.

"Red Crown declares Bandit; Watch Dog 1 is cleared, weapons red and free." After re-checking all friendly flight plans, the ship designated it an enemy aircraft and released Kid to engage and kill it.

Loitering at 38,700 feet, Kid eased the throttle past the emergency power detent. Quickly plotting a gentle intercept, he turned on course with an almost imperceptible turn. He forgot about the cold and existential thoughts, busying himself by coaxing every fraction of horsepower out of his engine and every pound of lift out of his wing.

"Zero eight zero for twelve," his metallic-voiced guide transmitted.

Re-plotting his intercept, he was satisfied. His course was 140; the bogey's, 160. By keeping him off of his wing, they would come together without maneuvering.

"Zero eight zero for three miles."

Straining to see the bogey, he turned his cockpit lights off and pushed his Hellcat further into an unknown realm.

"Merge plot."

They were now together in space. Altitude was all that separated them—how much, Kid did not know. He assumed higher and looked up through the polished canopy. A blue star caught his eye; it was different from the rest. Slightly changing course caused it to move. It was no star. It was the blue exhaust of the Recce bird. He forced his eyes to focus at a distance, and a hole in the stars appeared.

Kid stalked the black shape. Thirty minutes had elapsed; he didn't need to look at his MOBOARD to know they were close to the Southern Force. If the reconnaissance aircraft had radar it would find the fleet and radio its position. He had to make his move now.

The problem was, he couldn't. A mere twenty-five feet separated them but it might as well have been a thousand. Kid was surprised at how high he had already coaxed his Hellcat to climb; it would go no higher.

Then, he remembered a trick J.T. had taught him two years before. Kid began to slightly pump the control stick. Each time he pushed it forward the angle of attack and drag would reduce. The slight reduction gave him half a knot, which he immediately traded for altitude. Ratcheting himself up to the Recce bird, he could see that it was a Mitsubishi Ki 15.

His fighter was protesting. Each control input would cause the Hellcat to slide back. Making a split-second decision, Kid armed his guns and electrically charged the first rounds into the chambers of his six M2 Brownings. Feeling the thump as they charged, he pushed the nose over, gained a few precious knots, and then used them in an attempt to get the gun sight on the Ki 15. With his Hellcat buffeting heavily in resistance, Kid finally got the sight's piper on target and pulled the trigger.

At point-blank range, a single round left each of the six guns. And then they went silent—all remaining 2,394 rounds were jammed in frozen grease. But Kid's immediate concern was regaining control of his recalcitrant Hellcat. He soothed it back into balanced flight. He was just about to radio his failure to the fighter director when he saw an orange glow off his port side, level.

Easing his Hellcat toward the Ki 15, he quickly saw what the source was. One of the six rounds had severed either a hydraulic or oxygen line, causing a fire. Writhing in pain, the Japanese radio operator frantically battled the flames with a small CO_2 extinguisher.

Knowing his only defense was altitude, the Ki 15 pilot began a desperate climb. Kid Brennan closed on his tail, repeatedly trying to charge his guns to no avail. He had to knock this bird out of the sky before it climbed away. With no other option, he moved his Hellcat forward.

He flipped on his anti-collision light and moved even closer. The rotating red light bathed the Japanese aircraft in a one-second cycle. Strobing through the ten-foot propeller blades, the interrupted light made the blades look like giant swords swinging past his windscreen. Kid inched forward and tore into the rudder of the fleeing Ki 15.

The radioman's burnt face lit up in fear as the beacon made its cycle. Kid goaded the Hellcat forward and took another bite. Its heavy prop sunk into the rudder. Fluttering for a moment, the rudder separated, whisking just over his canopy. Amazingly, the Ki 15 continued normal flight.

Kid moved forward again. He stopped when he saw a yawing movement begin. Backing off and easing to the side, he watched as the yawing grew in frequency and severity. The tail began to swing wildly without a rudder to counter the oscillations. Tossed like rag dolls inside the cockpit, the crew was helpless as the aircraft began to plunge toward the ocean. Coldly, Kid pulled the gun's trigger to the first detent, activating the camera to record his kill. The tumbling mass broke apart as the speed built exponentially, igniting when it reached denser air. The night's dark events gave birth to an artificial falling star.

"Splash one Bandit," Kid transmitted into the night.

CHAPTER 22

A P-61 Black Widow streaked through the morning, its Pratt & Whitney R-2800-25 S Double Wasp engines propelling it at maximum power. Major Mark "Hass-man" Hass rolled the big fighter on its side to pull for the shot. The nose immediately began to wobble, making the shot impossible.

"Gunner, I can't get a bead," he transmitted. "Take the shot!"

"Standby, Skipper."

The gunner swung his tail-mounted gun pod, containing four 20-millimeter cannons, into the slipstream to attempt a shot. The movement caused the aircraft to buffet wildly as the bogey escaped. Hass-man fought to control the aircraft, yelling into the ICS.

"Align the guns with the fuselage—go parallel now!"

Rolling wings level, he snatched the throttles back to idle and neutralized the controls as the guns swung back into a trail position. Control of the Black Widow returned to normal.

Hass-man picked up his microphone and transmitted in a frustrated voice, "Knock it off, that's enough for this morning. Return to base."

Silently, the crew flew back to Orlando Army Air Field, well aware the P-61 had major design flaws. To make things worse, they also knew the skipper had committed the squadron to combat in Europe in two months.

Major Hass sat in the corner of their makeshift club. The hot steak and cold beer in front of him were untouched and trading temperatures. First

Lieutenant Jim Stoneman sat down across the wood plank table from his commanding officer.

"Skipper," he said, "the others had the same trouble, even in daylight. When you roll the Widow Maker, the nose uncouples and moves all over the place. You know what happens when the guns swing."

"Widow Maker?"

"Oh yeah, sorry, sir. That's what the guys are calling the P-61."

Hass-man nodded without comment. Along with the landing incidents it was becoming an accurate assessment of the Black Widow's performance qualities. Real concern that they would fail to be ready was beginning to creep into his thoughts. And he did not like the cold.

"Suggestions?" he asked.

"Forget the tail shot; pull for a normal guns kill. Shoot them in the face."

Hass-man shook off the second suggestion.

"It's the damn spoilerons," he said. "Some smart guy decided to turn this pig with spoilers on the wing instead of ailerons. It causes the aircraft to flop rather than rotate around the roll axis. Bottom line, it pulls the sight off of the target."

Both men fell silent, lost in deep thought. Stoneman pulled out a chart and began to draw out an intercept with a grease pencil. Hass closed his eyes and subtly moved his hands in mock flight.

"Sir, we can widen out the intercept a bit more and attack from a pure five or seven o'clock position. Of course, that doesn't solve the target tracking problem."

Hass-man opened his eyes slowly.

"I noticed if you unload the wing ," he said, "reducing the G toward zero, the aircraft rolls cleanly."

"Roger that," replied Stoneman. "I'll rewrite the tactical manual with those changes."

"Okay, Stony. Also add, when they sweeten up the shot, use rudder, not spoileron input."

06:05 Local, 21NOV (18:05 GMT, 20NOV)
Bunkroom 8, USS Suwannee

Kid Brennan sat at his small, fold-down desk, illuminated in the dark red night vision lights. He was writing a benign letter to Theresa. He didn't dare tell her what he had done, what he was capable of. He was sure that if she knew, she would never look at him the same way.

He heard and felt the air pressure change as the door opened and XO Stutzman stepped into the BK.

"Quite a show from the bridge, I heard."

Kid nodded in the eerie luminosity.

"Too close—"

"Yes, I saw your prop."

Both men knew it was not the propeller Kid was referring to.

"Pretty amazing," the older man said. "A one-round burst. That's what the report will show."

Kid shrugged and said nothing. Stutz patted his shoulder and left the bunkroom to Kid and his thoughts.

After pounding the Gilbert Islands for two more weeks, the Suwannee returned to Pearl Harbor. Once pier-side, the air wing was off-loaded to operate from Ford Island while the Suwannee continued to San Diego for re-work.

The air wing settled into a normal training cycle while LTJG David "Kid" Brennan and Theresa tried to do the same with family life. She had never looked more beautiful to him. David came home early one afternoon and found her crying.

"Theresa, what's wrong?"

Embarrassed at being caught, she tried to hide her tears.

"Nothing—"

"Talk to me," he said. "Is something wrong with the baby?"

"No, no, the baby is fine … it's just…." Her voice trailed off.

"Just what?"

She paused for a long time.

"Sometimes, I feel like you can't look at me."

David paused even longer, staring far away.

"Sometimes I can't," he whispered at last.

A tear welled in her eyes. He continued in a tone so hushed she could hardly hear him.

"You are so … good. And I have done things … terrible things—"

Theresa put her finger to his lips.

"You do whatever it takes to come home to us."

CHAPTER 23

1944
05:45 Local, 29JAN (17:45 GMT, 28JAN)
USS Suwannee, Marshall Island Chain

After weeks of intense training, the men of VF-27 received their Christmas wish. The word was out: they would transfer to the USS Princeton CVL-23 after one more line period on the Suwannee. A light carrier was the major leagues. Unlike the escort carrier Suwannee, Princeton could keep up with the big carriers. But first, Fighting 27 would start its year by being attached to Task Force 58, in the invasion of Kwajalein. Kwajalein was part of the Marshall Island chain; more importantly, it was part of Imperial Japan's outer defensive ring. It was considered Japanese soil; they would defend it to the death.

All hands were ecstatic except for Kid Brennan. Each separation was getting harder for him, not easier. Which ship took him away from Theresa didn't really matter to him. It had been a wonderful in-port. He'd spent his days with a mistress, the F6F-3 Hellcat, and his nights with Theresa. His attraction to her was beyond lust, even love. She had permeated his soul, changing his heart. Vengeance was no longer his center. Theresa and his unborn child had begun to quench its fire.

He wanted to stay frozen in that moment forever, but time would not stop. It marched on unmercifully, dragging him to war again. With each wave the Suwannee cut, it grew closer. Like the waves, each minute carried him closer.

Lost in thoughts of home, his world suddenly shook. He looked left to see a handler rocking the wing of his F6F-3, and the launch officer signaling him to pull his head out. Quickly, Kid ran up his PW R-2800 and saluted. Circling his flag impatiently, the launch officer exaggerated touching the deck with it as Stutz watched from his cockpit. Kid finally started to roll down the deck.

Rear Admiral Marc Mitscher had decided to use the twelve aircraft carriers in TF-58 in a new tactic. His plan was to completely sweep the skies over Kwajalein and Roi Islands in a single attack. Mitscher didn't want air superiority, he wanted air supremacy—complete control of the skies over the Marshall Islands.

VF-27 charged into the battle over Roi Island. Jazz led all sixteen aircraft to the merge with the Japanese Zeros. The morning erupted in tracers and flames.

Leading his own division, Kid felt tentative, confused. Heavy impact from 20-millimeter cannon on his armor plating suddenly panicked him. For the first time since he had stepped into a cockpit, he was scared.

Desperate, he snap rolled inverted and pulled into a split-S. Literally flying for his life, he accelerated away from the deadly fire. He continued to pull out of the bottom of the maneuver and began a zoom climb, knowing the Zero could not stay with him. Straining under the G force, Kid frantically looked around for his wingmen. They were gone.

Now pointed straight up, Kid again looked behind his Hellcat and was relieved to see a wingman slash into the fight and flame his pursuer. He could tell by the way the Hellcat maneuvered that it was XO Stutzman.

Bucking wildly, Kid's Hellcat began to fall to the ocean below. *What the hell is going on?* To his shock, he realized he had run out of airspeed and stalled his aircraft in the middle of the biggest dogfight he had ever seen. *I've got to get my head out!*

Kid neutralized the controls and pulled the throttle to idle to prevent a spin. Once pointed straight down, he regained control and jammed the throttle back to emergency. He reached his combat airspeed, snapped on six Gs, and turned back into the fight. Checking six, he saw the XO was still with him, covering his tail.

After pitching back into the fur-ball, Kid jumped a Zero. It was a high-deflection snap shot, left to right. He squeezed the trigger but nothing happened. He looked down and was shocked to see that he had not armed his guns. Just then, in his periphery, he saw the Zero explode—the XO did not miss.

ENDGAME

By 08:00 the last Japanese aircraft had been shot out of the sky. Nearly a hundred of them fell that morning. None would rise again to meet the Americans, and none had been flamed by LTJG David "Kid" Brennan.

After a shaky approach and landing, Kid retreated to his BK. He sat motionless at his fold down desk, staring at a framed picture of Theresa. XO Stutzman banged into the compartment.

"All hands muster in the ready room," he yelled.

As Kid began to stand up, the XO gently pushed him back into his chair and waited for the BK to clear. When the last aviator was out, he reached down and picked up the picture of Theresa. After whistling appreciatively, he yanked open a drawer and set the picture on some T-shirts and then closed the drawer.

"Back there," Stutz said, "you are David: a husband and, soon, a father. Out here, you are Kid Brennan, a fighter pilot and a killer."

19:05 Local, 18FEB (19:05 GMT, 18FEB)
Kate's Manor, Bowdown House, Greenham Common, England

J.T. and Irish were deeply engrossed in the finishing touches of the aviation transport section of Operation Overlord. D-Day was just a few months away; they had to cover three of the four sub operations: Tonga, Detroit, and Chicago. Each involved putting airborne troops behind enemy lines. It was a daunting operational task.

"Hello, boys."

Both men willed themselves not to jump.

"I really hate when he does that," Irish whispered to J.T.

"What's that?" queried Major Dan "Spike" Shanower, with a toothy grin.

"Oh nothing," Irish quipped back. "We were just discussing how long it had been since we had seen our favorite spy. I'm afraid we are no good for midnight jaunts anymore. Security issues. I'm sure you understand."

"Quite so, Irish. I'm here for planning purposes only, I promise."

"Really, I thought I made it clear we are just a tad busy—"

"Too busy to win the war?"

J.T. noticed the large attaché case handcuffed to Spike's wrist and waved him over. An hour later, Spike finished with a sobering statement: "One bomb could level London or New York. If we can take out this one target, it will buy us eighteen months—long enough for your plan to end this."

"Or for our bomb to be developed?" asked J.T.

Spike did not answer or move a facial muscle.

A more daunting target neither man had ever seen. It was in a tight box canyon at the foot of the Alps. A large overhang shielded the heavy water facility from carpet-bombing. One hundred triple-A guns sealed off the entrance to the canyon from even a suicide run.

"Geez, Spike," said Irish, "why don't you just ask us to cure the common cold?"

"So you can't help me?"

"I didn't say that," Irish snapped in response.

J.T. had remained silent, lost in thought. Finally, he spoke.

"I need to bring someone else in on this."

"Give me a name and command," said Spike. "I'll have him transferred here within a week."

"No need." J.T. smiled and glanced at his watch. "He will be down for cocktails in twelve minutes."

CHAPTER 24

05:45 Local, 24FEB (17:45 GMT, 23FEB)
Eniwetok Atoll

For eight days, Task Force 58 pummeled the Japanese bases on Eniwetok. All of VF-27's aircraft were assigned bombing missions, but it didn't matter much because not a single Zero rose into the sky to fight. Jazz's boys were starting to chomp at the bit. They were fighter pilots, not mud movers, and they resented the second string status. While no one dared to voice it near the CO or XO, both of them were acutely aware. Their next mission would make things worse.

A messenger delivered a note summoning LCDR Jasper to CAG's quarters. XO Stutzman was sitting next to him in the ready room when he received it.

"What's going on, Skipper?" Stutz asked.

"I don't know, but I suspect we won't like it. Call an AOM. I'll pass the word when I get back."

"Aye aye."

Twenty minutes later, obviously furious, Jazz returned. He picked up the metal folder that held the numerous daily messages and smashed it against the wall. Everyone froze in place as the metallic message board clanged to the deck, spilling its paper contents.

He struggled for composure but his crimson face left no one in doubt that he was mad enough to rip out spines. Finally, with his voice quivering in rage, he spoke.

"Put together a plan to shuttle our Hellcats to the USS Enterprise as replacements for her lost and damaged aircraft. We will return in Ducks and then the Suwannee will OUTCHOP (detach) TF-58 upon our return."

With forced calm, Jazz walked out of the ready room. He was unable to face his men after this final indignity.

20:15 Local, 25FEB (20:15 GMT, 25FEB)
Kate's Manor, Bowdown House, Greenham Common, England

Colonel Dobbs, Lieutenant Colonel Myers, and Majors Hass and Shanower hovered over charts spread on the massive table as Lieutenant Stoneman briefed them. Spike Shanower stood erect and tapped on a chart.

"So you think you can do this, Lieutenant?" he asked.

"Yes, sir," replied Stoneman. "Each P-61 will be armed with a single two thousand-pounder. We will do a low-level attack using our radar to break out the canyon. Zip in under their guns at three hundred knots. Our bomb release profile is to pull straight up as we close on the canyon's end. Release the bomb in the pull out and then continue to pull onto our backs in an Immelman to escape."

"Once we roll upright," he continued, "the aircraft will be pointed the opposite direction, fifteen hundred feet higher. We simply fly out the way we came in."

"At night?"

Spike turned to face Hass-man, but he let his tactics officer answer.

"Yes, sir—under the cover of darkness, five aircraft, thirty seconds apart," replied Stoneman.

"How about training?" Dobbs didn't sound convinced.

"We start today in Scotland—"

Hass-man took over the brief, sensing Spike's apprehension.

"Stony found a canyon that matches the target pretty closely," he said. We will do day runs first, then night full moon, and finally, total darkness."

"How long?" asked Shanower.

"Full moon is seven days out. It should give us two to three bright nights, and then we will go dark. We will be ready to go the darkest night of the cycle: twenty days, 03:48 time on target."

"What is your PK?"

"Probability of kill is a .67. The first three will have a maximum fusing delay. Last two, none."

"Why not?"

"Stony's major in college was geology; he got ahold of some old mining surveys and is convinced if we hit the overhang here," Hass-man tapped the survey, "we can drop it on the facility."

Spike walked toward the oversized fireplace. Its crackling fire was the only sound in the room. He stared into it and then turned to face the group.

"Okay," he said. "It's a go."

CHAPTER 25

06:00 Local, 16MAR (16:00 GMT, 16MAR)
Pearl Harbor

Tugs pushed the Suwannee into the channel where she transitioned to ship's propulsion. Her giant brass screws churned the oily water as the USS Arizona continued to bleed her fuel oil. On deck, Cue-ball and Andy hid waves to a very pregnant Theresa.

"She's about to pop," Cue-ball observed without moving his lips.

David stood next to her, taunting them. The rumors had turned out to be true: VF-27 was headed to the "Sweet P," CVL-23. Not only would they be on a fast carrier, on the Princeton they would have twenty-four brand new F6F-5 Hellcats—eight more than when they were on Suwannee. There was one more squadron metamorphosis: in violation of Navy regs, they had painted the VF-27 Tiger Cat face on their aircrafts' noses. Angry eyes on the engine cowl with a snarling mouth full of fangs below set them apart from every other squadron in the Navy.

It was an improved Hellcat. The Dash Five had a water injection system that increased horsepower to 2,200. The new engine was designated Pratt & Whitney R-2800-10-W; the W signified water-injected. Water injection would especially help in the hot climate of the Pacific. A new, bulletproof windscreen was incorporated, as well as a strengthened tail and a more aerodynamic nose cowl. But David's favorite improvement was the spring-loaded aileron control tabs. They made the ailerons much more responsive.

With the new aircraft came some new aviators, who had already started an intense training regimen. Kid had his own division and got busy teaching them how to fight. Theresa held squadron barbecues a couple times a week. She sensed that the aviators longed for home and normality, especially the young ones. When not entertaining an entire squadron's wardroom she kept busy converting a bedroom to a nursery. Neither worried nor thought about when the Princeton would take David away. They instead lived in the moment. Each day was to be reveled in.

23:58 Local, 17MAR (23:58 GMT, 17MAR)
Royal Air Force Station Greenham Common

Six P-61B Black Widows idled in the moonless night. Five would launch on one of the most secret missions of the war. The sixth was a turning spare, an extra aircraft already running, with systems checked, in case all systems didn't check. Their engines turned in anticipation of takeoff. They sat low on their struts, each weighted down with fuel and a two-thousand-pound bomb.

For three weeks they had practiced and drilled for this night, for this one mission. At the head of the line, Major Mark Hass sat watching his cockpit clock. In the RO position, First Lieutenant Jim Stoneman nervously ran bit checks, for a third time, on the Westinghouse SRC-720A radar. The internal tests again told him all systems were go.

When the second hand struck midnight, a pair of R-2800-25S double Wasp engines howled to life as Hass-man flicked on his external lights for a three count, then turned them off. His signal was to let the spare know his systems checked out and he was launching. Windows rattled across the base as the aircraft rolled at thirty-second intervals, until aircraft number five. He did not flash his external lights; instead, he taxied clear. Immediately, the turning spare flashed his lights to the tower observers and then rolled in sequence as the fifth aircraft's replacement.

In the tower, Spike, J.T., and Irish watched the blue glow of exhaust generated by the R-2800-25S engines disappear into the darkness. Spike turned from the window, lit a cigarette, and exhaled a long cloud of smoke, tinted red by the lights inside the control tower.

"Well nothing to do but wait," he said.

Five dark phantoms crossed the English Channel and slipped across the coast of France below the Luftwaffe's radar. In the rear cockpits, the ROs watched as the white line of the coast inched forward on their screens. Far shore brightening was easy to break out of the clutter. Now came the hard part—interpreting the radar prediction charts.

Their radar predictions were shadows drawn on topographical charts. The ROs shaded behind hills and highlighted the far shores of lakes and rivers to be crossed. Stony had picked radar-prominent turn points: dams, rivers, bridges. Now they had to match the screens to their charts. A tight timeline and precise flying would help. Each RO would pass corrections to their pilots via intercom.

Periodically, the ROs would switch the radar to air-to-air mode and run the tilt up to check their spacing with the aircraft in front of them. They had to check frequently because the air-to-air mode only had a range of five miles. Stony would scan all the way up to check for potential bogeys running an intercept.

Beads of sweat ran down Stony's face in the cool cockpit. Time compressed: two hours passed in what seemed like two minutes. Ultimately, this entire mission rested on his young shoulders. He alone had to find the canyon and orient the flight on the proper run-in heading, and then navigate inside a granite box—a very tight box—in pitch black, at 300 knots of indicated airspeed.

He wouldn't even get to catch his breath after the pitch and release point because he had to get them out too. Stoneman tweaked the gain on his SRC-720A radar set. He easily broke out a steel bridge from the ground clutter. Checking his timeline, he transmitted over the ICS.

"IP, five mikes out."

They were five minutes from the initial run-in point.

"Stand-by to mark on top IP," Stony began his litany. "Stand-by... stand-by... mark. Turn zero eight one, speed three hundred."

Hass-man jammed the throttles to military-rated power in response, accelerating the Black Widow to three hundred indicated. He eased the throttles back to maintain the speed exactly. In succession, all four of his wingmen accelerated on top of the IP.

"I'm painting the canyon, check right two degrees," Stony continued his target area commands.

In the trailing aircraft, the ROs took one last look at their spacing and then ran the tilt down, switching to air-to-ground for the attack run.

"We are on the attack run; select bomb."

Hass-man selected bomb on the makeshift panel.

"We are in the canyon; four right. Master arm on!"

In the front cockpit, Hass-man flipped the master armament switch and snuck a peek at the total darkness in front of them.

"Ninety seconds from release!"

"Sixty; check left two!"

"Thirty; hard right seven!"

Stoneman's voice raised in volume and octave after each call.

"Twenty; two back to the left!"

"Ten seconds out; stand-by to pitch!"

They were dangerously close to the end of the box canyon.

"Five… four… three… two… PULL!"

Hass pulled three Gs. When the pitch hit ten degrees nose up, Stoneman yelled.

"DROP!"

Pushing the pickle button, Hass felt the bomb release. After smashing on emergency power, he yanked back the controls to get six Gs.

Under the stress of the Gs, he transmitted over the ICS, "Bombs away."

He knew they were close to the overhang but resisted pulling harder, concerned the heavy fighter would stall if he yanked it too hard. As he pulled the Black Widow onto its back, the valley flashed blue for a microsecond. It was 03:48; their wakeup call was answered with uncoordinated triple-A and gunfire. Hass finished the Immelman by rolling upright, and then he pushed the nose back into the valley.

German guns lit up the boundary of the canyon, allowing him to visually see it on egress. Another flash of blue light filled the canyon, reflecting off the white snow. It temporarily blinded him.

"Give me a heading, Stony."

"Two left… steady up."

"Stony I'm flash blind, call my turn." A hint of concern was in Hass's voice.

"Ease your turn back to the right, STOP TURN!" Stony commanded.

"You are picking up a slight descent. Give me a bit of nose up trim."

Stony knew Dash Three would be under them a mere four hundred feet. Triple-A was going everywhere; some high, some low. The Germans even seemed to be shooting each other across the canyon. A third explosion bathed the valley as Hass-man's Black Widow cleared the rock walls at four hundred indicated.

"You are clear of the target area."

The OPLAN called for the aircraft to go back to the deck and egress low and fast. Hass-man had finally gotten his cockpit lights turned up so he could read the instruments. He wanted to check on his boys and began an arcing climb as a fourth bomb popped like a flash bulb. He turned to the right to keep the valley in view; the last bomb flashed blue, followed almost immediately by an orange eruption. Five had pulled up late and hit the overhang.

Major Mark Hass slumped in his seat, Stoneman's artificially generated voice filling his ears as they continued a slight climb. Being in the tail of the fuselage, he had seen the orange impact and instinctively, like Hass-man, knew what it was.

"Skipper ... Skipper! Get back on the deck. Turn two eight zero; two hundred on the speed."

09:58 Local, 18MAR (09:58 GMT, 18MAR)
Kate's Manor, Bowdown House, Greenham Common, England

By 10:00, the four surviving crews sat around the grand table in the expansive dining room. All the doors were closed and locked. A hearty breakfast sat in front of each crewman; none was touched. Instead, they sipped at India pale ales in silence. Spike quietly came through the door with J.T. and Irish close behind; they could hear it re-lock as the men sat down. Spike opened a simple manila envelope.

"First, gentlemen," he said, "deepest condolences. My HUMINT, human intelligence, sources confirm the fifth striker impacted the overhang."

He pulled a series of 8-by-10 photos out of the envelope and displayed them on the table. They were still wet.

"We got BDA, bomb damage assessment, from a Recce bird at sunrise." He pointed to the first one. "It appears we have a hit on the power station— technically a miss, but it is flattened."

He continued, waving his hand across the rest of the photos.

"We believe the other two delay-fused bombs were direct hits. But we can't really tell because our resident geologist was correct. A section of the overhang came down. The facility has been deemed a total loss. Good job, gents—this mission is complete."

The crews did not react, either out of grief or fatigue.

"Get some rest," Spike went on. "We will move you back to your base tonight."

All of the crewmen began to file out of the dining room. Spike asked Hass to remain in the room. He sat back down, folding his hands in front of him.

"Major, I'm afraid I will have to classify their loss a training accident."

Hass-man didn't raise his voice or react in any visible way.

"No," he said simply. "You call it a black project, secret mission, or whatever you want. Their families will receive Distinguished Flying Crosses and Purple Hearts."

With his statement complete, Hass-man headed for the door. Spike started to say something but J.T. tapped his arm and waved his head no. Spike nodded silently, giving way to the honors of the aviators. He knew it was not worth fighting.

Picking up an 8-by-10 showing the complete destruction of the heavy water facility, he studied it for a few moments and then tossed it on the table. He thought about rounding up families in the post-war chaos.

"Well, the easy part is over," he mumbled to himself.

J.T. and Irish both stared at him in disbelief. Spike laughed at their looks.

"Forget it, you don't want to know."

CHAPTER 26

06:00 Local, 29MAY (16:00 GMT, 29MAY)
USS Princeton, Pearl Harbor

L TJG David "Kid" Brennan felt the power vibrate beneath his feet as the USS Princeton churned the water to get underway. He had asked Theresa to stay home since it was so early in the morning and she was so pregnant. His mind wandered as he thought about becoming a father in less than a month. Rough Ryder elbowed him as they stood at attention, manning the rails.

"There she is," he said. Kid looked to where she always stood on the Ford Island Quay—she was indeed there, smiling and waving. He broke military bearing and waved back, not even trying to hide it. Then he blew an exaggerated kiss, causing her to laugh. All too soon, she was out of sight. When the formation was secured, he walked aft and stood at the ramp of the flight deck, watching Pearl slowly dissolve into the Pacific.

"You okay, Kid?" XO Stutzman had walked up next to him. Kid smiled big.

"I'm great. XO," he replied. "I can't wait to get back in the fight. It's time for the end game."

Stutz laughed. "Okay, killer—let's go get them!"

Thus began the most epic light carrier cruise of World War II.

16:38 Local, 02JUN (16:38 GMT, 02JUN)
Headquarters, US Strategic Air Forces in Europe

Major Hass sat calmly outside of General Spaatz's office, where he had been sitting for days. His Black Widows had not been cleared for combat and Hass-man was not leaving until he got an explanation. He suspected it was politics—Spaatz worked directly for Ike. General Eisenhower was trying to hold together the Supreme Allied Command. Hass-man figured the Brits were pushing the Mosquito as the preferred night fighter. After everything his men had gone through to get the P-61s on line, he had no intention of letting the brass ground them. Hass-man watched passively as an aide de camp entered General Spaatz's inner office.

"Is he still out there?" Spaatz asked when the door was closed.

"Yes, General, he hasn't moved. He doesn't even read any magazines."

"Damn it! Let the little shit in."

Major Mark "Hass-man" Hass, fighter pilot, strutted into the general's office. He snapped off a perfect salute and stood at attention in front of Spaatz's desk as if he had waited no more than fifteen minutes.

"Good afternoon, General. I'm Major Hass—"

"I know who you are and what you want, Major. So why don't we cut through the bullshit?"

"Okay, General," said Hass-man. "Let's. Why is the 422nd not operational?"

Ike had been leaning on Spaatz hard. He wanted one night-fighter, and wanted Spaatz to throw a bone to the RAF and pick the Mosquito. The problem with that was standing right in front of him. He had been briefed on the strike this guy Hass had pulled off. General Spaatz did not appreciate his aircraft being used on missions without being told. And he really didn't appreciate the smug look on that damn spy Shanower's face when he got the brief.

"Major Hass, I have responsibilities beyond a squadron or air wing, even the entire US Air Corps—"

"I thought we were cutting through the crap, General," Hass-man cut in. "I smell politics."

"You're damn right it's politics! The Brits want the Mosquito. It is their country—"

"Then we will not fly?"

"Never!" Spaatz pounded his fist on the desk in exclamation.

"Roger that, General," replied Hass-man. "You will have my resignation as commanding officer in the morning."

"It will be the end of your career."

"Ha! I'm here to win a war, not a promotion. Go ahead."

Not accustomed to being laughed at, the General fumed as Hass-man executed a perfect salute and about-face, strutting out exactly the way he had strutted in.

18:08 Local, 02JUN (18:08 GMT, 02JUN)
Royal Air Force Station Scorton

Major Hass, commanding officer of the Fighting 422nd, turned to face his crews. He had no intention of lying to them so he simply laid out the facts.

Once he was done, he asked, "Any questions?"

There were none from the shocked crewmen. They shuffled out in silence after being dismissed.

An hour later, one by one, the men entered his office, set their wings on his desk, saluted, and walked out. First Lieutenant Stoneman was the last in.

"They can keep us in the Army, Skipper," he said, "but they can't make us fly."

"Does this really mean that much to you guys?"

"Yes, sir. It does."

Hass-man nodded, saying nothing.

07:00 Local, 03JUN (07:00 GMT, 03JUN)
Headquarters, US Strategic Air Forces in Europe

At 07:00 Major Mark Hass barged into General Spaatz office, slapped down his letter of resignation and then dumped a bag of wings on the general's desk. Startled, the general spilled his coffee onto the letter.

"We quit," said Hass-man. "I'll be at the US press pool explaining to my old friends why."

CHAPTER 27

21:30 Local, 05JUN (21:30 GMT, 05JUN)
Royal Air Force Station North Witham

A flare shot from a catwalk on the control tower rocketed into the dark sky. Twenty C-47 Dakotas, loaded with three hundred Pathfinder Paratroopers from the 82nd and 101st Airborne divisions, began to roll, one aircraft after another. Colonel J.T. Dobbs flew the lead plane. Operation Overlord was under way. The Pathfinders would be the first American troops on French soil. They would set up the drop zones for the main airborne forces that would attack German defenses behind the beaches of Normandy. The press would dub it D-Day.

Circling until all twenty were aboard the flight, J.T. turned toward the Normandy Coast. Chaff aircraft flew slowly across the English Channel in front of the main force, dumping rolls of foil cut to different lengths. This chaff was designed to cause interference with the German radar. J.T. prayed it would work. Of course, it didn't matter now—it either did or did not. Either way, they were committed.

His flight maintained strict radio silence so they wouldn't give away their presence to the Germans listening. Suddenly, a flash of light caught J.T.'s eye. He turned quickly to see one of his wingman's engines erupt in flame.

"You got it!" he barked out to his co-pilot so he could watch the stricken aircraft fight for its life.

It burned brightly, and he could see that the propeller was not feathered. Inside the cockpit, the crew struggled to get the prop faired into the wind so they could maintain control. It would not react to the propeller lever's input.

Slowly at first, they fell back and then began to fall toward the water below.

J.T. could not dwell on his crew and the paratroopers who, no doubt, would have to ditch in the channel. Ahead, he could see air raid spotlights searching the sky. The Germans knew they were coming. To make things worse, clouds were in the area. Flak began to explode around them as they crossed the beach. His green pilots, having never seen it, began to try to maneuver around it. J.T. broke radio silence and demanded they maintain formation. It was too late: many had become separated in the clouds.

"Five minutes out," his navigator called over the ICS.

J.T. reached over and flipped on the yellow pre-jump light in the back. He heard the cadence of the jumpmaster begin immediately as he shouted over the roar of the engines and airstream.

"Get ready!"

Men who had been asleep were elbowed awake by their buddies.

"Left side, stand up!"

"Right side, stand up!"

Each soldier now stood in the cabin.

"Hook up!"

The paratroopers hooked their lines to a steel cable, closed the latch, and then put a pin into the hook to ensure that it would not open.

"Check equipment!"

Each man checked the parachute and gear of the man in front of him.

"Shuffle to the door!"

In the cockpit, J.T. felt the weight shift as the warriors shuffled to the rear of the Dakota.

"Stand in the door!"

The lead man of the first stick, or row of paratroopers, stood in the open door of the C-47. Exploding flak was in full view.

J.T.'s navigator called out, "One minute," over the ICS.

Seconds stretched as they bounced through the flak.

Finally, the navigator called, "Mark on top."

J.T. flipped on the green light at 00:15 and heard, "Go, go, go!"

Within seconds, the aircraft disgorged its troopers. Their parachutes blossomed immediately. Some of the other aircrews were caught by surprise and dropped late. The Pathfinders were scattered; some would not find their drop zones. Others were engaged by German troops immediately, and still others found their drop zones purposely flooded.

Again, it didn't matter. J.T. knew Irish was leading the first wave of the main airborne force across the channel now, a mere half-hour behind. The Pathfinders had to get their Eureka radio beacons up and broadcasting so Irish's wave could home in on them. They then had to mark the site with holophone lights. Eureka's accuracy was only good up to two miles; the lights were activated for accuracy. Unfortunately, many had gone down on the C-47 that ditched. Many more couldn't be activated due to the presence of German troops.

Irish was lead aircraft of four-hundred-plus troop carriers. He was well aware that sixty percent did not have navigators on board. He could also see the clouds ahead and knew what was coming. Flak was everywhere as he approached DZ D; regardless, Irish put his troops on the drop zone accurately. His flight had stayed together through the clouds. Being a realist, he knew most would not.

J.T. had turned back to England and was crossing the channel at maximum cruise speed, headed for RAF Greenham Common. He would lead the first C-47 wave, towing Waco gliders. The gliders held the heavy weapons the paratroopers would need to defend against tanks and hold the positions they were taking.

At 01:51, he found himself watching another flare climb into the pre-dawn sky as he eased the throttles up on his R-1830s. He moved them gingerly so he would not prop-wash the glider attached to his tail by a tow cable. Howling at emergency power, the engines seemed unable to move the two aircraft. Finally reaching sixty knots, J.T. gently raised the tail. He could feel the Waco pilot fighting to keep the glider on the runway. Then he felt it lift into the air. He kept his wheels on the runway to get as much air speed as he could before nudging his C-47 into the air.

Once established in a climb, J.T. told the copilot to reset the power for a max power climb. His most experienced pilots were on this mission; the rendezvous went much smoother. On time, they pushed for the coast. J.T. led his fifty-two C-47s, towing fifty-two Waco gliders, on a mission code-named Chicago. Mission Detroit launched with fifty-two Waco's right behind them.

As they approached the Normandy coast, he could see operation Neptune was not going as planned. He had memorized his plan and could see by the firefights that many units were out of position. But he had to let it go. These fifty-two gliders had to be dropped on target. Checking his Eureka beacon, he could see that it was functioning perfectly. He kept it right on the nose, broke out the landing zone lights, and turned toward them. J.T. knew all surprise was lost.

"Chicago, stand-by for release … release," he broadcast in the clear.

At 04:00, fifty-two gliders were dropped and descended to the DZ. Ninety-two percent would be on target, an unqualified success. Detroit only put sixty-two percent on the DZ but both contained heavy weapons, and the overall missions of immediate support were achieved.

* * * *

Irish and J.T. sat in the operations office drinking coffee. They were exhausted and discouraged. Their plan had turned into an unmitigated disaster. Irish reached into a bottom drawer, pulled out a bottle of whiskey, and poured some into J.T.'s cup, then his own.

"What a friggin' goat rope," he said. "What happened?"

"Clouds, flak, green crews—the fog of war, Irish."

"I hope Ike doesn't have us shot."

"Oh, I wouldn't worry about that, boys."

Both men were too tired to flinch at Spike's latest unannounced arrival.

"You have another cup of that?" he asked.

Irish poured Spike a special coffee and then sat back down next to J.T. Both watched as Spike sipped at it, smiled, and then gave them both an appreciative nod. As he savored the concoction, he set down the folder he was carrying. It was clearly labeled Top Secret.

"Ike was quite pleased with Neptune's results."

"Excuse me?" said J.T.

"He expected, planned, for much worse," Spike explained. "Paratroopers are a special breed. Ike anticipated that they would take the initiative and reconsolidate."

He tossed the folder to Irish.

"Check it out for yourself," he said. "Most of the objectives were achieved. Never underestimate the American soldier. Our hosts did, to their own peril."

Irish shared the folder with J.T. They were pleasantly surprised by the results.

"Chin up, lads. The Allies are on the offensive."

21:13 Local, 06JUN (11:13 GMT, 06JUN)
USS Princeton, South Pacific

Oppressive heat drove the ship's crew up onto the flight deck at night.

ENDGAME

They made the best of it, showing movies and setting up huge barbecue pits that grilled hundreds of hotdogs and hamburgers. Kid, Rough, and one of the new guys relaxed in the warm breeze, watching a Daffy Duck cartoon and waiting for the main feature to start.

The new guy stood up and excitedly proclaimed, "This war thing's not so bad. I'll go get us some sliders."

Without taking his eyes off the screen, Rough asked Kid, "Were we ever that clueless?"

"I hope not. That nugget is too daffy to be scared."

They both smiled.

"New call sign," Kid said.

"Daffy, I like it. Done," replied Rough. "Do you think he will like it?"

Both men laughed.

CHAPTER 28

06:00 Local, 12JUN (20:00 GMT, 11JUN)
Over the Philippine Sea

Guam rose out of the grey Pacific as VF-27 flew toward her as Jazz led all twenty-four F6F-5 Hellcats into battle. A rising sun had reached the Hellcats, accentuating the vibrant colors of their painted, tiger cat faces. Kid looked left; Rough Ryder was on his wing with his nugget pilot, Whitey. Looking to his right, he could see the smiling face of his wingman, Daffy. Even the new call sign did not dampen the young pilot's enthusiasm. Kid smiled to himself. *Man, that boy is just not right.*

Task Force 58 had a force of fifteen aircraft carriers. TF-58 was divided into five groups; Princeton was in 58.3, which also included the carriers Enterprise, Lexington, and San Jacinto. VF-27 was attacking in a classic pincer; Enterprise's VF-6 was attacking from the south. Kid was amused that many of their old aircraft no doubt were in the air while they flew brand-new Dash Fives.

J.T.'s words from almost two years earlier flashed through his mind: In a fighter's cockpit there is only the fight, only your wingman and the enemy. Nothing else and no one else exists. You must protect one and the other kill.

Jazz bumped up the speed to near redline. Kid looked ahead and saw why. Black dots, at least fifty of them, were visible ahead. He was filled with anticipation of the fight; he signaled his flight to arm up their guns and then charged his own. As expected, the dots grew into Zeros. Jazz slashed Fighting 27 through the middle of their formation, guns blazing.

The clean Pacific morning turned dirty in a single pass as Zeros erupted in flames, trailing black oily plumes. At the merge, every aircraft seemed to turn in a different direction. Kid rolled hard left and dove on two divisions below him. He twisted his flight of four Hellcats into position behind the trailing flight of Zeros. At max range, he opened up. All four maneuvered weakly before exploding in flames.

Pulling up into a steep climb, he enticed the second division of Zeros to follow; they did. Once they fell away in their futile attempt to reach his Hellcats, Kid simply rolled inverted and dove after them, catching them quickly. Twenty-four .50 caliber machine guns let loose a firestorm of glowing lead. A mixture of orange and black smeared across the blue canvas of the ocean below.

Kid blew through the carnage, accelerated to three hundred knots, and then pitched back up into the hornets' nest. A section of Hellcats were defensive, chased by three Zeros. Kid turned his flight hard right and reengaged, flaming all three almost immediately. Quickly changing course, he saw a section of Japanese fighters roll in on his flight.

"Whitey, break left; Bandits left seven."

Whitey reacted instantly to the command, turning so hard he ended up in the lead position when the rest of the flight turned. It put the Zeros in between them.

"Whitey, weave."

Whitey reversed his turn and dragged the Zeros right in front of his waiting wingmen's guns. They filled the sky with tracers. The engagement ended in two simultaneous fireballs. Every time Kid glanced right to check on Daffy, he was in perfect position and had a huge smile.

Movement drew his eyes to the ocean: two Zeros were trying to escape. Snap rolling inverted, he gave chase. Whitey, still in front, did not see the move; Rough stayed with his young wingman. Kid and Daffy pursued the Zeros who were diving for the surface. They caught the fleeing Japanese pilots just above the ocean. Plainly inexperienced, they didn't even maneuver. Kid and Daffy flamed the wingman and were peppering the lead when it suddenly and violently nosed over into the Philippine Sea.

Kid yanked on a hard turn to check his own six. He had to assume the two Zeros were not maneuvering hard because they were waiting for wingmen to shoot Kid and Daffy off of their tail. Kid's six was clear but they were in a bad spot, on the bottom of a vicious dogfight. Any Zero could roll in on them from above and flame them.

Looking up, Kid was awestruck by the aerial battle raging overhead. Aircraft were raining down like the embers of spent fireworks. It was astounding: columns of smoke rose from Guam, juxtaposed against trails of dark smoke plummeting and white parachutes gently descending throughout the scene. Kid took it in in a fraction of a second. It would stay seared in his memory for life.

He and Daffy were most certainly sitting ducks. Accelerating to his best maneuvering speed, he bugged out of the fight. He pointed away from the melee and began a climb while scanning behind his flight. At eight thousand feet, he turned back into the fight and sped up to three hundred knots. He figured the fur ball was at least as low as he was by now. He got a quick fuel check from Daffy and figured they had enough fuel for another pass.

Scanning the horizon for targets, he realized the sky was eerily empty; the fight was over. Only a moment ago a hundred aircraft clashed in an epic fight to the death. Now, only the smoke columns on Guam remained. Kid turned for the Princeton.

07:00 Local, 13JUN (21:00 GMT, 12JUN)
Imperial Japanese Navy Headquarters, Manila

Admiral Soemu Toyoda reviewed the after-action reports from the air battle over Orote Field on Guam from the day before. He already had a report of naval bombardment from American battleships on Saipan from earlier in the morning. The gaijin's plan was beginning to crystallize in front of him. Imperial Command had anticipated the Americans would move methodically from the outer islands toward the inner line of defense.

They were not. Instead, they were engaging in an island-hopping campaign while simultaneously attacking the Japanese means of defending and supplying the islands that were skipped over. The U.S. fleet would sweep his aircraft from the skies and sink his ships; the garrisons passed would die on the vine. American marines would seize islands and operate them like giant aircraft carriers, putting the long range B-29s on them. A fiery hell would rain down on Japan unless he stopped them now in the Marianas.

He was no fool; the plan to inflict huge casualties upon the Americans so they would sue for peace had failed. They just kept coming, kept building, kept innovating. He must stop their offensive and consolidate a line of defense. Admiral Toyoda initiated his plan to stop the American fleet:

ENDGAME

Operation A-Go. He ordered an attack fleet to assemble and sortie against the Americans, and all available land-based aviation assets to Guam.

On 16 June, Vice-Admiral Jisaburo Ozawa rendezvoused his fleet of five heavy and four light carriers, with five battleships and their escorting cruisers and destroyers, off the coast of the Philippine Islands. Ozawa turned due east to meet the American 5th Fleet west of the Mariana Islands and destroy them.

Admiral Nimitz, Commander-in-Chief Pacific, warned Admiral Spruance, Commander 5th Fleet, they were underway toward his forces. CINPAC staffers had broken the Japanese code in 1942, and they had not changed it. Spruance's 5th Fleet was divided into two forces, the invasion fleet and TF 58. Task Force 58 was divided into five groups in battle formation: TG-58.7 had seven battleships and was on station, furthest west. TG-58.4, with three carriers, was north of them. TG-58.1, TG-58.2, and TG-58.3, all containing four carriers, were oriented in a line north to south, positioned between the Marianas and TG-58.7/TG-58.4. Eight heavy cruisers, thirteen light, fifty-eight destroyers, and twenty-eight submarines sailed in support of the capital ships.

On the night of the 18 June, Vice Admiral Marc Mitcsher, Commander of TF-58, requested permission to sail west and meet the enemy. Spruance was concerned that the fleet sailing toward them was a diversion, meant to draw the battle fleet away from the invasion fleet. He feared another Japanese fleet would make an end run to destroy the invasion force; thus, he ordered Mitscher to hold station.

05:50 Local, 19JUN (19:50 GMT, 18JUN)
Over the Philippine Sea

A lone Zero found TF-58 at 05:50 and radioed its position to the Japanese command. Orote Field on Guam began to launch aircraft for a strike. As they circled over the field, US radar detected their presence and launched fighters from the Bella Wood, in TG-58.3, to attack. Sweet P was also in TG-58.3; Kid watched them launch while sitting in Alert-5 in the cockpit of his aircraft.

He switched over to Red Crown frequency and listened to the fight. It was a replay of the fight on 12 June. A shocking revelation had been made during the post-mission debriefs of the first fighter sweep. These Japanese airmen were not the same. Instead of tigers, the Japanese aviators were lambs led to slaughter.

Kid was listening so intently he had not noticed that the Princeton had turned into the wind. A recall to Bella's Hellcats, broadcast over Red Crown, bewildered him until he saw a flurry of activity on the deck of Sweet P. Big props began to sweep as engines fired up. Kid robotically went though the start sequence and then sat calmly, waiting for the signal to launch.

Climbing into the morning, he was surprised to immediately get a hot vector from the fighter director. They were not being allowed to circle and rendezvous; instead they were being sent directly to the fight. Kid knew this meant the Japanese were close. He closed his canopy and pulled down his goggles. After he set power for a slow cruise to get his chicks aboard, he armed and charged his guns.

All around him, Hellcats rose from the decks of twelve carriers. He knew that to the north, three more carriers were launching theirs as well. Hundreds of fighters were in sight, all climbing to the west. They would have the midmorning sun at their backs. Things couldn't be better for them.

At seventy miles, the Japanese circled to re-group their formation. Those ten minutes allowed the Hellcats to attack. Because of the expedited launch, Kid found himself in the lead of at least two squadrons; his division was intact. But he could see others were mixed. Some were even composed of aircraft from different squadrons. It didn't matter. Due to standardized training, an effective and far superior force sped toward the sixty-nine Japanese strikers.

Coming into sight, Kid could see sixteen Zeros providing cover from above the strikers' formation. His wave of Hellcats was at a higher altitude; he would attack the fighters coming out of the sun. They would not have a chance. A devastating first pass announced the arrival of the Hellcats. The Zero fighter cover was neutralized by Kid's attack. Engaged with a superior force, they were instantly defensive. The bombers were on their own.

Wave after wave of Hellcats tore into the Japanese strikers. Most of the strikers were Zeros loaded with bombs. Once jumped by a Hellcat, they would jettison their bomb and fight. This effectively neutralized them as bombers. The sequence of the morning was a bomb falling away followed by the Zero spinning to the ocean in flames.

Kid's two squadrons had decimated the Zero cover and then turned to attack the rear of the strikers' formation as they flew toward TF-58. Hellcats were already swarming them. The Japanese aircraft were outnumbered, outclassed by the F6F, and flown by inexperienced crews. It was an airborne slaughter. Kid dove into the conflagration with his guns blazing. His biggest concern was accidentally shooting one of his fellow aviators.

Kid jumped the trailing flight of Japanese Aichi D3A Val bombers, flaming one at max range. So many aircraft were jammed into the tight airspace that he had to pull up to avoid a mid-air collision. On a high perch slightly aft and to the right, he watched as his kill plummeted with at least twenty others to the ocean below. Seeing an opening, he rolled inverted and pulled back into the fight, flaming another. With each pass, his wingmen also added to his kills. Finally, there simply were no more Japanese aircraft to shoot. Kid could see more falling in the distance.

Of the sixty-nine aircraft in the first attack, only a few made it as far as the group of battleships. None penetrated to a carrier group. The USS South Dakota took a direct hit from one of the bombers, sustaining casualties but staying in the fight.

"Ninety-nine; all Hellcats snap vector two seven five; multiple Bandits."

Fighter control had addressed all the aircraft with the ninety-nine call. Kid knew it had to be a second strike. Turning his flight back to the west, he glanced at his watch. Thirty-one minutes had passed. He began a climb and got a fuel check from his flight; they were all good on gas. Kid pressed toward the enemy. Scanning left and right, he saw that again he was leading a force of squadron strength or more.

Ahead, contrails pointed at the Japanese flight. Its size almost took Kid's breath away. There were at least a hundred aircraft coming toward him. Glancing right, he saw Daffy's smiling face, nodding enthusiastically at the attackers. Kid smiled and gave him a thumbs-up.

They crashed headlong into the flight. Kid shot the strike's leader in the face at the merge. It disintegrated as he flashed by. Contrails were so heavy the ships below could watch the fight as it moved closer. Waves of Hellcats crashed into the Japanese until seventy were splashed.

Kid's guns were empty before his fuel reached bingo. Four kills in a single mission. He had heard one of his fellow pilots call it a turkey shoot over the radio. It truly was. With his ammunition expended, Kid returned overhead the Sweet-P and waited for it to turn into the wind for recovery. Suddenly the ship's guns exploded in fury; he was startled at first, hoping they had not mistaken his flight for the enemy. Then he saw a couple of torpedo bombers, running on the surface, drop their weapons: *Oh, no!*

Kid craned his neck and watched the torpedoes trail harmlessly into the wake. It was a near miss for the Princeton. He could not believe that not only did the Vals make it through the Hellcats, they made it through a wall of flak.

Kid got to watch the next dogfight from his cockpit, chained to the deck of the Princeton. He felt vulnerable; even so it didn't quash his appetite. He consumed his entire box lunch while watching the swirling contrails above. When the white contrail turned black, he knew it signified a kill.

At 13:00, VF-27 launched to CAP overhead Orote Field on Guam. Jazz was back out front; Kid was exhausted and welcomed being in the pack instead of leading. The day finished the same way it had started, in a swirling dogfight. Kid recorded his fifth kill of the day when Jazz jumped the fourth wave of Ozawa's forces, who had been unable to find TF-58, and diverted to Orote to refuel. Even though outnumbered two-to-one, VF-27 downed thirty of forty-nine strikers and damaged the rest.

13:50 Local, 19JUN (03:50 GMT, 19JUN)
Twenty Nautical Miles Southeast of Saipan

Cue-ball floated lazily on the trade winds as he headed for his patrol station. Canopy open, he enjoyed the cool air at eight thousand feet. Totally relaxed, he had his elbow out as if he were home in St. Louis driving a cab, not piloting a brand new TBF-1 Avenger. His radioman was highly amused by his pilot's relaxed demeanor. Cue-ball was fun to fly with and one hell of a dive-bomber pilot. He tapped the tail gunner behind him and pointed to their pilot. The tail gunner keyed the ICS.

"Comfy up there, Ensign?"

"Absolutely, Dougie. I am a man of leisure, a genius of comfort."

They were both still laughing when Cue-ball descended through the overcast and suddenly snapped the Avenger inverted and pulled four Gs. He slid the lever forward to close the canopy and armed his depth bombs as the bomb bay slowly opened. With the Wright R-2600-20 howling at full power, Dougie instantly armed the tail gun and searched for bandits.

"What you got, Ensign?"

"Submarine. Stand-by for drop."

Below them, Imperial Japanese Navy submarine I-184, the Sensuikan, was desperately crash-diving. Lieutenant Commander Rikihisa had seen the TBF Avenger slip beneath the clouds and ordered the dive. Covered with saltwater that flooded in as he pulled closed the hatch, he held on as the nose of I-184 pointed to the ocean bottom.

ENDGAME

Cue-ball watched as the submarine slipped below the surface. He instantly put his aim point ahead on the submarines track. His persona, even his voice, changed as he fell upon I-184 like a bird of prey. Balancing the aircraft perfectly with rudder and aileron, he ensured the bombs would fly true to their target. Cue-ball actually found the gun sight a distraction; he could perceive the spot in the windscreen that didn't move. That is where the bombs would hit. At exactly 830 feet, he released two depth bombs and pulled out.

Both bombs impacted over I-184; the overpressure caused by their explosion breached the hull forward of the sail bridge. Water flooded into the submarine, sweeping her crew up and smashing them into steel bulkheads before drowning them as it sought every space. Weight became the enemy of the boat as millions of pounds flooded into it, pulling I-184 deeper. She was plunging into the Marianas Trench when the water pressure crushed her entire hull, compressing the oxygen until it combusted.

IJN Sensuikan's crewmen were all dead long before the sonar operator on the USS Suwannee recorded the impact on the floor of the trench in the ship's sonar log. Above, a debris field blossomed on the surface as the Avenger circled. Cue-ball's mood turned melancholy, watching the debris, mixed with bodies bobbing in an oil slick.

Later that night, Andy Levine found Ensign Paul "Cue-ball" Bement, recent nominee for the Navy Cross, sitting alone in the Suwannee's Wardroom. He was picking at the chicken adobo on his plate. It was a strange, almost neon color. Andy sat down next to him.

"Did you ever wonder what makes it that color?" he asked.

"I don't think we want to know."

They sat silently, comfortably, for a long while as only friends who had been tested together could. Finally Andy spoke.

"Busy day, I heard."

Cue-ball shrugged.

"Navy Cross?"

Again he merely shrugged, then answered quietly.

"I killed a ship and its entire crew today."

"They'd have killed us—"

"Oh, I know," Cue-ball replied. "Hey, I'm not about to jump overboard or anything. But did you ever think of the repercussions?"

"David lives with them, Paul, every day."

By the day's end, not only the Sensuikan was on the bottom: Ozawa's flagship Taiho, the newest and largest IJN carrier, as well as the carrier Shokaku and 350 aircraft had joined her. American submarines had sunk the IJN carriers.

Mitcsher moved west during the night to find the rest of the Japanese fleet and destroy it.

CHAPTER 29

05:30 Local, 20JUN (19:30 GMT, 19JUN)
USS Princeton, Philippine Sea

Dawn broke, as it always did in the South Pacific, with the purity of a raw splash of color. Kid had a fleeting thought of the son who had been born to him as he killed men the day before. A single line in a message sent from Pearl had announced the birth. He forced himself to focus. First in line to launch, he watched the launch officer, who stood cross-armed watching the yardarm, waiting for the signal.

Kid saw movement behind him; Daffy was holding his hands as if they were guns and shooting them like the Yosemite Sam cartoon they had watched the night before. Daffy's animation and big, goofy grin caused Kid to start laughing as the launch signal was run up. He was still laughing as he rolled down the deck and into the dawn.

Guam's grey cliffs rose vertically out of the light brown beach. They were capped with incredibly dense jungle. While beautiful, the scene had a sinister quality of foreboding. As he watched, waiting for Zeros to rise from Orote and fill the sky that wrapped the enchanting cliffs, they erupted. Plumes of brown, black, and orange, preceded by white flashes, laced the ridgeline. Kid was struck by the contrast between the cliffs' natural beauty and the sudden, destructive force of man. Sixteen-inch naval guns continued to pound the coast.

A war raged right in front of him; he literally had a front-row seat. And yet he was bored because he was only an observer. Vengeance still coursed through his veins. War was not a spectator sport. Now, he was nothing more than a voyeur.

Kid Brennan blasted his Hellcat past the bow of the Princeton and curtly kissed off his wingmen. Rolling onto his left wingtip, he pulled on five Gs and yanked the throttle to idle in frustration. Frustration, born of yet another flight where the ordnance tape over his gun ports stayed in place—not a single shot fired.

His big propeller and the high G slowed his Hellcat dramatically. Throwing down the gear and flap handles at the abeam position, he kept turning to final approach. His circular pattern put him on centerline behind the ship. Kid pushed up the power of his R-2800 as he rolled wings level on a very short final. The LSO flashed him a cut signal and he settled onto the number two wire.

Still in a funk as he flung open the ready room door, Kid was met by half of the squadron rushing out. He grabbed Rough Ryder by the arm and stopped him.

"Where is everyone going?"

"CVIC," replied Rough. "Mitscher just launched the Northern Task Force's air groups. They found the Japs!"

"How far?"

"Three hundred miles," Rough said as he moved down the passageway.

Kid looked at his watch and shouted after him, "It will be dark by the time they get back!"

He quickly got out of his flight gear, threw it on his ready room chair, and then hustled down to CVIC. Princeton's aviators were sitting quietly, listening to the hum of the radio.

"Red Crown holds two groups bearing; two three five and two three zero from bull's eye."

Bull's eye was a pre-briefed latitude and longitude; it allowed the radar operators to give the bogey's position without giving away the striker's. The fighter director picked a point north hoping to pull the Zeros away from the strike. It worked: the Zeros showed their bellies and the Hellcats tore into them.

"Red Leader, bogeys two o'clock high, turning north."

An excited voice broke through the static.

"Okay boys, arm 'em up."

An east Texas drawl responded.

"Short bursts, in close. Don't waste ammo."

Engaged with the Hellcats, the Zeros, that only numbered thirty-five, could not defend their fleet. They were Ozawa's last experienced fighter pilots but, hugely outnumbered, they fell to the Hellcats' guns. Avengers found the Japanese carriers and attacked in waves with bombs and torpedoes. Hiyo was attacked and sunk with two oilers. Zuikaku, Junyo, and Chiyoda were damaged by bombs. Twenty American attackers were shot down.

As the naval aviators of TF-58 turned toward the darkness, the fires that burned behind them signaled the end of Imperial Japan's naval aviation—it presaged the end of empire. Had the US naval aviators known, they still would not have given it a second thought. Their concern loomed beyond, in the darkness, deeper into the Pacific night.

Kid glanced at his watch and looked around the room. Sweat-glistened faces turned away from the silent speaker and looked at their feet. Envy turned to doom and guilt, hanging in the stifling space like a foul odor.

Making eye contact with Rough, Kid nodded to the hatch. Once in the passageway, he spoke quietly.

"Let's go get something to eat. It is going to be a while."

Kid pushed his beef roulade around with a fork. They were nicknamed Nairobi trail markers due to their remarkable visual similarity to what was left behind by a passing caravan of camels.

"Kid, do you think they have a chance?" asked Rough.

Slicing off a chunk of beef, Kid popped it into his mouth and then responded while trying to cool the morsel with an inhale of breath.

"Nope."

20:00 Local, 20JUN (10:00 GMT, 20JUN)
Flag Bridge, USS Lexington, Philippine Sea

Vice Admiral Marc Mitscher agonized over what to do. His air wings were almost an hour away and it was already quite late. In the dark they could not find the fleet, let alone find the carriers to land on. Had he risked the entire task force to submarines and night bombers or let his aviators fall into a black sea without a chance?

Each revolution of the clock wound the tension tighter. His staff left him alone on the fly bridge; this decision was his to make alone. At 20:45, the first aircraft returned and chaos began to reign. Unable to determine even ship types, aircraft began trying to land on destroyers and support ships as their crews desperately zigged and zagged to dodge the planes. Radio calls of aircraft running out of fuel quickly followed, adding to the confusion.

"Top Cat Lead; Dash Four is ditching, out of fuel."

"Roger, good luck."

"Red Leader is outta gas, boys. You're on your own."

"Godspeed, Skipper."

Mitscher heard the calls echoing from the bridge and looked up at the circling bedlam. He made his decision and walked into the flag bridge to issue a simple message.

FLASH MESSAGE
DTG: 20JUN2209
FROM: COMTASKFOR 58
TO: TASK FORCE 58
SUBJECT: RECOVERY
TEXT: TURN ON THE LIGHTS.
MITSCHER SENDS
FLASH MESSAGE

22:10 Local, 20JUN (12:10 GMT, 20JUN)
USS Princeton, Philippine Sea

VF-27 was all assembled in the ready room; the movie had been canceled. CVIC was piping in the strike frequency over the squawk box to the ready rooms. All hands listened intently as their friends and fellow aviators ran out of gas, calmly announcing it as they fell away from their formations. Suddenly, the 1MC blared out at full volume.

"NOW HERE THIS. TURN ON THE LIGHTS. MITSCHER SENDS."

Cheers erupted throughout the ship as TF-58 lit up like a Christmas tree. They would now have a fighting chance. Spotlights were pointed straight up as beacons to the returning strikers; destroyers shot starburst rounds into the air.

"What a beautiful sight," was broadcast over the frequency as the naval aviators descended to the well-lit carrier decks.

Any port in this storm of confusion would do. There was no way to determine which flattop was which; they simply landed on the first one they found. Each carrier had accidents that were pushed over the side, and the landings continued. By 23:00, the recovery was complete. Eighty aircraft had run out of gas and ditched but over the next few days, many aviators would be recovered. TF-58 ruled the Philippine Sea.

Admiral Ozawa was ordered by Toyoda to withdraw. Admiral Toyoda had all of the after-action reports, including Guam. They were shocking: three carriers sunk; out of Ozawa's 473 aircraft, only thirty-five could fly; another two hundred land-based aircraft were destroyed. Even more disturbing was the effectiveness of the new Hellcat: five hundred of his aircraft fell to its guns while less than two dozen were claimed by his fighters.

Toyoda walked to his window and gazed into the night. It was over, and not just the battle—the war. He had warned of this in 1941. He had adamantly advised against taking on the Americans and their industrial might. It was no consolation being correct. Now they must fight for the best terms possible in surrender.

In the coming weeks, Admiral Spruance would be criticized for not being more aggressive early in the battle and finishing off the IJN Fleet. His caution and concern that the carrier force was a diversion would prove prophetic. With all of its aircraft shot down and most of its aviators dead, the carrier fleet of Imperial Japan was defanged.

CHAPTER 30

08:30 Local, 01JUL (13:30 GMT, 01JUL)
OSS Headquarters, Navy Hill Washington DC

Major Spike Shanower sat across a steel table from his Nazi captive. He opened a folder, clearly stamped Top Secret and slid it in front of Colonel Gerhardt. The German's hands left sweat prints behind on the cool table as he nervously picked up each photo, convinced that by seeing them, he had just been sentenced to death.

"So?" Spike demanded.

"It is done," the German responded, his voice cracking in betrayal.

"How long?"

"A year, maybe more."

"Good," Spike replied. "The war will be over by then. The Allies landed in France last month."

Colonel Gerhardt's forehead receded in astonishment. He knew this was the beginning of the end for the Third Reich. His thoughts returned to his personal predicament, now certain that his fate was sealed. There would be no further use for him.

"And now what, Major?" he asked with trepidation.

"The end will come quickly."

Gerhardt closed his eyes. He tried to visualize his wife and daughter but could not. Everything he had was gone; soon everything he was would also be gone. Strangely he was at peace with it. He had seen so many atrocities, so much death. Hiding in his work had not been a sanctuary. He knew that by being a part of it, he must also be held accountable. And so it would be.

"We will need to move quickly in the chaos," said Spike, reading his body language.

Gerhardt opened his eyes in question and Spike spoke again.

"Get a list of your personnel, with locations, together. We must beat the Russians."

Visible relief flushed across the German's face. Spike smiled.

"What, did you think I was going to shoot you?"

"Oh, no, Major—"

Spike held up his hand to stop him. He then calmly crossed his hands and looked into the former Nazi's eyes.

"Hans, you and your team are going to be Americans now. We don't operate like that."

He got up and left, leaving the new immigrant to his thoughts.

16:30 Local, 02JUL (06:30 GMT, 02JUL)
Sydney, Australia

Colonel Sean "Thumper" McDonald slept soundly on the clean white sheets of a hospital bed, a luxury he had not enjoyed for months. His blissful slumber was rudely interrupted by a kick to the footboard of his rack.

"Are you going to sleep for the rest of the war?"

Thumper opened his eyes, focusing on a buxom nurse, arms folded under her chest. Her provocative pose was accentuated by a familiar smirk. He smiled in return.

"Brenda, you are a sight for sore eyes!"

"And you are just a sight," she said. "Where have you been?"

"The Canal and other garden spots, all at a loss for luxury supplies—like food, for example."

"Well, get out of that bed and let's see if we can fatten you up."

Thumper dressed hurriedly while Brenda watched with a wry smile. His uniform was about three sizes too big. He looked to be twenty-five pounds lighter than when she had last seen him in India, early in the war.

"Marine Corps?" she noted. "Weren't you in an Army Air Corps uniform the last time I saw you?"

"Indeed," he said, "a temporary condition necessitated by our secret little project, 7Alpha. However, upon my return to the States, Uncle Sam's Misguided Children decided they just couldn't make do without yours truly."

"No doubt," Brenda replied with sarcasm and added, "promoted to full colonel, no less."

She watched as Thumper buttoned up his uniform shirt.

"That, my dear, is more a function of attrition than merit." Thumper hastily tied a knot in his tie. "Let's put the war behind us and a steak and beer to the front."

"I suppose that is exactly what you need, Colonel—perhaps some personal exercise later."

"Outstanding! I look forward to my rehabilitation."

Colonel Sean McDonald USMC and Major Brenda Walker US Army Nurse Corps, were married twelve days after they reunited. A week later, he left for Espiritu Santo to stand up the brand new Marine Air Group 11 and get back into the shooting war.

CHAPTER 31

17:00 Local, 13JUL (06:00 GMT, 13JUL)
Eniwetok Atoll

For millennia, monotony and boredom were plagues commanders had fought with fielded troops. Gambling and most sports were invented between campaigns by bored warriors. Modern warfare made the battle all the harder because troops no longer had to forage for food. America's industrial base was pumping out ships, planes, tanks, food, cigarettes, and even beer for the boys overseas.

Industrious sailors adapted. A shot from a CO_2 extinguisher chilled their beer, and hardwood from pallets made good charcoal. The VF-27 Tiger Cats had moved to the beach of Eniwetok, laying claim to a screened structure with a corrugated steel roof. It was promptly named The Taj, short for Taj Mahal. The name was a stretch but the roof kept the afternoon rain off, and the screens kept the bugs at bay. Riotous beer parties and continuous poker games filled the nights. Swimming, fishing, and baseball filled the days. All events were sprinkled amply with beer from the States.

Jazz finally had to put his foot down to keep his boys from becoming lushes. After a top-secret meeting with the other COs and CAG, they set mandatory calisthenics at 07:00 and training at 16:00 every day except Sunday. Happy Hour would not start until 17:00. It kept a lid on the craziness and allowed the Intel guys to keep everyone briefed on latest tactics, aircraft, and the war in general.

Boredom, however, was not so easily slain. Each day was a carbon copy of the last—events, menu, scenery, even the weather was the same. It was the nature of war, no different from ancient Rome. Trading chariots for Hellcats, or galleys for aircraft carriers, changed nothing.

Mail call was the only break in routine. Theresa sent Kid pictures of his son in her daily notes—mere images that could not be held or hugged. It depressed him. He was sitting alone waiting for the mail when Rough Ryder banged through the screen door.

"Hey, snap out of it, it's 17:00!" He grabbed a beer and tossed it to Kid. "You got a church key?"

Kid produced one from under his T-shirt; it dangled from his dog tags. Hammer Ferriso walked in, passing mail around the room.

"Kid, mail call from Texas." Hammer tossed a box onto his lap.

Kid trapped it with his elbow as he popped two holes in his beer can with the opener. Boxes traveled much slower than letters, due to space. Kid's mother always sent cookies, so her news was always old—months old. Ripping open the box, he pulled out the letter and then passed the stale cookie crumbs around the room. Suddenly, he gurgled out a hoot as he passed beer through his nostrils.

"What's so damn funny?" asked Rough.

"My little sister ran off and joined the Woman's Auxiliary Ferry Squadron."

By 20:00, VF-27 was a six-pack past sober. Kid repeatedly offered toasts to his sister and laughed. He wondered who taught her; Irish was now in England. Besides, he wouldn't test his mother's patience twice. Neither would Jon. Kid would just have to wait to find out.

"Attention on deck," yelled an anonymous voice.

Jazz pushed through the screen door, its long spring snapping it back in place. CAG was with him. The two men moved to the center of the room. A fire extinguisher loudly shot its contents over two beers chilling them. Rough tossed them to the senior men.

"Skipper, CAG—incoming," he yelled.

Each man caught his beer and popped it open with a church key. CAG raised his to the crowd of junior officers.

"To the fighting 27th!"

"To the 27th!" all hands yelled back and guzzled down their beer. As flying beer cans tinkled onto the wood-slatted floor around CAG, he raised his hand.

"Gents, I'm here to congratulate the Hammer: he's going back stateside."

All the pilots gathered around LTJG Tom "Hammer" Ferriso and poured beers over his head. CAG handed him a set of orders to be an instructor in Pensacola. He had a shocked look on his face as the men demanded a speech.

"CAG," he said, "I don't want to go."

Everyone laughed and CAG grabbed him around the shoulder.

"Son you've done your part," he said. "You are an ace, and the Navy needs you to teach the next wave. Intel is telling us that is why the Japanese expertise has fallen off so sharply; we've killed them all. We need our best in the training command."

Skipper Jazz stepped forward.

"Okay, boys," he said. "Liberty expires at 22:00. We get underway first thing tomorrow."

10:10 Local, 14JUL (15:10 GMT, 14JUL)
New Castle Army Air Base, Delaware

A TA-6 Texan popped and pinged as its hot engine cooled in the almost equally hot breeze. Kaitlyn Brennan squatted on the wing, retrieving her helmet bag and kneeboard from the cockpit. Her instructor leaned over and whispered into her ear. He did not anticipate the response.

Uncoiling like a cobra, she struck him with both palms square in the chest, propelling him off the wing. He landed flat on his back. While he struggled for air, she pounced on him, straddling his chest. He leaned forward in an attempt to get air into his lungs, but she punched him squarely in the nose. With the threat neutralized, Kaitlyn jumped to her feet and strolled away as if nothing happened.

Major Nancy Love sauntered by, unnoticed until she spoke to the hapless instructor pilot. She couldn't help laughing at the young lieutenant as he struggled to find air and lost blood from his nose.

"Three brothers," she said. "I'd leave that one alone."

02:10 Local, 15JUL (02:10 GMT, 15JUL)
Over the English Channel

Major Mark Hass eased the piper of his gun sight onto the flaming rocket exhaust. He was careful not to wag his wings with the spoilerons; he sweetened up the picture with rudder only. After shutting his eyes, he pulled the trigger on his eight 20 millimeter guns. Each barrel flashed white ten times a second as they spit the heavy rounds at the V-1 rocket.

After a five-second burst, he opened his eyes as the rocket exploded four hundred feet in front of him. Flash-blinded, he couldn't read his instruments. The aircraft flew unbalanced while he fumbled around the cockpit trying to find the switch for the new thunderstorm lights.

"Everything alright up there, Skipper?"

The bright white lights flicked on.

"It is now, Stony," Hass replied. "It will be an hour before I get my vision back. Let's RTB."

Stony radioed fighter control that they were returning as Hass-man turned toward England. After turning up his red instrument lights all the way, he eased down the brightness of the t-storm lights.

"So tell me, Skipper," said Stony, "how pissed was the General when you handed him that bag of wings?"

"Not nearly as pissed as when we won the fly-off competition against the Mosquito."

Both men laughed.

10:10 Local, 15JUL (02:10 GMT, 15JUL)
Mindoro Island, The Philippines

Sergeant Donnelly made his way up the trail to the lookout point. Captain Dave Butler sat still, intently surveying a Japanese patrol craft through high-powered binoculars. "You were right, Dave," said Donnelly. "They're gone."

"And the camp?"

"Stripped clean of everything—ammo, food, nothing left."

Butler handed Donnelley the binoculars, motioning to the entire horizon.

"Notice something different?" he asked.

"Yeah, they are all going the same direction."

"Yep, check out how low in the water they are, too."

"What is going on?" asked Donnelly.

No longer concerned with being seen, Butler stood up and stretched his back.

"They are setting a defendable perimeter," he said.

"Why?"

"Invasion. Break radio silence and report the movement. Stand by to copy orders—we will be on the move."

CHAPTER 32

11:00 Local, 20JUL (16:00 GMT, 20JUL)
New Castle Army Air Base, Delaware

Laura Brennan sat through yet another winging ceremony. The words spoken were different and yet the same. She had sat through her husband's ceremony, those of two sons, and now a daughter's. *Daughter.* This war would change the country forever. It was clear to her that America had turned the tide of war and would very soon be the world leader. It was also clear to Laura that all of America's citizens were needed in order to win. Social changes were coming. One of them stood right in front of her.

She sat lost in her thoughts until it was time to pin on Kaitlyn's wings, Women's Auxiliary Ferrying Squadron pilot wings. Nicknamed WAFSs, they were attached to the 2nd Ferrying Group at New Castle. C.R. Smith's WAFS program was commanded by Nancy Love, who handed Kaitlyn's wings to Laura.

"Brennan is a natural," she said. "You should be proud."

"She gets it from her father," Laura replied. "I know he would be as proud as I am."

05:45 Local, 24JUL (19:45 GMT, 23JUL)
Tinian, Marianas Island Group

Palm trees swayed in the soft breeze as dawn broke on the island. The only sound was the gentle lapping of the surf on the sandy beach. Even the birds had not yet awoken. On the ocean's horizon a series of flashes flickered like heat lightning. A few seconds later, the island turned inside out and upside down. Dirt and sand filled the air; palm trees flew, roots first, into the morning air. Silence was a concept lost as sixteen-inch shells weighing nineteen hundred pounds arced in from the sea and shook the island to its core. They left craters fifty feet wide and twenty deep, defoliating the jungle out to four hundred yards with each explosion.

High overhead, VF-27 led three squadrons in a fighter sweep and then set up CAP (combat air patrol) stations for Japanese fighters that never came. TBF-1 Avengers circled with bombs and rockets, waiting to pounce on survivors of the naval bombardment. Amphibious ships birthed landing craft that formed lines and approached the beach full of marines from the 2nd and 4th divisions. Kid marveled that anyone could survive, let alone return fire. But return fire the Japanese did, putting twenty-two rounds of six-inch shells on the USS Colorado alone, killing forty-four sailors.

Tinian's flat terrain allowed it to be stripped clean by the weapons of man. Kid watched as the jungle was blown and literally burned away. Marine Corsairs dropped a new weapon called napalm; it was ghastly—a firebomb that spread like flaming water on impact. A week later, it was over: eight thousand Japanese were dead and the Princeton was headed back to Eniwetok. The denuded island was already being transformed into the world's biggest aircraft carrier. B-29 Superfortresses would now be able to reach mainland Japan.

Admiral Nimitz and General MacArthur had competing plans for the invasion of Japan. Nimitz's plan called for an invasion of Formosa; a Chinese island with extensive air defense. MacArthur had promised he'd return to the Philippines and wanted to keep his word. Both plans would sever the supply lines of fuel to the Japanese war machine.

In a compromise, a plan was developed to first neutralize the aviation assets on Formosa and then invade the Philippines. Bull Halsey's Task Force 38 would be sent to destroy the Japanese aircraft and bases. After replenishing at Eniwetok, TF-38 would sortie against the enemy on 2 August.

Colonel McDonald had arrived on Eniwetok the night before. He and Kid had been invited to dine with Vice Admiral Halsey in the Flag Mess. Kid hated "forced fun" but it was great to see Thumper. Halsey presided over a relaxed mess; the conversation was lively. Everyone present was highly amused at David's account of his sister slipping off to join the WAFS. It was also apparent that the admiral's staff was talking around a plan to end the war.

ENDGAME

On 10 September, Task Force 38 launched strikes on Mindanao Island's northern airfields. They were effective but the fleet did not slow its pace to re-attack. Instead, it steamed north, headed to its real target: Formosa. The Philippine attacks had been a diversion.

06:52 Local, 21SEP (21:52 GMT, 20SEP)
Manila Bay, The Philippine

VF-27 flew over Corregidor and then over the open Manila Bay. The historical significance was not lost on Kid; he hoped that the American POWs somewhere below could see the US Navy's finest fighter squadron overhead. Looking to his right, he got a Daffy smile from his new section leader. After a couple of more experienced men were rolled stateside, the squadron had been re-shuffled. Rough Ryder got his own division, and Kid picked Daffy as his new section lead.

Fighter sweeps were being flown all over the Philippines, and Jazz had drawn the plum, Manila. Everyone knew that the Japanese would put up a maximum effort.

"Tiger Cat lead; bogeys left ten o'clock low."

Jazz rolled in on the Japanese. Within a few short minutes of a swirling dogfight, thirty-eight Japanese Zeros were blasted out of the sky by VF-27's twenty-four Hellcats. Daffy had racked up five kills in the single mission; his grin was irrepressible.

07:32 Local, 21SEP (22:32 GMT, 20SEP)
Mindoro Island, The Philippines

Soft morning sunlight filtered through the trees. Captain Dave Butler leaned against a tree trunk watching a dogfight rage. It had begun strangely silent, just trails of white clouds crisscrossing and making circles. Occasionally there was a flash of orange and then black smoke, followed by a vanquished fighter spinning out of the bottom of the fight. It gradually descended en masse within earshot. He could hear the engines' growl and the bark of guns.

Below him, Donnelly made his way up the switchback path to his high perch.

"Amazing sight, don't you think?" Butler said when he arrived, pointing to the air combat.

Donnelley looked up.

"Yep, it sure is."

"Would you like to do it, Paul?"

"No thanks, Dave—no place to hide."

Butler chuckled.

"You didn't walk all the way up here to chat," he said. "What's up?"

"They want us back on Luzon."

Butler's stomach involuntarily constricted. It meant going back into the heart of darkness they had barely escaped.

"Why?" he asked at last.

"They want us to take a look-see."

"They do realize the entire Japanese force is there," replied Butler.

"I believe that is exactly the point, mon capitan."

"Your French stinks, Sergeant."

"Aw," said Donnelly. "Now you're hurting my feelings."

CHAPTER 33

05:45 Local, 12OCT (20:45 GMT, 11OCT)
South China Sea

Halsey had slipped Task Force 38 into the South China Sea undetected. At dawn, he launched all his Avengers and Hell Divers at the Japanese airfields on Formosa. Half of the Hellcats were held back for fleet defense. The Formosa raid was such a total surprise that a counterattack was not initiated. VF-27 didn't see a single enemy aircraft as they circled on their CAP station. That night, Toyoda initiated Sho Go 2, the plan to defend Formosa.

Dawn broke quietly on the South China Sea. VF-27's Tiger Cats sat in Ready Room 1 in full flight gear. The fighter pilots were on an Alert 15—that meant airborne in fifteen minutes. Still early morning, the ready room was already a sauna. The men packed into the space, listening to CAG's briefing.

"Gents, we do not anticipate a day like yesterday," he said. "No doubt the Japanese will respond in force—"

Before he could finish his brief, they could all feel the ship heel to port as it turned into the wind.

"Launch all fighters!" the amplified words rang out over the squawk box, jolting the men into action. "I say again, launch 'em!"

Within five seconds, they had cleared the room and begun scrambling to the flight deck. Overhead, engines began to rumble to life as plane captains fired them up and then jumped out to make room for the pilots. It didn't take long. Eight minutes after the launch call, Stutz rolled off the end of the bow.

Kid's flight was next off deck. Once airborne and cleaned up with gear and flaps raised, he kept full power on his Hellcat as he turned toward

Formosa. His radio came alive.

"Red Crown holds; multiple bogeys, multiple groups. Check in with your lineup."

Stutzman looked left and right. Kid's flight of four was on his right, Rough's four on his left.

"Stutz flight is checking in with twelve Hellcats," he radioed.

"Stutz flight, snap vector: three, zero, zero."

"Declare," Stutz demanded.

"Bandits; Stutz flight is cleared, weapons red and free."

"Arm 'em and charge 'em, Tiger Cats!" Stutz commanded.

"Update?" was his next brief transmission.

"Bandits twelve o' clock, level, for seven miles," Red Crown control responded.

Kid saw the first wave. He had never seen so many enemy aircraft in the air at one time. He cleared his throat and then transmitted.

"Tally ho: multiple Vals slightly low, Zeros high; left eleven-thirty."

"Tally," Stutzman responded calmly, and then turned the flight of Hellcats directly for the enemy. "Let's shoot the Vals in the face on the first pass."

Stutz put his piper on the lead bomber and let loose a short burst, flaming the Val at the merge. His men followed suit, and half of them scored. Post merge, he pulled up into the Zeros, who seemed confused. Ten fell to belly shots before maneuvering.

"Save ammo," he ordered. "Kill them quick and re-engage the Vals!"

They had to get to the Vals before they could reach the fleet and drop their bombs. Kid couldn't believe how easily they dispatched the Zero fighters. As the last few fell to Hellcat guns, he rolled steep onto a wing and got sight of the Vals starting their bomb runs.

At their max diving speed of 240 knots, the D3A2 Vals were run down quickly by the Hellcats. Kid closed with more than a hundred knots of excess speed and saw the Type 92 tail guns come alive, hurling 7.7 millimeter rounds at his flight. At three thousand feet, he let loose in return. Vals and their parts filled the dawn, accentuated by fire and smoke. Flashing through the pieces, Kid pushed hard to avoid an engine tumbling past his cockpit, propeller still spinning.

Pulling up hard to reposition for another attack, he watched as Stutz flight tore into the Vals. When they pulled off, Kid rolled inverted and pulled back into the fight to finish them off.

"Red Crown holds a second wave; three, zero, five. Angels high, distance thirty."

Kid turned his flight to face the second wave. He saw an explosion off his right wing; the cruiser Canberra had taken a hit. Re-motivated by vengeance, he ripped into the second wave with the same results.

Aircraft rained down like the Marianas turkey shoot. It was obvious that Japan had expended all of its experienced aviators in past battles. Their inexperience sealed their fate when the few survivors returned with wildly inaccurate claims of victory. These claims convinced Formosa's commander to send the rest of his air assets to finish off the invasion fleet of the gaijin. It was a disastrous decision.

By the next morning it was apparent that the previous day's battle had decimated the Japanese navy and land-based aircraft. Kid was part of a CAP that dispatched a small raid, as Halsey began to withdraw TF-38 before the Japanese fleet arrived.

Returning to the Princeton, Kid detected movement far below his Hellcat. A Zero was running in fast and low. Kid dove for it at full throttle but couldn't catch it. He watched in shock as the Zero dove deliberately into the carrier Franklin.

Once on deck, he went directly to CVIC to report the incident in a debrief.

"He was probably hit and just dove it in, Lieutenant," the intelligence officer replied.

"I don't think so, sir. I didn't get a shot off," replied Kid. "He snuck in— there was no triple A."

"I wouldn't worry about it. Probably just one nut."

Kid looked at Stutz, who had listened intently to the report. He could read the concern in his eyes.

Halsey's mission to crush the Japanese air forces on Formosa was a huge success. Five hundred Japanese aircraft fell compared to only eighty-nine from TF-38. Even more damaging, Toyoda was convinced the invasion fleet had been driven away and Halsey's carrier force was withdrawing due to losses.

08:45 Local, 14OCT (23:45 GMT, 13OCT)
Luzon Island, Philippines

Butler could feel it closing in around him, from every side, every angle.

He knew eventually they would be swept away, defenseless, unable to resist. His unit was deep in the Zambales mountains, positioned between Angeles and Olongapo. Manila Bay was to the southeast and also close, too close. From here, with the aid of the Filipino guerillas, he could monitor the naval and ground forces of Manila and Subic Bays as well as the aviation assets at Clark Air Base in Angeles.

"You were right, Dave," said Sergeant Donnelly, but he got no response. "Captain Butler?"

"Huh—what, Paul?"

"You were right. They are setting up in the mountains, fortified with classic fallback positions."

"Yeah, I knew they would."

"How?" asked Donnelly. "That breaks their Bonsai tactics. It's new."

Butler was lost in deep thought for a few moments and then drew a rough map of the South Pacific in the dirt. At the top was Japan. Next were Okinawa and the Philippines with Malaysia at the bottom of the line. He tapped on all the open area around his chain of islands.

"This is about the navy, Paul. Malaysia has the fuel oil and raw materials the war machine of Imperial Japan needs."

Then he drew a line through the Philippines perpendicular to the islands.

"If we control the ocean enough to put troops on the PI, it's over. The Allies will cut off the fuel supply to the Imperial Navy."

"But why is the Jap commander giving them the beach?"

"Two reasons," said Butler. "How many islands in the Philippines chain?"

"About a million," Donnelley replied sarcastically.

"Exactly. Lots of beach to cover."

"What's the second reason, Captain?"

"This isn't the A-team, Paul," he said. "They are in Burma. In fact, a lot of them are dead. A defensive position is inherently stronger. The command just wants to hold out until the IJN gets it done."

"We need to tell Allied Command, don't we?"

Butler nodded his head slowly.

"We are trapped up here," said the sergeant, looking around. "They will come after us, won't they?"

Again, Butler nodded. "Once we start transmitting," he said, "they will come."

ENDGAME

Colonel Sean "Thumper" McDonald hooked up with his Marine Air Group 11 on Emerau. His boys had looked at him with suspicion until a mission a few days earlier. A Japanese destroyer had been found camouflaged right on the shoreline of Babelthuap Island. His boys had been tasked with sinking it. VMF-122 rolled in first, and got close, but other than blowing the camouflage off, they were not effective. Thumper led a section from VMF-114; he rolled in after the misses and put one dead center, sinking the ship.

Today, they were headed back to Babelthuap for a strike on the northern tip of the island. Thumper was leading the strike, this time flying with VMF-122. They flushed an A6M2-N Rufe, a Zero on floats. Thumper kissed off his section and transmitted, *Go get him, boys.* He knew it would likely be the only air-to-air kill these young guys would get; the real war was well north. Peleliu was about protecting the flank and was already shaping up as the bloodiest mistake of the war.

It was supposed to be over in a few days but they were into the fifth week. Bloody hand-to-hand combat was becoming a norm. The First Battalion, First Marines sustained seventy-one percent casualties. Captain Evert Pope's company, trapped on bloody Nose Ridge, fought with knives, fists, and rocks. Of the entire company, only nine survived.

Internally, Thumper was furious; there was no reason to take this island. He kept his thoughts to himself and put up all the aircraft he could to cover the infantry. This was where MAG 11 would end their war, in a backwater nightmare. He also knew that they were not even close to done. Many more young men, some of them his, would die on this bloody rock.

Peleliu was a microcosm of hell: rocks, even the air, burned with napalm. Men tore at the flesh of others with bare hands. *Dante must have been a Marine,* he thought.

CHAPTER 34

05:00 Local, 20OCT (20:00 GMT, 19OCT)
Leyte Gulf

Avenger, Helldiver, and Hellcat propellers began to turn in the pre-dawn darkness. Barely visible in the dim, flight deck lighting, they began to flicker to life. An optical illusion made them appear to spin backward momentarily until they came up to speed. Kid Brennan's flight was the first ready. After getting a thumbs-up signal from his wingmen, he sat back with a rare opportunity to take in the scene.

Sweet-P, as the USS Princeton was called by its crew, tilted hard to starboard as she turned into the wind. Aircraft, safely chained to the deck, clung to her like insects. All around him, ten-foot propellers swung like giant swords as flight deck crews darted between them.

Princeton steadied her deck. Handlers signaled the chain gang to pull the tie-downs. With heavy chains accumulating around their teenaged shoulders, they went from aircraft to aircraft. Chocks were pulled next, and the aircraft in front of Kid launched. He moved forward and spread his Hellcat's wings, then launched into the dark toward another routine day of death and destruction.

Sweet-P had been assigned air to ground. The fast attack boys wanted the Zeros for themselves—bridesmaids again. Half of the VF-27's Tiger-cats climbed their Hellcats to altitude and then circled on CAP stations. All the rest, Kid among them, pressed toward targets on Leyte.

Admiral Toyoda was still acting on the intelligence that insisted Halsey was withdrawing TF-38 due to the drubbing TF-38 had gotten off of Formosa.

ENDGAME

Imperial Command was shocked when Halsey put a thousand aircraft over the Philippine Islands. Once the landing craft hit the beaches of Leyte, there was little doubt. Toyoda activated Sho-Go 1 and sortied the entire Imperial Japanese fleet in the defense of the Philippines. If his plan failed, he knew it would be the end for Japan.

None of this mattered to Kid as he rolled in on his assigned target. He robotically armed his bomb and then charged his fifties. Centering the runway in his bombsight, he didn't react to the glowing golf balls that rose toward him. They started in slow motion and then streaked by his canopy with amazing speed.

It was a routine bomb run, on a routine target, on a routine mission. On his routine pull out, a golf ball found its mark. Smashing into cylinder number six, the large-caliber round blew it off the engine. A cloud of fuel flared around the cowl and then extinguished. Noise from the damaged engine filled the cockpit at a debilitating decibel level. Kid was slapped out of complacency. He fought for control and his life.

His Hellcat was vibrating so violently that he didn't bother to try and read the instruments. *Turn to the sun. Turn to the sun! Get feet wet, get feet wet!* The thought screamed through his overloaded mind over the din. Pointing to the sun, Kid eased the throttle to lower the noise and vibration. He tried to use his mirrors to glance aft but they shook to the point of being useless. Kid turned to look aft and saw a smoke trail. Heat at his feet verified that he was indeed on fire.

Even with his Hellcat on fire, he had no intention of bailing out over Japanese territory. Movement overhead demanded his attention; he was relieved to see his wingmen in a defensive weave of protection.

Clawing his way over the beach, he centered his vibrating windscreen on a destroyer. He watched the flash of its guns as his engine began to disintegrate. It was bombarding the beach he had just crossed. Noise, acrid smoke and tracers attempted to render his brain useless.

On board the USS Johnson, Lieutenant Commander Ernest E. Evans, the ship's captain, watched the dying Hellcat turn toward his vessel.

"Gunner, cease fire. Cease fire all guns!"

His commands reverberated throughout the ship as they were repeated over the 1MC.

"Engines all stop. Stand by to launch the starboard whaleboat."

Flames began to lick at Kid's feet. The engine had brought him as far as he dared. Pulling the throttle to idle, he next snatched the mixture to idle cutoff. Mercifully, the noise ended but not the flames. Turning the fuel shut-off valve with his left hand, he grabbed his fire extinguisher with his right and shot it at his feet as he blew the canopy back. With noise, vibration and fire all secured, his mind and eyes could finally focus. Incredibly, the Johnston had gone dead in the water and its whaleboat was launching. Plumes of water began to rise around her as the Japanese gunners zeroed in. Skipper Evans calmly watched from the fly bridge as the Hellcat dropped below one hundred feet.

"Launch the starboard whale boat."

"Resume shore bombardment."

The officer of the deck nervously scanned the waterspouts erupting around them.

"Skipper, shouldn't we get underway?" he asked.

"Negative, Mister Jenkins. Stand fast—we can sustain a hit better than our whaleboat."

"Aye aye, Captain."

Kid was getting close to the Johnston; he scanned from airspeed to altitude, slowing the Hellcat as he descended. Eighty knots, forty feet… eighty knots, thirty feet … twenty feet … he shifted his scan to outside only as he cushioned the landing with a slight flare. Skipping twice, the prop of the Hellcat dug in and brought the aircraft to an abrupt stop. His shoulder harness dug in as deep as the propeller did the same into the calm ocean.

Coming to a halt nose low, Kid unstrapped quickly as the aircraft began to sink. Free of the cockpit, he ran down the wing to the whaleboat pulling up to his port wing. He jumped into the small boat, and the boatswain's mate didn't wait for him to hit the hull's bottom before jamming its engine to full throttle.

On board Johnston, the skipper calmly ordered all ahead slow.

"Make turns for five knots."

"Stand-by to recover whaleboat starboard station."

Slicing through the saltwater, the whaleboat set up an intercept course with starboard side station. Its yardarms swung out over the ocean as they approached.

"Gunner, secure the aft five-inch gun."

The ship's rear gun immediately stopped firing as the whaleboat slipped under its extended barrels.

"Make turns for seven knots. Corpsman to the starboard station."

On board the whaleboat, the boatswain's mate aligned with the Johnston as his crew snapped hooks to the bow and stern.

"Hoist the whaleboat, starboard side."

Winches yanked the boat out of the water its spinning propeller, breaking the surface with a final wisp of sea water, before the boatswain shut down the engine. Skipper Evans watched as it cleared the water and then walked back into the bridge.

"All ahead full!" he commanded. "Gunner, commence firing aft five inch. Navigator, resume base course."

Then, Skipper Evans gave control of the ship back to his OOD.

"Mister Jenkins, you have the con."

"I'm Ensign Jenkins," the younger man responded, "and I have the con."

All hands in the bridge yelled in unison.

"Mister Jenkins has the con."

There was now no question who was controlling the ship, and there was also no question who commanded it. Skipper Evans sauntered back onto the fly bridge to observe the bombardment's accuracy. From the whaleboat his corpsman, who had examined Kid, signaled with a thumbs-up. The skipper nodded and turned his attention back to the beach.

LCDR Evans intently studied the shore through his binoculars until he heard a voice behind him.

"Sir, Lieutenant Junior Grade Brennan requests permission to come aboard."

The skipper continued to hold the large binoculars on the impact area until a series of explosions. After evaluating the hits, he turned to face Kid while the guns barked out another round.

"Granted, Lieutenant. Welcome to the Johnston."

"It is the most beautiful ship in the Navy, Captain."

"Indeed it is, Lieutenant; stand-by one." He turned to watch another salvo impact on target. He spoke without looking up. "You are not even wet."

"No sir, your crew was kind enough to pluck me from the wing."

"Looked more like a swan dive from here."

All the ship's guns launched another round of shells. Skipper Evans faced Kid again.

"I was in a bit of a hurry, sir," said the pilot. "No worse for wear—except my shoes are a bit singed."

"Well, we will get you a nice pair of black ones."

Aviators wore brown shoes, one of the ways they liked to differentiate themselves from the surface Navy. "Black shoe" and "brown shoe" were slang terms for the different warrior communities.

"I'd be honored, Captain."

"Excellent, why don't you strike below and send a message to your ship. Don't forget the ice cream—my crew prefers chocolate."

"Aye aye, Skipper. And thank you, sir."

07:00 Local, 21OCT (20:00 GMT, 20OCT)
Guadalcanal

The 2nd Battalion of the 29th, 6th Marine Division was standing tall, at attention. They were turned out in full combat gear. Lieutenant Colonel James Russell was also at attention facing the battalion: centered perfectly, twenty paces out. To his left was Command Sergeant Major Michael Paillou. Russell's adjutant, Major Tom Jameson, marched front and center and saluted.

"Sir, 2nd of the 29th, 6th Marines is ready for combat inspection."

"Very well, Major. Post," Colonel Russell replied, returning the salute.

Major Jameson fell in behind Paillou, and the three men marched down the line to inspect each one of their marines. The ranks stood resplendent in their new combat web gear, topped off with camouflage helmet covers. Each was armed with M-1 semi-automatic rifles and bayonets. To the casual observer they looked battle ready. To Sergeant Major Paillou, they did not.

First in line of the inspectors, he set upon them like a tsunami. If a helmet wasn't cinched tight, he'd slap it askew.

"A mortar concussion will knock that off."

He tugged hard on web-mounted gear; any loose attachments were snatched off and thrown to the deck. Pulling out canteens, he'd shake them, and if there was any noise, to the ground they went.

"All the way full, or all the way empty."

Bayonets were pulled; dull ones went to the deck.

"You gonna bludgeon someone with that?"

Lieutenant Colonel Russell followed the fury calmly, as if nothing out of the ordinary had preceded him. Methodically, he stepped from one marine to the next after the storm had passed.

"Are you getting enough chow, Marine?"

"Sir, yes sir."

"How about you, son, are you staying in shape?"

"Sir, yes sir."

Slowly, they wound their way through the entire battalion. By the time they finished, Paillou had the parade field looking like a junkyard. Complete, they reassembled front and center.

"Sergeant Major?" Russell demurred to Paillou.

"Sir, I would like the enlisted men to stand fast."

"Very well," replied Russell. "Major, have the officers secure to my tent, in combat gear. Dismiss the battalion."

Major Jameson looked as green as his gear. This had not gone well. Paillou stood at rigid attention, glaring at his battalion. Every man felt the CSM's eyes on him.

"Officers," Jameson said, "muster immediately in the commanding officer's tent. Dismissed."

"Marines, stand-fast!" Paillou bellowed, and then did not move a centimeter as the officers left the parade deck. He watched with his peripheral vision until all of the officers were out of earshot, his voice suddenly shattering the silence.

"You look like shit. Your gear is rigged like shit. Therefore, you will fight like shit! Look around you." Not a man moved, fearful it was a trap. "Look to the deck!" Paillou's baritone voice compelled them. "Do you see that gear adrift?" There was no response. "I said, do you see that gear adrift?" he demanded in no uncertain terms; they had to respond.

"Sir, yes sir."

"That gear does not serve the Corps if it is lost in the surf. We need it to fight. Your buddy's gear on my parade deck means he screwed the US of A, who paid for that gear. He screwed the Corps, who needs that gear to fight. He screwed you because now he will have to depend on you, or even worse, you will die because you can't depend on him."

Paillou stood glaring in disgust at his marines. "Sergeants, my tent. Dismissed." Each of his sergeant's throats visibly gulped.

06:13 Local, 22OCT (11:13 GMT, 22OCT)
New Castle Army Air Base, Delaware

Kaitlyn turned away from the pilots gathered at the operations counter and stared out the window through the morning mist at the P-51 Mustang.

She cradled a telephone receiver in the crook of her neck while she jotted down her flight plan. In the receiver, she could hear the phone ring on the other end and was relieved when she heard a familiar cowboy drawl answer the operator.

"Yes, ma'am, I accept the charges. Kaitlyn Brennan, what are you doing up so early?"

"I'm sorry to wake you, Captain Smith. I need your help."

"What's up, honey?"

"Well you know I'm a WASP now?" asked Kaitlyn.

"I heard about that," Smith replied. "Thought I was gonna be skinned alive by your mother for teaching you to fly—"

"Sorry about that," she interrupted. "I'll get to the point: I have an assignment to deliver a P-51."

"A Mustang?"

"Yes, sir."

"Holy cow. Did you get a check-out?"

"Just a manual," she replied. "Last night."

"Bastards," he said. "They are trying to get you to quit—sorry about the language."

"That's okay. What should I do?"

"Okay, Kaity girl, here is what you do," said Smith. "First, that machine has more power than you will ever need. Just mosey on down the runway and set 36 inches of manifold pressure, more than enough. Second, that Merlin engine is water-cooled, so keep an eye on the temp. Also, controls are twitchy. Lastly," he continued, "do not get slow on approach, I've read it has nasty stall characteristics. If you do get in trouble, do not jam on the power. That big prop and all that horse power will roll you on your back faster than a jackrabbit."

Kaitlyn was scribbling notes furiously.

"You got that, sweetie?" he asked.

"Yes, sir."

"Good, one last thing. Have fun!"

She laughed out loud, drawing the attention of her chauvinist observers, and hung up the phone. After a few more notes, she walked up to the operations counter and slapped down her flight plan. Confidently, she strode out to the Mustang as her onlookers crowded around the windows to watch the show.

Kaitlyn's heart pounded but her voice did not betray her when she accepted clearance for takeoff. As she pulled onto the runway she felt the eyes of the entire air base on her. After one last glance at her notes, she eased the throttle of the P-51 forward, stopping at 36 inches on the manifold pressure gauge. Even at the reduced power setting, the acceleration was like nothing she had ever experienced. With the tail up, she rotated effortlessly, raised the gear, and slipped gracefully into the overcast sky.

06:11 Local, 22OCT (21:11 GMT, 22OCT)
USS Johnston, Leyte Gulf 23

Kid sat in the combat information center, reading an after-action report from the submarine Darter. It reported two Japanese heavy cruisers sunk and one damaged, after Darter and Dace launched a torpedo attack in the Palawan Passage. He plotted the passage on a chart, right in the middle of the Philippines.

"Sir, you better get out of the Chief's chair."

"Oh sorry, I don't want to piss of the ship's chief—"

"No, sir—The Chief."

Kid looked at him confused, until the petty officer laughed.

"Lieutenant, Skipper Evans is Cherokee and Creek. He sits there in the mornings."

Kid jumped up just as the skipper came through the hatch.

"Good morning, men. Anything on the message boards?"

Skipper Evans and Kid discussed the torpedo attacks and plotted the known Japanese positions. It was obvious to both men that something big was afoot. After contemplating the chart for some time, the ship's captain stood up and issued orders.

"Signal the Princeton," Evans told the petty officer. "Tell them we are bringing back their wayward son. I think he will be busy very soon."

Two warships cruised in the mid-morning sun separated by a mere thirty yards—one large, one small. Between them hung a boatswain's chair, dangling from lines that were pulled tight or slackened depending on the ocean's swells. Kid Brennan sat in the metal-framed seat—cage would be a better description—shiny black shoes sticking out the bottom.

Aviators had gathered on the Princeton side of the rig to watch as Kid came over from the Johnston. They were highly amused by his predicament, and when one of them noticed his new black shoes, he began a chant.

"Dunk him, dunk his black shoes!"

The cheers and jeers grew louder as Kid got closer to the water. Skipper Evans had watched from the port fly bridge and gave his own order from there.

"Do not get my shoes wet."

A reverse tug of war started: as the sailors of Princeton let out slack in the line, the crew of Johnston would pull it taut—they won. Finally, the most harrowing experience of the previous three days was over and Kid arrived on the hangar deck of the Princeton. After strapping on ten gallons of chocolate ice cream, the crew of the Sweet-P hauled the chair back to the Johnston's victorious crew.

XO Stutzman had watched the operation, laughing and joining in on the catcalls to dunk Kid. He walked up to the junior officers, who were still giving Kid a hard time.

"Nice shoes, Mister," he teased.

"Hi, XO," said Kid. "They are nice. I think I'll keep them. Sorry about my Hellcat."

"No need to sweat it. We got you another. Go see the doc and get an up chit. You are on for a 05:00 launch tomorrow."

CHAPTER 35

08:01 Local, 24OCT (21:01 GMT, 23OCT)
USS Princeton, Leyte Gulf

Kid had watched the sunrise from the flight deck, another watercolor scene that unfolded in front of his eyes. He now climbed his Hellcat into the painting. The contrast between intent and the beauty of this day struck him. The dichotomy was stark. Natural splendor of island and ocean, God's majesty, was juxtaposed against man's steel weapons of war that stalked among the magnificence.

Their very presence warped time itself. Wooden boats, powered by paddle or sail, had been the norm just a few short months ago. Now, giant steel ships the size of cities and capable of launching flying machines plied the waters and fought fantastic battles. It was as if Orwell's Martians had landed in the South Pacific, not at Grover's Mill.

Not just Martians had landed but Venetians as well, and they now engaged in titanic battles in full view of the earthlings. Collateral damage was as cruel as it was pervasive. Mankind adapts to survive and so, too, had the islanders. They now knew to get out of the way when the aliens fought.

Kid circled in the middle of this cosmic intrusion, an existence that despite his best efforts had become monotonous. He was unaware that he was part of an invasion that had upset the natural order of the islands. Because of the depth and breadth of the violence they were able to inflict on some islands, they were being worshiped as gods. Oblivious, to the aviators and sailors it had all become routine. They too had learned to adapt and struggled to stay on edge.

Kid had learned his lesson more than once; even so, his thoughts were not of the grand universe at war. His thoughts were of his little part of the world: Theresa and his son, Charles Henry Brennan IV. They filled his morning, not the bombs and artillery he saw in the distance. He slowly circled on the gentle winds of the South Pacific, wondering when he'd see them again.

"Ninety-nine Hellcats, snap vector three-zero-zero; multiple bandits."

Tapping his shoulder, Kid signaled his wingmen to hang on while he pushed the throttle of his R-2800 to military power. Waves of Japanese strikers were inbound from Clark Field on Luzon. TF-38 Hellcats smashed into each wave of fifty strikers with such fury it didn't seem even remotely fair. Commander David McCampbell, CAG of Air Group 15, shot down nine in a single flight.

Glowing rounds filled the morning air around Kid as wave after wave attacked. His guns emptied, he knew the fuel tanks of his wingmen were close behind. His flight, having scored five kills, made its way back to the Sweet-P to re-fuel and re-arm.

Arriving overhead the Princeton, they began to orbit. Kid watched the ongoing recovery, waiting for a chance to sequence into the landing pattern. Then, out of a thick cloud, a Yokosuka D4Y "Judy" suddenly appeared and let loose a five-hundred-pound armor-piercing bomb. It hit between the elevators and penetrated both the flight and hangar decks before exploding.

Secondary's rocked Sweet-P and she turned into an inferno. Kid was stunned. It had happened in a blink, not a shot fired in self-defense. He sat astonished at the destruction a single aircraft's bomb had done to his ship. A wing waggle caught his attention: Daffy flashed a hand signal showing a very low fuel state. Time to find a new home for his flight.

Scanning the horizon, he realized the other close carriers were all CVEs, escorts that were too small for Hellcats. He had to find an old friend: the Suwannee. After twenty-two fuel-burning minutes, he saw her familiar deck and dove down as she turned into the wind. He cut in front of two flights that circled overhead, taking his own flight straight into the break.

After trapping onboard, his flight was pulled forward, then re-fueled, re-armed, and launched immediately. Kid looked at his watch; it was just after 11:00. His flight circled on BARCAP for three more hours before returning to the Suwannee. On deck, they were re-fueled again and told to CAP over the Princeton before launching on their third combat flight of the day.

Kid's flight was circling over Princeton by 14:48; it appeared the fires were under control. Alongside Sweet-P, the cruiser Birmingham was helping fight the fires with her hoses as well. He continued to circle and listened to the radio reports from the battle in the Sibuyan Sea. A Japanese task force was being driven from the area.

At 15:23 the Princeton exploded with such force it rocked Kid's flight. Gaining control of his aircraft, he looked down at his dying ship. The Birmingham was obviously severely damaged and was withdrawing to save itself. By 16:00 Sweet P was lost; the order to abandon ship was given. At 17:50 the Reno shot a salvo of torpedoes into the Princeton and she sunk with 108 of her crew. On board the Birmingham, 233 lay dead on her deck.

Kid turned toward the Suwannee as the blood-red sky announced the coming night. The sun's last remnants began to disappear. Flames on the burning ships had been extinguished by their crews or the flooding ocean. Serenity descended on the Philippine Sea; all hands knew it would not last past the next dawn.

As the sun set, Vice Admiral Kurita re-entered the Sibuyan Sea headed for the Straits of San Bernardino. Halsey, convinced Kurita had been defeated, moved north to crush the Japanese carrier force off of the island of Samar.

05:45 Local, 25OCT (20:45 GMT, 24OCT)
USS Suwannee, Leyte Gulf

Intel briefed the combined squadron of the fantastic naval victory the night before in the Surigao Strait; in fact, Japanese ships were still being sunk. He added that the last thrust of a three-pronged attack was being repulsed by Halsey's TF-38 off Cape Engano at daybreak. They were engaging the last of the Japanese carriers to finish them off.

VF-27 was looking for vengeance; their ship had been sunk. To add insult to injury, the Tiger Cat faces on their aircraft had been ordered painted over. They knew this was the swan song for the Fighting 27th. Their ship was gone, half their airplanes had gone with it; VF-27 would be pulled back and reconstituted. Most likely they would be broken up as pilots were reassigned.

Kid flicked on the battery switch, and the Hellcat's DC gauges twitched to life. He depressed the primer button and watched the fuel pressure move to 20 psi. Satisfied, he pushed the starter button and counted three blades as the big prop rotated, and then pushed the mixture lever to full rich. Coughing to life, the big R-2800 shook the entire airframe before steadying out in a guttural lope. Kid bumped the throttle to warm the oil and cylinder heads.

The familiarity of the routine was comforting, something he could control. Not much in the past few days had been within his control. The men of VF-27 wanted to get back into the fight but had gotten more than they bargained for. Things change.

06:44 Local, 25OCT (20:44 GMT, 24OCT)
USS Johnston, Leyte Gulf

Johnston was the northernmost picket ship in Task Unit 77.4.3. The call sign for the lightly armed force was Taffy 3. Operating on her own, the Johnston was essentially a lookout. A young sailor scanning the horizon with "Big Eyes" binoculars from the fly bridge suddenly stiffened. He turned toward the bridge and reported in a loud, nervous voice.

"Multiple surface units, in battle formation… they have pagoda-shaped superstructures!" He emphasized the last statement.

Skipper Evans had been dozing lightly in his captain's chair, letting the officer of the deck maintain position. He rarely left the bridge, even taking his meals there. Jolting instantly awake after the report, he made his way out onto the fly bridge. The lookout stood aside as the skipper swung the Big Eyes on their mount toward the ships and quickly focused them. The giant binoculars revealed a very large surface action unit coming out of the dawn haze. All the capitol ships had the unmistakable pagoda structure of the Imperial Japanese Navy. Without looking up, Evans issued his first order of the day.

"Sound General Quarters! Stand by for war at sea!"

"GENERAL QUARTERS, GENERAL QUARTERS; ALL HANDS MAN YOUR BATTLE STATIONS. GENERAL QUARTERS, GENERAL QUARTERS," rang out over the 1MC and echoed through the ship.

Sailors and officers scrambled to their pre-planned positions for war. Captain Evans stepped back on the bridge and continued a string of orders.

"Comm O, break radio silence, transmit in the clear: Japanese task force, consisting of: battleships, heavy cruisers, cruisers and numerous support vessels, north Taffy 3. Bearing three six zero degrees at fifteen miles. Steaming towards main force Taffy 3, at a constant bearing, with a decreasing range. Johnston is engaging."

Evans scanned the surface action group, settling his binoculars on the closest large ship, heavy cruiser Kumano. He quickly plotted an intercept course to the enemy as his lookouts called out the ship types and numbers.

"Helmsman, set course zero one zero, flank speed."

He walked across the bridge and picked up the microphone of the 1MC and spoke to his entire crew, calmly and to the point.

"This is the captain. A large Japanese fleet has been contacted. They are fifteen miles away and headed in our direction. They are believed to have four battleships, eight cruisers, and a number of destroyers. This will be a fight against overwhelming odds," he continued, "from which survival cannot be expected. We will do what damage we can. That is all."

Well within range of the Japanese guns, a wall of waterspouts erupted in front of the Johnston. She didn't flinch as she charged alone toward Kurita's entire fleet—an armada of four battle ships, six heavy cruisers, two light cruisers and eleven destroyers. All five of her five-inch mounts returned fire with over two hundred rounds.

"Arm all torpedo tubes. Torpedo Officer, target the lead cruiser."

"Aye aye, Captain."

"Helmsman set an evasive course. Activate the smoke screen. We must cover the carriers."

The ocean upended as Johnston closed within range in a zigzag pattern. The entire Pacific seemed to be in the air during her five-minute run. Bursting through a wall of water, the Johnston turned hard at full speed, lining up on the Kumano.

"Port and starboard tubes fire! Port one torpedo away. Starboard one torpedo away."

Torpedoes splashed into the ocean on both sides of the ship. Their propellers, already spinning at maximum RPM tore at the water as they built speed.

"Salvo, port and starboard tubes!"

"Ten fish in the water, Captain, all swimming true."

Ten torpedoes, in a perfect spread, closed on the Kumano.

"Right full rudder. Duck into our smoke."

Minutes later, after emerging from the smoke screen, Skipper Evans observed the damage to the Kumano. Her bow was completely blown off and she was retiring from the fight. As Johnston turned to re-engage, three fourteen-inch shells from the Konga simultaneously crashed into her amidship, followed by three six-inchers from the battleship Yamato. Johnston was rocked by the impacts. The hurricane windows on the bridge imploded. Blood flowed on the deck.

"Skipper, steering is out!"

Evans got to his feet and looked at his bloody left hand. Two fingers were gone. Undeterred, he continued to issue orders as fire swept toward the bridge.

"Shift the conn to aft steering; secure from the bridge."

The bridge crew ran aft to the fantail. A hatch was opened in each deck, allowing Evans to shout orders directly to the rudder room where sailors pounded the rudder into position with sledgehammers. Seeing a low rain squall, he conned the Johnston into it to perform damage control.

On board his flagship, Admiral Sprague watched the heroic Johnston and crew. He issued a simple order as he withdrew the escort carriers south.

"Small boys attack."

Informed of the order, Skipper Evans re-attacked. Unable to keep up with the USS Hoel, Heerman, and Roberts, with only one of her two engine rooms operating, Lieutenant Commander Earnest E. Evans saluted them as they steamed past the Johnston and toward the enemy on their own suicide charge. Suddenly at 08:20, a battleship appeared out of the smokescreen only seven thousand yards away, closing on the CVEs. Evans attacked it immediately, scoring repeated hits to its superstructure as the Japanese shells fell around the Johnston to no effect.

Observing the CVE Gambier Bay, one of the unarmored and slow escort carriers under fire from a cruiser, Evans attacked, putting four direct hits into it. Evans shifted next to a squadron of destroyers moving at flank speed toward Sprague's line of retreating CVEs. Again, the Johnston attacked ferociously, first the lead and then the second Japanese destroyers in line, until the entire squadron retreated to launch torpedoes at her.

Engaged against the full squadron of destroyers and numerous other ships, the Johnston's luck finally ran out. With the Imperial Japanese Navy circling and firing at her, at 09:30 she lost her last engine and went dead in the water. Unable to maneuver or return fire, at 09:45 Skipper Evans gave the order to abandon ship.

Kid Brennan saw the end from overhead. He knew it was the ship that had saved him. He attacked with an anger he had not felt for months. Four hundred fifty aircraft joined the fight with whatever they had—bullets, depth charges, bombs, even drop tanks full of fuel.

Admiral Kurita was shocked by the fury and bravery of the picket ships and aircraft. The unbridled ferocity of what he assumed was just the lead element unnerved him. He could not lose the central fleet. Certainly, once Halsey's main force engaged, they would be destroyed.

With victory in his grasp, he ordered the central force to withdraw as a lone destroyer closed within a thousand yards of the Johnston and fired the final death shot into her hull. Floating on rafts, her surviving crewman watched as the Japanese captain saluted the sinking Johnston. Hoel, Samuel B. Roberts, and the Gambier Bay joined her at the bottom of Leyte Gulf. Of Johnston's 327 officers and crew, only 141 were saved. Skipper Evans went down with his ship.

Sho-Go 1 was a complete failure. Rear Admiral Oldendorf's bombardment group of battleships had caught Admiral Shima's southern force in the Surigao Straits and destroyed it. Admiral Halsey's Task Force 38, successfully decoyed, had nonetheless destroyed the northern force, and even though Kurita successfully withdrew the central force, only one of his capitol ships was battle-worthy. The Imperial Japanese Navy was defeated. Even worse for the Japanese, they were cut off from their war machine's life blood, oil. Admiral Toyoda knew that not just the Battle of Leyte Gulf but the entire war was lost. The once mighty Imperial Japanese Navy could not even defend the home islands now.

09:54 Local, 25OCT (21:54 GMT, 24OCT)
Luzon Island, The Philippines

Butler scanned Clark Field, watching Japanese aircraft take off. Something bothered him, but he couldn't put his finger on it. He turned to Donnelly after he finally realized what was different.

"Why are they launching as singles?" he asked.

Sergeant Donnelly scanned the field and overhead with powerful binoculars.

"It doesn't make any sense," he replied. "They are not forming strike groups."

Donnelly scanned again, watching their direction of flight. Small formations and single aircraft departed, all headed toward Leyte Gulf. It was non-standard; if nothing else, the Japanese forces were standardized. Very regimented, in fact, to a fault. They were inflexible when the plan fell apart. This made no sense.

"We need to tell the brass, don't we?" he said.

Butler looked worried. They were limiting transmissions due to the close proximity of the Japanese. He had no doubt they were aware of the presence of fighters in the mountains and would use direction finders to try and find those with radios.

"Yes, this is non-standard," he replied. "We need to get the word out."

Vice Admiral Takijiro Onishi had unleashed his *tokubetsu kōgeki tai,* or Special Attack Force. The world would come to know them as Kamikaze: aircraft employed as missiles and driven into the heart of American ships with fuel and bombs onboard. Their guidance systems would be human. Kamikaze translated to "Divine Wind," heralding to a time in history to when Kublai Khan's Mongol invasion fleet was miraculously destroyed by typhoons. Onishi released a storm of metal, fuel and explosives.

CHAPTER 36

09:58 Local, 25OCT (00:58 GMT, 25OCT)
Leyte Gulf, The Philippines

Kid Brennan trapped on board the Suwannee and taxied past a hole in her wooden deck being quickly repaired by carpenter's mates. He was directed to keep his engine running. Purple shirts wrestled fuel lines to his Hellcat. Red shirts cranked nine yards of .50 cal into his guns as his R-2800 lazily loped. A lieutenant appeared on his wing with water and a box lunch.

"What's going on?" asked Kid. "I thought the Japs were retreating?"

"Hell has been released," replied the officer. "They are coming in as singles on suicide runs. The bastards already got the St Lo. And damn near got us!"

He nodded to the large hole in Suwannee's deck as her guns came alive in a convulsive chorus.

Looking to the sky, both men saw the Zero diving out of the clouds at full speed. To Kid, the gun sight seemed centered on his Hellcat. Both he and the lieutenant froze, transfixed by the desperate act. Besides, there was nowhere to hide.

Kid was sure at that moment he would never see his son, never see Theresa again. As the thought dulled his mind and deadened his soul, a wing blew off the Zero and it spiraled into the ocean just off the port bow, throwing up a huge spout of ocean. Wiping the stinging salt water out of his eyes, the lieutenant signaled the fuelers and ordnance men to stand down.

"Go with what you have—launch now!" he demanded and then slipped off the wing, immediately giving Kid the signal to launch.

With the gear still retracting, Kid was already in a hard turn toward the beach. His wing tip was barely twenty feet off the surface; even so, he held the nose down to accelerate. Reaching 350 knots, he jerked the stick and zoom climbed. At two hundred knots, having reached fourteen thousand feet, Kid scanned the horizon, straining to see the crazed attackers.

A Val's wing flashed below him in the sunlight as it rolled in on a destroyer. He quickly did a split S and chased it down. Glowing rounds of ammunition filled the sky around him as both the Val's tail gunner and the destroyer opened fire.

This is absurd, Kid thought, triggering his own six guns. *Has the entire world gone mad?*

It was not the .30 caliber tail gun that was unhinging him, it was the large caliber triple A, shot by one of his own navy's ships. *Concentrate! Gun sight to target! Piper to impact point.*

Not sure whose weapons had done it and not caring, Kid pulled off aggressively as the Val disintegrated. Rolling inverted so he could scan below his aircraft, he saw a second Val and dove on it, dispatching it in one burst as he roared past. Pulling on a hard turn, he desperately tried to fly toward the beach and engage the enemy further out.

He couldn't. They seemed everywhere, scattered individuals. A Zero appeared, diving on an escort carrier. Kid flamed it in a head-on pass and had to push the stick violently to fly under the debris. After giving chase to another Zero whose inexperienced pilot simply flew into the water, Kid's guns went silent.

He arrived overhead the Suwannee at 12:38 and orbited, waiting to sequence into the landing pattern. Then, out of nowhere, an A6M2 Zero dove through the marshaling stack of Suwannee's aircraft waiting to land, toward her deck. With the Suwannee unable to shoot due to the US aviators overhead, the Zero hit the deck just as an Avenger snared the number two wire. Both aircraft burst into flames, quickly spreading to nine others.

Kid couldn't believe what he had watched. With the conflagration burning and no ammunition, he recovered on the Santee. After a quick turn he was airborne again, flying cover over the Suwannee. Overhead his stricken ship, he joined on a squadron mate who passed Kid the flight lead.

As suddenly as they had appeared, the Kamikazes were gone. Kid scanned the sky. It was empty of aircraft tracers and smoke trails. Calm had returned to the air and airways but not the surface of the Pacific. Ships burned everywhere.

ENDGAME

Suwannee's crew worked feverishly to put out the fires and repair the flight deck. Kid looked north; clearly Taffy 1 was steaming to join Taffy 3. No doubt they would give chase to the Japanese fleet. The Suwannee was withdrawing south. Just after 16:00, Hellcats began to launch from Suwannee as she turned into the wind. With his relief airborne, Kid descended and landed.

He sat, staring blankly forward, unable to get out of his aircraft. Finally, he noticed Cue-ball standing next to his Hellcat, tears streaming down his cheeks. Kid turned his head looking at the scar on the flight deck and then turned back to Cue.

"Andy?" he asked.

Cue-ball nodded slowly as fresh tears rolled down his face.

The Suwannee was retiring to lick her wounds. Below, on the hangar deck, 107 of her crew lay dead—but she had fared better than many other ships that were now on the bottom of Leyte Gulf. Imperial Japan's Navy may be out of the war, but the Suwannee would be back.

CHAPTER 37

06:18 Local, 28OCT (21:18 GMT, 27OCT)
Sierra Madre Mountains, Luzon Island

Captain Dave Butler moved fluidly and with purpose through the dense foliage. He would close within a few yards of a Japanese position, take notes, and then withdraw to the jungle. For two days he had been on his lone mission, mapping the enemy's defensive positions. He had gathered all the intel he needed from just a couple of observation points and begun the journey back to the rally point.

Butler had run out of food the night before. He was now living off the jungle just as Rubio had taught him. Sitting silently among the huge ribbons of roots, he disappeared into the base of the indigenous tree. He dug at the soft soil and unearthed some yellow grubs. Popping them into his mouth quickly, he kept them down with a chug of black water and then continued his trek up the mountain.

06:38 Local, 28OCT (21:38 GMT, 27OCT)
The Philippine Sea

Soft red light emanated from the overhead fixtures of Bunk Room 10. A single white fluorescent light illuminated Andy's desk. Cue-ball and Kid sat quietly "sanitizing" his personal effects. There was nothing to sanitize: Andy Levine was who he was, a gentle soul. They boxed it all, with his uniforms on top, and then took it to VB-27's ready room. Bombing 27th's quartermaster gathered it up, without a word, to ship home. Kid looked at his watch.

ENDGAME

"We'd better get topside," he said. "It starts in a few minutes."

Despite the heat, all hands were turned out in their dress whites, standing at attention in perfect formation on the freshly painted deck. Before them, 107 shrouded shipmates lay on stretchers. Chaplains moved among them giving blessings and quietly saying prayers. Finally, the ship's CO said a few words, followed by the command chaplain. A small platform had been erected with hinged boards slightly larger than the stretchers. An American flag was attached at the inboard end, and the outboard end hung over the port side. Ten at a time, the stretchers were loaded onto the platform, marines fired a volley, the inboard end was lifted slowly, and ten shipmates slid from under their flags into the welcoming ocean. Their presence was like the scar in the deck: forever hidden but never forgotten or fully healed. After all were buried at sea, "Taps" sounded.

Suwannee's melancholy crew put into Kossol Roads in the Palaus as the pastel, tropical sky came again. Kid watched the anchor drop, thinking of his friend and wondering when his grief would end, waiting for the stars.

05:08 Local, 28OCT (09:08 GMT, 28OCT)
Nova Scotia

Winter had seized the North Atlantic. A thick marine layer blanketed the ocean and shoreline for thousands of miles. Stable air would ensure that it stayed for weeks and also provide a smooth ride at altitude.

Kaitlyn Brennan scanned the endless white horizon she had just climbed through. It was forbidding. She had no illusion of survival in the harsh environment if the Merlin engine purring in front of her quit.

She led a flight of four P-51 Mustangs, holding position on the right wing of a B-17 Flying Fortress. On the pathfinder's left wing was another flight of four Mustangs. All nine brand-new aircraft glistened in the sun high above the white cloud layer.

Kaitlyn couldn't believe that she and seven of her girlfriends were flying the best fighter in the war. They were flying from the USA to the UK and would land right into the war. This was unthinkable just a few months ago. It would change things, she was sure. Kaitlyn couldn't have known that already, men behind the scenes were conspiring to kill the WASP program and put her back in her place. But here and now, her innocence and naiveté allowed her to think she was on top of the world.

Onboard the B-17, its all-male crew was less concerned with social change than finding Keflavik, Iceland. In fact, the closer they got to their ultimate assignment in the 8th Air Force, the more the novelty of having eight pretty girls flying off their wing wore off. They were on the longest leg of the journey; it gave them ample time to contemplate daylight bombing. As the latest of many replacement crews from their base, it didn't take a PhD to figure out what lay ahead in England.

Captain Wilson sat in the left seat of the B-17, sipping coffee from a thermos lid. His radioman tapped on his right shoulder, holding a slip of paper. The twenty-one-year-old aircraft commander took the offered paper as the radioman gave the highlights.

"Ceiling of a thousand feet, with a nasty crosswind!"

"Great, thanks, Sparky. Pass it to the girls."

Kaitlyn, as overall Mustang lead, listened and then transmitted a response.

"That wind gust is out of a Mustang's crosswind limit. We will circle and wait."

"No can do, ma'am. Forecast to get worse."

Wilson took his mission to get all of these aircraft to the UK to heart. He had no intention of dropping them off above the overcast and wishing them luck. He briefed the flight that he would bring four at a time below the clouds and line them up with the airfield.

Forty knots of wind, with gusts to sixty, weather-vaned the aircraft; they approached sideways. Kaitlyn could see the runways out of her side windscreen. Of course, the gusts were between the runways, guaranteeing a crosswind; this would be a varsity landing. She called for half flaps over the radio after detaching from the B-17. She turned downwind and flew a wide pattern. Holding extra speed, she fought the hammering wind all the way to the runway, plunking it on in a three-point landing. She fought all the way down to taxi speed and cleared the runway.

Kaitlyn was worried; Texas had prepared her for strong wind but she wasn't sure about her wingmen. She turned her Mustang so she could watch her flight. Number Two was rolling out already; Dash Three battled all the way to the deck but made it. But the pilot must have taken out the wind correction—the aircraft lifted its left wing suddenly, pointed into the wind, and left the side of the runway and buried itself in a snow drift.

It happened so quickly that Kaitlyn could hardly comprehend what had just happened. Then, movement caught her eye. She looked up and saw her fourth wingman struggling in a steep angle of bank. Its nose was cocked up, airspeed obviously dangerously slow. Kaitlyn stabbed at her microphone button.

"Go around! Go around!"

Too late. The Mustang pitched up abruptly, entering a spin as its Merlin engine roared in futility. All of its magic wouldn't save the aircraft or pilot. Kaitlyn sat helplessly as her aircraft was wracked by the gusting wind, watching the virgin snow burn.

21:18 Local, 28OCT (13:18 GMT, 28OCT)
Sierra Madre Mountains, Luzon Island

Butler rendezvoused with his team at the designated spot. They quickly ate a light meal and then set up the portable wireless and generator.

"Okay, boys," he said. "As soon as we hit the key we are giving our position away. So we will transmit our SITREP and beat feet. Be ready to move."

Kowalski began to crank the generator, quickly bringing it to full power. Butler watched as the power needle centered.

"Stand-by to transmit."

Rubio was at the transmitter.

"Troops dug in, high ground, Sierra Madres Range, stop."

"Conceding all low territory, stop."

Rubio continued tapping as Butler let him catch up.

"Main force intact and fortified, stop."

"Captain Butler US Army sends—"

Donnelly grabbed Rubio's arm, stopping the last message from being transmitted.

"Do you really need to put your name on it?" he asked.

"I have to authenticate, Paul. Our codes are expired."

Rubio looked directly at Donnelly. Slowly, he let loose of the Filipino's arm. After the message was finished, they rapidly broke down all the equipment and double-timed into the night.

* * * *

A young second lieutenant barged into General Yamashita's headquarters far below. The general's chief of staff looked up coldly at the intruder.

Yamashita continued to study a large map spread out on a table.

"General-san."

"Speak."

"A message has been intercepted—"

"Did you decode it?"

"It was sent in the clear—"

"Then disregard it."

"But, sir!"

All eyes in the room stared in astonishment at the break in military bearing. Even Yamashita glared in surprise. First bowing deeply, the lieutenant continued.

"It was sent by Butler-san… the one who executed our patrol—"

The General held up his hand.

"Yes, I know. What did he transmit?"

"Our positions and troop strength."

"This is a disaster!" his chief of staff huffed.

"It changes nothing," said the general. "Do you think MacArthur would not have noticed? Do you think he would have thought we vanished into thin air?

Yamashita turned to another member of his staff, a young infantry major. He spoke to him in the familiar.

"Yoji, I cannot have a unit, no matter the size, maneuvering behind my lines. Especially providing intelligence."

"I shall take care of it personally, General-san."

Major Yoji took the young second lieutenant by the arm and escorted him from the office.

"Major, I have more to report to the general," the lieutenant protested.

"He has no time to waste on the details of one small unit. He must plan for the clash of entire armies."

"Forgive me, Major."

"No need, you have done your job. Tell me, Lieutenant—"

"Tatyana, sir."

"—Tatyana, were you able to triangulate a position?"

"Yes, Major."

"Outstanding. Show me."

Tatyana enthusiastically explained how he had contacted another station and between the two, DF'd a location on the highest peak in the Sierra

Madres. Yoji studied the map.

"May I go with you to kill the gaijin?"

"They are gone, my young friend," the major replied. "Butler knows we hunt him."

Again, he looked at the map and then pointed to a peak further down the chain.

"He will go there so he can transmit. We will beat him there. Can you prepare a portable direction finder and be ready by morning?"

"I will be ready, Major!"

10:25 Local, 28OCT (13:25 GMT, 28OCT)
Keflavik, Iceland

Kaitlyn sat in the cockpit, still in shock from what she had witnessed. The B-17 bounced onto the runway. Behind it, two fires marked the impact point of a Mustang from each flight. She looked up to see a giant of a man leaning over her. Even though he was kneeling on the wing, she could tell he was more than six feet tall. His eyes were ice blue, hair blond, his complexion ruddy from the wind.

"Hey, little sister, are you all right?"

"Those were my friends…"

"I'm sorry, honey," he said. "Happens a lot up here. Better get inside; a front is moving in."

Forty-eight hours later, on a crystal-clear day, a B-17 and six P-51 Mustangs rolled down the runway for England.

CHAPTER 38

09:10 Local, 03NOV (00:10 GMT, 03NOV)
Sierra Madre Mountains, Luzon Island

Yoji lay in wait for days. An occasional update from his prey to Allied Command had allowed him to track their progress. Cleverly, they did not follow along the ridge and they kept transmissions short. They were so brief that, had Yoji's listening stations not been dedicated to only Butler and his men, they would have been impossible to track.

This American was no fool. Unfortunately for him, Yoji knew where he was going. Of this, the Japanese major was certain. It was as if the jungle accepted him as a co-conspirator. He felt it. Lying beneath the foliage, he had noticed it was similar to his homeland's on Okinawa Island. It comforted him, welcomed him, embraced him.

Two days had passed since he had radioed the second patrol to start pushing Butler-san to him. He'd ordered a silent approach but made the unit large, knowing stealth would be impossible. Yoji wanted Butler-san to hear them and know their numbers; he would run right into the trap.

Butler moved with trepidation. The jungle taunted him, toyed with him as the Japanese pursued. Clearly elite troops, they were surprisingly quiet for their number. They were also quite obviously hunting him and his team. Yet it was the jungle he feared.

Butler was on point, leading his men down a wild boar path. Sensing something, he held up his fist; Rubio moved up to his right flank, Kowalski to his left. They moved as one, muzzles searching for targets, so fluid and lithe that they were almost on top of Yoji before he noticed them.

The jungle convulsed in Butler's face. Without thought, his body reacted. His right index finger squeezed the trigger as his arms, in full control from his brain, aimed in precise counter fire. Instinctively, his torso sought refuge on the rotting jungle floor. Rubio did not return fire, falling dead from a grievous face wound. Kowalski emptied his Thompson into the jungle; he was losing discipline in his fire. Butler glanced over to see that he had been wounded in the chest and fallen into the crook of a small tree. It held him up, exposing him to the withering fusillade. He was unable to extricate himself, and his chest erupted in spurts of crimson from repeated wounds. Butler's Thompson was soon alone in returning fire.

Donnelley and the remaining men moved forward but were flanked by Yoji's men in a classic L-shaped ambush. Twenty minutes into the fight, Donnelley's group began to take fire from the pursuing force's scouts. Even though he was nearly encircled, Donnelley didn't hesitate. He made his way forward to support his comrades.

Butler dug in his elbows as he pushed himself back, but each time, the jungle floor gave way. His body began to fail him; uncoordinated rounds fell from his submachine gun. His vision began to tunnel. *What is wrong with me?* Looking forward, he saw that he had left a trail of blood, now being absorbed by the soil. He felt himself being transported. He began to fade.

"Dave, Dave!"

Butler opened his eyes and squinted, trying to focus toward the sound of Donnelley's voice. Paul was dragging him into a shallow crevice as bullets crashed into the trees around them. Then he saw Butler's chest wound.

"Oh, no! *No, no, NO!*"

Donnelley awkwardly tried to put pressure on the wound with a bear hug while also attempting to keep his friend out of the continuous fire.

"Sorry, Paul," said Butler.

Sergeant Paul Donnelley sobbed as the jungle shrieked in perverse joy. The gunfire intensified from behind them as the main pursuit force engaged. One Filipino and two Negrito Indians grabbed Donnelley by the collar and dragged him down the hill.

"Sergeant, we must go," the Filipino said. "Everyone dead."

All four survivors slipped down the hill and into the jungle as the Japanese started to fire at each other. Ten minutes later, Major Yoji ordered ceasefire. Moving cautiously forward with his pistol extended, he shot Rubio and Kowalski each once in the head. He noted the wireless transmitter that had spilled out of Rubio's pack. Guardedly following a blood trail, he finally saw the worn boots of Captain Butler. The way they lay, he knew that he had been dragged.

Tatyana appeared beside him, startling the major. Both men moved forward. They could see the captain's rank on the bloody collar. Holding his pistol on Butler, Yoji slowly reached over and snapped off his dog tag chain. Carefully, almost with reverence, he pushed one of the dog tags between Butler's front teeth, slipping the other in his front pocket with the captain's bars.

"Another great victory, Major!" Tatyana drew his sword and moved toward the corpse.

"No, Tatyana. It would dishonor us. He was a great warrior. Bury him."

CHAPTER 39

Suwannee limped into Pearl Harbor. Her exhausted crew manned the rail to pay honors to the Arizona. Kid looked but wasn't even sure if Theresa had gotten the Red Cross message he'd sent after the Princeton was sunk, telling her he was back on the Suwannee. Then he saw them. His eyes welled with tears at the sight of his son for the first time.

Kid waited nervously for the Suwannee to be tied quayside. He and Cueball were the first down the gangway. At first, they couldn't find Theresa in the crowd; finally, Cue saw her.

"There she is, David!"

Moving through the bystanders, Kid stopped in front of them. Charles Henry Brennan the Fourth peeked around his mother's leg. He held onto Theresa's dress, standing behind her in a brand new little sailor suit. Kid kneeled down and held out his arms. Gripping hands full of his mother's dress to steady himself, the toddler ducked behind her. Kid stood, still with his arms out. Slowly, his son looked out again and then smiled.

Kid reached out and picked up his boy, who looked nervously back to his mother as Cue-ball beamed in the background. After staring at his father intently, the little boy turned and reached for his mother. Theresa moved close and hugged them both. Cue started to slip away.

"Paul where are you going?" she asked.

"To the BOQ. You all need to be alone."

"Don't be silly—"

"I'll swing by tomorrow."

Kid and his family slowly walked to their car. A flash of guilt hit him as he thought of Andy. Theresa seemed to sense it and engaged him quickly in light conversation as they got into their Chevy. Today would be about happiness.

* * * *

After weeks of discussion, the pilots of VF-27 not transferred stateside were folded into VF-40 on the Suwannee. VF-27 would be re-constituted under a new CO. Jazz transferred, as did most of the experienced pilots. Kid, Rough, and the XO stayed, along with some of the nuggets.

Suwannee had returned to the West Coast for repairs and refit. VF-40, along with the rest of the air group, stayed at Ford Island and after a period of down time, began to work up for another deployment. This would be the final thrust at Japan, starting with Operation Iceberg, the invasion of Okinawa.

David and Theresa settled into daily life as much as they could with yet another combat cruise looming in the future. They lived for the moment and enjoyed watching their little boy grow. At the squadron, David had become a hard taskmaster. As a flight lead, he did not accept anything but perfection. His favorite phrase was, "You will fight like you train."

08:00 Local, 02DEC (08:00 GMT, 02DEC)
Royal Air Force Station North Witham

Kaitlyn Brennan entered Colonel J.T. Dobbs's office with trepidation. She had made up her mind, set her jaw, and would not back down. Irish was briefing J.T. and looked up as she entered; immediately, he sensed a showdown. He recognized the glare; he had seen it in her father's eyes for years. A shit-storm was blowing in.

"How's my favorite WASP?" he asked.

"Angry, Lieutenant Colonel, very angry."

Now, J.T. looked up from the reports.

"Spill it, Kaitlyn," he said. "What's wrong?"

"The Army, in its infinite wisdom," she said, "refuses to transport my fallen squadron mates from Iceland. They are quite literally on ice."

"What? Why?"

"Because they are not officially military, and that is unacceptable. They died serving their country."

J.T. looked down at the message he had just gotten, back channel, from C.R. Smith. The entire WASP program had been canceled, as of no later than 20 December. Jackie Cochran had a showdown with Congress over militarizing her WASPs. Kaitlyn's current issue was one of the main reasons she had demanded it. She had issued an ultimatum: militarize the WASP program or stand it down. Congress had chosen the latter.

J.T. fell silent, looking a bit sick to his stomach.

"Irish," he said at last, "configure a C-47 with long-range tanks and enough stretcher racks for the ladies in Iceland. Release it to Kaitlyn and her crew, and cut some orders for a return flight to CONUS via Iceland."

"Yes, sir," replied Irish, "I will send a navigator with them too."

"Kaitlyn," said J.T., "we need to talk."

Irish beat a hasty retreat knowing what was coming next.

06:10 Local, 07DEC (09:10 GMT, 07DEC)
Keflavik, Iceland

Kaitlyn and her crew stood at attention and saluted as the big Icelanders easily handled the petite body bags. In addition to her squadron mates, another WASP had been abandoned in Iceland; she too was put on a stretcher rack. Quietly, they made their way to the cockpit and did the pre-flight checks. Within twenty minutes they launched, the last WASP crew to cross the Atlantic.

CHAPTER 40

1945
07:00 Local, 23FEB (17:00 GMT, 23FEB)
Pearl Harbor

Weeks ticked away, then months. All too soon the Suwannee slipped back into Pearl Harbor. It loomed over them like a dark cloud for a week, waiting patiently to take David away from his family and back to war. As they glided into the channel, Kid could see Theresa. He waved but she had her face down, clutching their baby, sobbing.

For the next six weeks they would island-hop back to the front. Former war zones were quiet backwaters now: Tulagi, Eniwetok, and Ulithi. Even the Philippines were now conquered. VF-40's young nugget aviators were full of nervous anticipation; they wanted into the fight. The salty aviators were in no big hurry to get back at it. They knew that the Suwannee's air group would be given air-to-mud bombing missions. No zeros, just bullets—and lots of them—pointed at the sky.

05:00 Local, 01APR (20:00 GMT, 31MAR)
Okinawa

Landing craft stretched line abreast for hundreds of yards, approaching the Hagushi beaches in waves. The XXIV Corps, US Army and III Marine Expeditionary Force bobbed toward the western coast of Okinawa. It was L-Day for Operation Iceberg. In the phonetic alphabet, each letter was assigned a name so there would be no confusion when communications were difficult: A-able, B-bravo, etc. L was love, an irony not lost on the warriors storming the hostile beaches of Japan. Second of the 29th, 6th Marine Division, was in the first wave.

"You know what day it is, Colonel?" Sergeant Major Paillou smiled at Lieutenant Colonel Russell, a Pall Mall cigarette dangling from his lower lip.

"Easter Sunday."

"True, but it is also April Fool's Day."

Russell grimaced as Paillou flashed an amused grin.

Overhead, the constant bombardment from the Navy's big guns suddenly stopped. Paillou pulled himself up high enough to see that the beach was close. He turned to the men in their landing craft and shouted over the drone of the diesel engine.

"Saddle up, boys—here we go!"

Crashing to a halt on the shore of Japan, the Mike Boat's flat bow dropped, giving the marines a platform for running onto the beach. Paillou led out of the right side; Russell, the left. Running at full speed, both knew something was out of the ordinary. They reached the first line of dunes and turned to watch all of their men join them.

Huge casualties had been expected. D-Day in France saw a virtual slaughter on the beaches. There was no noise except the droning of the landing crafts' engines as the second wave hit the beach.

"Do the Japanese celebrate April Fool's Day?" Paillou asked as Russell looked up.

"Here they come," he yelled. "Get your heads down—incoming!"

Seven Zeros had just begun to roll in on the marines below when sixteen Hellcats slashed through their formation. Flaming debris spun toward the beach below, all of it Japanese. A swirling dogfight ensued until seven mounds of flaming aluminum dotted the Hagushi beaches. Kid Brennan split-S'd out of the fight and buzzed the beach right over Paillou and Russell, waving his wings, signaling all clear.

"What now?" asked Paillou.

"We will let the third wave secure the beach," Russell replied. "Let's move inland, Sergeant Major. Radioman, pass the word: no resistance, 2nd of the 29th moving inland."

"Aye aye, Skipper," said Paillou. "Get on your feet, Marines, let's move out."

Moving inland, the marines began to receive harassing fire. They developed a tactic of peeling off small patrols to engage the fleeing Japanese, and then rejoining the column at the rear as it quickly moved inland. Within hours, the combined force seized Kadena and Yomitan airbases.

General Buckner called together his staff and the commanding officers of his units in a bombed-out hangar on Kadena Airfield. Maps were hastily spread out, radios chattered in the background, and USMC F-4U Corsairs landed on the runway as the men filtered in.

"Gents," Buckner said. "I'm damn sure we didn't surprise them—any ideas?" Russell stepped forward.

"General, they withdrew to a defensible perimeter on the Philippines. I suspect they are doing the same here."

"Makes sense," Buckner replied. "Well then, there is no point sitting around on our cans. Execute phase two immediately."

Having secured the center of Okinawa, 6th Marine Division turned north as the Army's 96th and 7th Infantry Divisions wheeled south. Both units continued to be harassed but did not meet with any real resistance.

11:00 Local, 01APR (02:00 GMT, 01APR)
USS Suwannee, Pacific Ocean

VF-40 and VT-40 aviators were being debriefed in CVIC. Fans whirled but did little except move around the hot, stale air. Each debrief had a common thread: there was little to no resistance. Few targets on the ground were observed and, except for the seven Zeros, nothing in the air either.

While each aviator ate a box lunch, Intel briefed the second event. All hands present seemed very nervous. They were waiting for the other shoe to drop. Where were the Japanese?

"Okay, gents," Intel continued the brief, "we are in support of a feint. The 2nd Marine Division is going to do a diversionary landing on Minatoga Beach here on the southeast end of Okinawa."

He pointed to the map with a wood pointer. "We need to make it look real so they don't move their reserves north. Our boys are moving through central Okinawa like crap through a goose. We have Corsair squadrons on deck Kadena already."

LCDR R.D. Sampson, CO of VF-40, let out a low whistle in response.

"How long is this going to last?" he asked.

"I don't know, Skipper. But the big guys upstairs are nervous."

"Well, you can imagine our concern," Sampson quipped, to the laughter of the aviators.

"Roger that, sir. Targets of opportunity around the landing area is the mission. We have loaded your aircraft with the new five-inch rockets. Should be exciting."

"No doubt."

Four F6F-5 Hellcats crossed the beach just below the overcast at twelve hundred feet. They should have been sitting ducks. They should have been getting shredded by triple-A. But they weren't even receiving ground fire from small arms. Kid flew section lead for LCDR Sampson; the extra weight and drag of the five-inch rockets felt strange.

They caught a couple of tanks moving away from the beach inland. Skipper Sampson rolled in on the trailing tank and unleashed a barrage of rockets. Smoke trails filled the air as they spiraled into and around it. Kid quickly armed his rockets and let all six go at once. The intel officer was right—it was exciting. Kid's favorite part was watching them impact. After strafing empty buildings until their guns were Winchester, out of ammo, the flight RTF'd. This eerie order of battle continued for three more days.

13:20 Local, 04APR (04:20 GMT, 04APR)
Okinawa

All hell broke loose on the fourth day, as the 96th Infantry Division approached the city of Shuri on highway number one. The typhoon of steel had started on land. At sea, it was already underway—Kamikazes were sinking at least a ship a day and damaging numerous others. As the 96th engaged the fortified positions on what would be known as Cactus Ridge, the 7th encountered equally fierce resistance on the Pinnacle, a thousand yards southwest of Arakachi.

The 6th Marine Division pushed up Ishikawa Isthmus and engaged the northern Japanese force, codenamed the Udo Force. It was a running battle as the marines aggressively marched north.

LCDR Sampson circled over the advancing marines, leading a flight of two. Once he was sure of the FEBA (forward edge battle area) he rolled in, looking for targets of opportunity. Getting sight of three trucks, he unleashed four rockets, two from each wing. They streaked toward the trucks, causing one to erupt in an orange fireball. Sampson's wingman, Bugs, rolled in and got tally on a fourth truck as Sampson reset. Rocketing the original three trucks, Bugs then pulled off, radioing Sampson its location. When he didn't get a response, he turned and watched as Sampson's Hellcat, enveloped in a fireball, fell to the earth. Unknown to the aviators, the rocket launches had blown off the tail cone of a five-hundred-pound bomb. When Sampson dropped the bomb, it did not fly true; instead it bounced off his right wing and fuselage, exploding before falling clear. Flaming debris continued to rain down. There was no parachute.

A subdued VF-40 sat in the ready room, waiting for Stutz to come back from CAG's quarters. LCDR Sampson had been a favorite of the men, a great leader and pilot. His death was a blow to morale. When Stutz finally came in, nobody noticed that he wore a command pin and the oak leafs of a lieutenant commander, not even when he turned at the front of the ready room to face his pilots.

"Kid, front and center." Kid looked up and saw the new rank, confused as to why he was being called on deck.

"We all just moved up," Stutz continued, "whether we like it or not. Kid, you have been given a battlefield promotion to full lieutenant. You are now the executive officer." Stunned silence filled the room. It was real. The skipper was officially gone. His billet had already been filled. The Navy would go on. The war would go on, no matter who was lost. It was a sobering realization for all of them. Stutz shook Kid's hand and showed him to his former seat in the front. It had a big XO embroidered on the back.

"Okay, gents," Stutz went on, "there is some good news. We are being pulled off the air-to-mud mission. Suwannee is heading south, VF-40 will CAP over the Sakishima Islands. These Kamikazes are ripping the fleet to shreds—we will stop it." Reaction to the news was understandably nil. Skipper Stutz then waved to an aviator who had been standing in the back forward. "We also have a new guy reporting in. Robbie, introduce yourself." Kid looked up to see his buddy from flight school smiling at him. He jumped up and gave his old friend a bear hug.

"Still at the head of class, eh, Lieutenant Brennan?"

"Great to see you, Robbie, I'll put you in my division."

"No offense, XO, but I'm cross-decking from another ship. I have a few kills of my own—any chance I can get my own flight?"

15:22 Local, 07APR (07:22 GMT, 07APR)
Okinawa

Lieutenant Colonel Russell kneeled over a large map of Okinawa.

Sergeant Major Paillou squatted next to him. All of the officers of the 2nd of the 29th, 6th Marines, were formed around them in a circle.

"We need to seal the Motobu Peninsula," Russell told them. "The 22nd is heading north. HQ believes the bulk of Japanese forces are on Motobu."

"How's the rest of the battle going?" Paillou asked, rubbing the week-long stubble on his chin.

"The Army has run into a buzz saw south—over a thousand casualties already. We need to secure the north so that all assets can be moved in support."

"When do we move onto Mobotu?"

Russell looked at his watch.

"In thirty-eight minutes."

"Great."

* * * *

Sixteen-inch shells pummeled the Japanese positions for an hour before the marines moved forward. Incredibly, they didn't seem affected, as withering machine gunfire came from the rocky enemy positions immediately. Paillou rolled onto his back, grabbing the handset from his dead radioman.

"Alpha Four, Alpha Four; this is Alpha One: I need mortars on hill 2402." Paillou tossed the handset down and waved forward a flamethrower.

A young private struggled forward with the bulky tanks strapped to his back. He flopped down next to Paillou, rolling onto his back to protect the highly volatile bottles.

"They have to be in caves," Paillou said. "No other way they would've survived that naval bombardment."

"You want me to flame the cave, Sergeant?"

"No. You and I are going up there when the mortars stop. Stay close and be ready to move."

He rolled away from the private, grabbing the handset and yelling cease-fire over the din. In an instant Paillou was up, pulling the young flamethrower onto his feet and pushing him forward. They reached the first Japanese position as the gunners were emerging from a tight tunnel. Paillou opened up with his Thompson machine gun, dropping them at the entrance. Throwing himself against the side of the hill he tossed a grenade into the cave and rolled away as it blew.

"Get up here! Fill the entire cave with gas."

"Without firing it up?"

"Affirmative. Shoot the entire load in there except for one burst."

Paillou stacked the Japanese bodies in the entrance of the cave and then calmly checked his watch. After ten minutes he pulled one of the bodies out of the cave and moved behind a large rock, pulling the private behind him.

"Put a flame into the cave and then duck."

Squirting a short liquid flame at the cave resulted in the entire hill seeming to erupt. A whooshing sound was followed by a huge concussion. Blowtorches shrilled all over 2402, and then the hill fell silent.

"Holy cow, Sergeant Major!"

* * * *

Russell found his command sergeant major leaning against the mouth of the cave, smoking a Pall Mall. Marines were crawling out of the cave, .45 caliber pistols at the ready.

"You're a little old for this, aren't you, Mike?"

Paillou shrugged and then deeply inhaled the blue smoke.

"I thought you were coming up here to assess the situation," Russell said.

Paillou exhaled calmly.

"I did sir; it was AFU."

Russell laughed as one of the marines reported.

"It's weird, Colonel. Some of them don't look touched, but they sure as hell are dead."

Russell turned to Paillou, eyebrow raised in question.

"Moonshine, Colonel."

"Say again?"

"Always was a little left in the bottle. Roll it around the inside and drop in a match; makes a rocket engine. I figured it would be an unpleasant ride from the inside."

05:00 Local, 08APR (20:00 GMT, 07APR)
USS Suwannee, Pacific Ocean

Kid watched as Robbie's Hellcat rolled; he had given him the lead. He just wanted to hang on Robbie's wing and not have to think for a while. Kid ran up his engine to thirty-six inches when the launch officer pointed at him.

ENDGAME

He cycled the electric prop to full pitch and then jammed on full throttle when the LO touched the deck. Pumping out all 2,200 horsepower, the Duel Wasp propelled him down the deck as it dipped in the heavy seas. Suwannee's bow pitched up as Kid reached the end, hurling him into the predawn sky.

Heavy and slow, he had a boot full of rudder kicked in to keep the F6F-5 straight. The supercharger whistled as it compressed air, boosting the pressure in all eighteen cylinders and raising the horsepower to peak output. It strained against the three blades of the Hamilton Standard propeller. Kid held the controls with fingertips, gently inviting the machine to stay in balance, maximizing its acceleration rate. With each additional knot of airspeed, the controls felt firmer and more responsive. Like a beast awakening from hibernation, his Hellcat was coming back to life.

Now joined together, the four Hellcats began a high-speed climb. Kid was the section leader with Bugs on his wing, and Rough on the other side of Robbie as Dash Two. Looking past the lead aircraft. Kid watched the huge cumulus nimbi clouds in the background. Thin bolts of lightning licked at the atmosphere, free of the clouds, like the tongue of a serpent. Large flashes jumped cloud-to-cloud. Internal throbbing lit the large storm clouds like paper lanterns.

Kid realized for the first time in quite a while that he was enjoying flight. In tactical formation, he and Rough were in an undeclared contest to see who could maintain the most precise position while scanning the sky for Kamikazes. Their flight was now the only thing that stood between the insane martyrs and the Suwannee.

They floated effortlessly through the valleys formed by the great clouds. Behind them the sun rose, coloring the lanterns. Kid was so taken by the scene he hardly noticed Robbie roll inverted. When he realized it required four Gs to maintain position, Kid was pulled back to the dark side of flight. The duality of flight returned when he awoke from the dream into the nightmare.

Drop tanks fluttered by. Kid matched Robbie's configuration by blowing off his own. He armed his weapons and looked past his lead for the enemy. Robbie's guns came alive, barking out death as he flamed a Val and, without releasing the trigger, walked the stream of bullets onto another with similar result. Red, glowing bullets stopped as the aircraft and men disappeared below, plummeting to the surface of the ocean. All evidence of the violence would sink with them while the Hellcats climbed back to their perch, sparkling in the morning sun.

216

20:15 Local, 08APR (11:15 GMT, 08APR)
Okinawa

Lieutenant Colonel Russell sat cross-legged in a small pup tent as the darkness surrounded it. Sounds of war crashed in the distance and close. He used a red-lensed flashlight as he read the after-action report from the US forces in the south. Paillou joined him.

"You sent for me, sir?"

"Yeah, look at these."

Sergeant Major Paillou took the reports, reading them as he lit a cigarette with his Zippo.

"Fifteen hundred casualties—"

"It gets worse. Keep reading."

"Cactus Ridge and the Pinnacle were just outposts?"

Russell nodded slowly.

"Affirmative," he replied. "The main force is a line centered on Shuri. And they are dug in deep."

"Great," said Paillou. "I guess we know where we are going next."

By 13 April, the 22nd Marine Regiment reached the northern end of Okinawa, turned south and with other 6th Division units, converged on Aha, securing it on the 18th. Motobu Peninsula fell to the 29th by the afternoon of the same day.

16:15 Local, 18APR (07:15 GMT, 18APR)
Okinawa

Yae Take was a burned-out moonscape. The last stronghold of the Japanese on the Mobotu Peninsula had withstood incredible bombardment, but in the end, simple fire had proved too much. Like ancient Roman legions, the Marines had used liquid fire to dislodge entrenched troops. Napalm fell from Corsairs and Avengers, while on the ground, flame-throwing tanks and men filled the caves with horror. Russell and Paillou walked among the carnage. The smell of death was overpowering. A young corporal walked up to them.

"Sir, you shouldn't be up here," he warned. "We still got suicide Japs in spider holes."

Paillou detected movement among the rocks and bodies—an emaciated

ENDGAME

Japanese soldier sprung to his feet, rushing toward them. Paillou drew his .45 and shot the soldier three times before the grenades he was holding blew up. Paillou's world went silent, then faded to black as he felt himself falling.

CHAPTER 41

06:00 Local, 19APR (22:00 GMT, 18APR)
Overhead Okinawa

Red, orange, purple—every tint of the rainbow painted the sky as Kid drifted through the clouds of another omnipresent sunrise. It was overpowering, pushing away the carnage that surrounded him. Only the brilliance of color and thoughts of his family entered his private sunrise. His flight had been diverted to support the troops on Okinawa, but even the mission, for now, was miles away.

06:05 Local, 19APR (21:05 GMT, 18APR)
Naval Field Hospital, Okinawa

Navy corpsmen and doctors scurried about, checking on patients. Clean, white bandages contrasted sharply with the grimy men they covered. Paillou looked at the tubes leading from his arm and then shouted at one of the passing personnel.

"Corpsman, where am I?"

"Okinawa still, field hospital. We had to pull half a junkyard out of you, Master Sergeant."

"Where is my CO?"

"Over here, Mike." Russell waved a bandaged hand from across the aisle. "We medevac'd last night. You were out for most of it. How's your head?"

"Hurts like hell. How are you?"

"Same as you. We will be out of the fight for a while."

"And the corporal?"

"Not a damn scratch."

They both laughed through clenched teeth.

07:05 Local, 19APR (22:05 GMT, 18APR)
Overhead Okinawa

Kid's flight had circled, waiting for a mission to be called by a forward air controller. After a few minutes, he was assigned to investigate reported troop movement on the south end of the island. After detaching his section, he and Daffy flew down to the southern edge of Okinawa. Putting Daffy into high cover, Kid dove down to get a better look.

He saw movement on the cliff's edge and armed and charged his guns. Something was strange—they were just standing on the cliff's edge. As he got lower he could see they were civilians. He eased his finger off the trigger, dropped lower, and slowed down. Flying level with the cliff, he looked over just as a woman jumped.

Shocked at what he witnessed, Kid made fleeting eye contact with another woman as she jumped with a baby in her arms. Watching them land like rag dolls on the rocks below left no doubt of their fate. The Technicolor horror was beyond description. For him, the war was over. It would rage on, and hundreds of thousands more would die, maybe even him. But it didn't matter. His war, his private war of vengeance, was over. It ended on the cliffs of Okinawa.

~ The End ~

EPILOGUE
The Typhoon of Steel

Okinawa, the bloodiest battle of the Pacific Theater, waged on until June. Japanese commanders committed Seppuku (ritual suicide) in the end. A hundred thousand Japanese and sixty-two thousand American casualties were the result of the conflict. Its scale is staggering: the Japanese lost 7,800 aircraft. It foreshadowed an epic struggle on mainland Japan, with predictions of one million U.S. military casualties.

And on the hard-fought island of Tinian, a pair of bombs was being readied....

ABOUT THE AUTHOR

Leland "Chip" Shanle Jr; Lieutenant Commander, USN (Ret.) is a contributing editor to *Airways Magazine*, and an award-winning writer in both fiction and non-fiction. His first novel, *Project 7 Alpha*, won the Military Writers Society of America's (MWSA) Gold Award for Historical Fiction in 2012. In addition to writing articles on aviation, he has written screenplays and has been an aviation/military technical adviser on five major motion pictures including *Pearl Harbor, Behind Enemy Lines, xXx: State of the Union, The Day After Tomorrow* and *Stealth*, as well as for a television series pilot which, as of this writing, has not yet announced. His production company, Broken Wing LLC, is featured in Discovery's Curiosity Series Documentary: *Plane Crash* in the USA, Channel 4 in the UK and Prosieben in Germany.

He is a member of The Society of Authors in the United Kingdom and the MWSA in the United States, and has remained an active member of the Society of Experimental Test Pilots (SETP).

Project 7 Alpha, American Airlines in Burma, 1942 was the first in his World War II Aviator Series, and he now follows it up with *Vengeance at Midway and Guadalcanal*. The third in the series, *Endgame in the Pacific*, is scheduled for release in 2013. And he is hard at work finishing his fourth, *A Race With Infamy*.

Chip was born and raised in St. Louis Missouri, attended Chaminade College Prep Class of 1977. After High School he joined Naval ROTC at the University of Missouri, Columbia. Upon graduation in December of 1981, he was commissioned an Ensign in the United States Navy. A month later he married Laura L Cantrell and they set out on their Navy adventure together.

Chip received his Masters from Embry Riddle Aeronautical University and also graduated from the Naval War College CCE. He flew 16 different naval aircraft in 10 squadrons; including the F-4 Phantom II, EA-6B Prowler and TA-4J Skyhawk. Attached to CAG (Air Wing) 5, 11 and 1. He cruised on the USS Midway, America and Lincoln. He flew 80 missions over the war torn skies of Bosnia, Somalia, and Iraq. An Airline Transport Pilot and Certified Flight Instructor; he has flown numerous civilian types from the Cessna 150 to the Boeing 767-300. Currently he is rated in 767, 757, 727, MD-80 and Sabreliner series aircraft.

Closing out his Naval Aviation career in 1998 with 600 carrier landings (200 night) on 11 different carriers, Chip, his wife Laura, and their four kids moved home to St. Louis. He now flies for American Airlines and concentrates on his writing.

CPSIA information can be obtained at www.ICGtesting.com
Printed in the USA
LVOW13s2301170314

377830LV00005B/170/P